BASED ON A TRUE STORY

NO PAVED ROAD TO FREEDOM

A DRAMATIC AND INSPIRING STORY OF HUMAN STRUGGLE AGAINST OVERWHELMING ODDS

By Sharon Rushton

Soaring Reader Press

Soaring Reader Press
www.soaringreader.com
www.nopavedroadtofreedom.com

COVER AND INTERIOR DESIGN BY HEIDI LOWE

ISBN 978-0-9831304-0-6

Library of Congress Control Number 2011901088

Author's Note

THIS STORY BEGS TO BE TOLD, especially now that those involved can tell it without fear. Prior to 1990, a negative perspective of communist Romania could not include names of individuals still living there. Those mentioned would have faced persecution.

No Paved Road to Freedom is based on the life of Cornel Dolana. I first heard about Cornel Dolana from his son, Cornel Dolana Jr., whom I know as Corey. When Corey mentioned he was Romanian, I asked if he or his parents had immigrated. His answer was the beginning of the most enlightening and penetrating story I had ever heard.

A few days later, Corey introduced me to his father. The handsome, silver-haired man spoke in a very thick Romanian accent as he summarized his experiences in Romania and his escape attempts. His determination captured my soul. I knew without a doubt I had to write this book.

From hundreds of hours of interviews over several years, I incorporated the highlights as well as the many details of Cornel's experiences. The dialog is reconstructed from his recollection of what could have been said. While Cornel could not give me specific dates, I was able to match much of what happened to him to historical records.

Most names used in the book are real; some have been changed for various reasons.

ACKNOWLEDGEMENTS

I THANK COREY DOLANA FOR making me aware of his father's pursuit of freedom. I thank Cornel and his wife, Mimi, for spending endless hours sharing the joys and hells of his life. Mimi told me nightmares often plagued Cornel after our interview sessions.

Writing this book would not have been possible without the wonderful support of my friends and family. I appreciate the encouragement of my loving and supportive husband, James Rushton and son, Chris Rushton. I thank my mother, Velma Betz, and sisters, Janet Betz and Diane West, for always believing in me.

I appreciate the assistance of Marissa West, Bob and Becky Knopf, Michael Hayes, Christy Abbatello, Brandi Rushton, Paul Cuccolo, Keith Sutton, Jim Casada, and Barb Gigar.

I thank Jan Adamczyk of the Slavic Reference Service for responding to my questions about Yugoslavia.

Very special thanks go to Kaeli West, Kenny Kieser, and Kent Hayes for providing extensive and invaluable guidance.

I'm grateful to reviewers Lavinia Stan Ph.D., Andy Cline, Ph.D., Jane McCasland, Ph.D., and Nan Stark who volunteered suggestions for fine tuning the manuscript. Stan, an expert in Romanian communist studies, also provided essential insight which improved the accuracy of the book.

Thanks are not quite enough to describe my appreciation of Deborah Johnson's contribution to this book. I refer to her as my angel.

CORNEL DOLANA'S IMMEDIATE FAMILY

Father Marin Dolana (born 1902)
Mother Oprita Dolana (born 1901)
Brother Ion (John) Dolana (born 1926)
Sister Florica Dolana (born 1928)
Brother Aristotel Dolana (born 1930)
Cornel (Cornica) Dolana (born 1938)
Brother Georgica Dolana (born 1939)

GLOSSARY OF ROMANIAN AND YUGOSLAVIAN WORDS:

burghez: category of upper class
burghezi: people of upper class
canepa: a crop raised for fibers to make ropes and to weave into fabrics
chiabur: category of middle class
chiaburi: people of middle class
militia: communist police
militianu: communist policeman (singular)
militieni: communist policemen (plural)
Noroc: "God Bless" or good luck
politia: police
Securitate: Secret Service of communist Romania
Sluzba drzavne bezbednosti (SDB):
    Secret Service of communist Yugoslavia
Slibovitch: a brand of liquor
tata: father
tuica: homemade liquor

EUROPE - 1940

ROMANIA - 1941

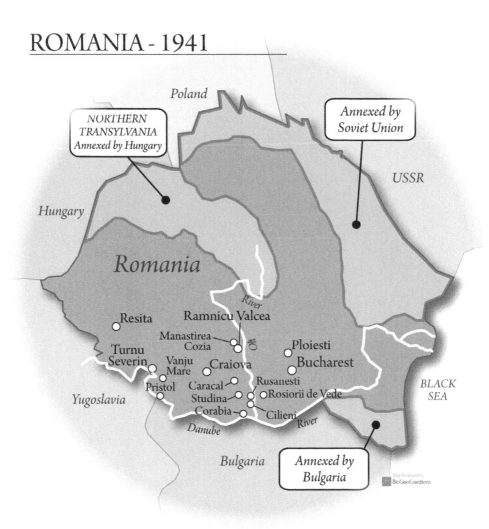

No Paved Road To Freedom

September 1959

CORNEL DOLANA STRUGGLED in the cold, swift waters of the Danube River. His survival hinged on his swimming skills and endurance. His numb hands and feet meant he had been swimming a long time, so he couldn't be far from the Yugoslavian shore. The darkness prevented him from seeing the shoreline, but any landing would do as long as it was not back on Romanian soil.

The twenty-one-year-old gasped for breath as he felt something drag him under. Panicked, he kicked furiously and clawed with his hands, but the river would not let go. He felt his body being pulled deeper, and he struggled harder. The river held him. Cornel, starving for air, feared he was being forced into a deep, dark grave.

His father's words, "You can't fight a whirlpool!" came to him. He commanded his body to stop resisting. His muscles obeyed and loosened up. At first, he felt the whirlpool pull him deeper, but then the water seemed to relax its hold and release him. He kicked and clawed to the surface.

He broke into the cold night air, inhaling deeply while stretching his neck up to avoid swallowing the rushing river water. He forced himself to breathe slowly and tread water to stay upright. The current pushed and pulled at him. He was confused. He had to start swimming again, but which way? He knew the whirlpool could have turned him around. In which direction was Yugoslavia?

Darkness was the only thing he saw, the rush of the river the only sound he heard. He made his choice, ordered his arms to pump and legs to kick, and set out. Each stroke was a cold agony. He felt enveloped in the force of the current as it pushed his body downstream. He fought panic that the river might be carrying him back toward Romania. His body had given all it could. Cornel could feel fatigue strangle his muscles.

He could not let freedom slip away and dismissed the thought that he might not be making any headway toward the Yugoslavian shore.

I'm strong, and the river already said it wouldn't take me today, he said to himself. He forced his body to swim. Compelling desire to survive as a free man kept him going.

Bushes brushed against his hands. Startled, he jerked but then felt his legs touch slimy rocks. Relief washed over him as he realized he was in shallow water. He grabbed the rocks and looked up. The sky was pale. If dawn was near, then he had been swimming five hours, much longer than he had thought it would take to cover a mile-wide stretch of the Danube River.

A sound made him turn his head. Terror engulfed him as his eyes focused on three AK47s aimed at his head. In the silhouettes against the half-dark sky, the soldiers' uniforms appeared to be Romanian. Cornel wanted to weep; *I must have swum the wrong way when I came up from the whirlpool.*

He had started dreaming and planning in his early teens for a better life, one free of communism. Now, shivering from the freezing temperatures and fear, he thought, *That's the end of me!* He braced himself for a bullet.

PART ONE

Rusanesti, Romania

CHAPTER 1

Spring 1941

MARIN AND OPRITA DOLANA and their five children lived in the southern Romanian village of Rusanesti de Jos.

In the spring of 1941, Marin told his family he would soon be leaving to fight in a war. His three-year-old son, Cornel, didn't comprehend the complexities or dangers of war, but he understood that his father would not be home for a long time. Cornel decided to spend every minute with him and became a miniature shadow to his six-foot-tall father.

One day Cornel's Uncle Costica stopped by to ask Marin to go fishing. The two men grabbed their large fishing net as they left the yard. Cornel tagged along as they headed for the Olt River.

"Cornica, you'll have to stay out of our way if you come with us," Marin said. The family always called him "Cornica" which meant "little Cornel."

Cornel's little legs tried to keep up with the long strides of the two adults as they walked past the church and cemetery and along the rough path of the prairie. The men stepped around a pile of warm cow dung, but Cornel couldn't resist and jumped into the center of it. He paused a minute to let it ooze around his tiny calloused feet and then ran to catch up with his father.

At the river's rocky edge, they removed their clothes and without flinching, they stepped naked into the chilly water. Snowmelt, from where it flowed through the Carpathian Mountains, kept the quarter-mile-wide river refreshingly cool. Seventeen miles down-river from Rusanesti, the southeastern-flowing Olt River joined Europe's second longest river, the mighty Danube.

"You can swim downriver from us," Marin told Cornel.

The two men moved upriver from Cornel and ran the seine through the light current. The net came up empty. Cornel swam up and grabbed on just as they moved it to the other side of the river. When the netting went tight, Marin saw Cornel hanging onto it.

"Cornica, hang on. We'll pull you to calmer water." Marin shouted. Just as he said the words, the current swept Cornel into a whirlpool. The net went limp.

"Cornica!" Marin and Costica screamed, but he didn't come up.

"Grab hold and pull. Hurry!" Marin yelled to Costica after they repositioned the seine. Their first sweep caught the lifeless boy in the net, and they dragged him to the edge of the river.

Every nerve in Marin's slender body shook in panic. He grabbed his son's ankles and twirled him around in circles, going faster and faster as terror seeped in.

"Marin, stop!" yelled Costica. Marin kept circling, and Costica yelled louder. "Marin, stop! Let him down and see if he's breathing."

They laid Cornel on his back. When the boy began coughing, Costica sat him up.

The moment Marin knew his son would live he started to yell at him. "What were you thinking? You could have died. You haven't learned about whirlpools. You can't fight a whirlpool. If you do, it will pull you into its belly. You have to relax and go with the flow of the current."

Cornel, still shaken, looked up at his father. "I'm sorry, *Tata*."

Marin continued to scold his son as they put on their long shirts and walked home. When they entered the kitchen, Marin told his wife what happened.

"What were you thinking Cornica?" Oprita asked. "I'm not sure you should get supper this evening. Now we don't have any fish because they had to look after you instead."

They let Cornel recover from his experience in his room and gave him time to think about the consequences of his actions. Oprita felt two hours was enough punishment for a three-year-old, and she longed to hold in her arms the little boy she almost lost.

"I'm sorry, Mama." Cornel said as she entered the room.

She walked over and wrapped her arms around him. Tears ran down her slender face.

"Are you hungry?" she asked.

Cornel shook his head. He held her hand as they walked into the center room and joined the rest of the family at the table.

It was soon time for Marin to say his good-byes. Romania had tried to remain neutral in 1939 when World War II first broke out, even giving up land to stay out of the war. However, the country couldn't avoid the conflict between German dictator, Adolf Hitler, and Soviet Union leader, Joseph Stalin. In September 1940, Romania's Prime Minister, Ion Antonescu joined forces with Hitler's Third Reich, and Romania's men were called to war. In late spring 1941, Marin had to report for duty.

Marin asked his oldest sons, John and Aristotel, to look after their sister, Florica, and their two younger brothers, Cornel and Georgica.

"I'm not sure how long I'll be gone. Your mama needs you to be on your best behavior and to help all you can while I'm gone,"

Marin said to all of his children. They exchanged hugs. Marin and Oprita held each other for a long while.

Cornel wrapped his arms around his father's leg and held on tightly. Marin looked down at him and said, "You be good to your mama." He uncurled Cornel's grasp and held him in his arms. As he put him down, he said, "I'm going to miss you."

Everyone cried as they watched Marin walk away, worried they might never see him again.

Early Summer 1943

WITH MARIN STILL AWAY, the family continued to labor more than ever to make up for his absence and the lack of conveniences of rural life. Villagers had no electricity, no running water, no indoor bathrooms, no stoves, no grocery stores.

There was no access to doctors, so they had to deal with their ailments as best they could. Once, Oprita had to assist with the delivery of a baby, since women had to rely on each other for such occasions.

With no tooth brushes or toothpaste, they occasionally cleaned their teeth with salt or ashes from the fire.

Their clothes were all handmade, each crafted from fibers of the crops they harvested or from the furs and skins of animals they raised.

All young boys and girls in the village wore similar knee-length shirts and no undergarments. Shoes were special commodities. Children always went barefoot; they were given their first pair of shoes when they entered the seventh grade. Older children and adults owned shoes but used them sparingly; they did not want to wear them out, so even the rough field work was not an adequate reason to wear shoes.

The Dolanas felt fortunate that they didn't have to worry during hard rains even though the relatively flat terrain of the region could flood easily. They had a brick home in the area of Rusanesti that benefited from a few feet rise in elevation. Some villagers had mud homes that would disintegrate in the floods.

Just like their neighbors, the Dolanas worked together to live off the land. They ate only what they produced. They respected the land and found a purpose for everything. Nothing was wasted.

Daily chores left little time for play, but five-year-old Cornel and his friends made the most of every moment. Using their creativity to make toys and invent games, they made balls out of cow hair by spitting on the hairs and rolling them in their hands until the ball was at least four inches in diameter.

When they could get one, a pig's bladder made their favorite ball, but it lasted only a few games, and they'd have to go back to the hair ball that didn't bounce. Most of the time they kicked the ball around and tried to get it into a goal made of sticks and rocks.

If those games didn't work, Cornel always knew he could rely on the large piles of cow manure. He liked jumping off the barn and sinking into the warm manure, a feeling only a child could appreciate. The smell always let his mother know where he had been. She'd greet him with buckets of water or order him to the Olt River.

All the children enjoyed swimming in the river, but none more than Cornel. No whirlpool could keep him away. He was undaunted by his previous experience and determined to become a better swimmer.

One day the children stopped their play on a side street when they heard a deep rumble.

"Something big is heading to the village," someone yelled.

They ran to the main street. All they could see was a cloud of dust billowing over the trees. The ground shook. The noise grew louder. Cornel and Georgica spotted a massive machine.

Their eyes grew wide as a long line of military tanks lumbered toward them. Everyone in Rusanesti used horses and wagons for transportation, so the children had seen few motorized vehicles, let alone tanks. Some children ran home, but most were curious enough to stay put. They stood transfixed as the machines came closer. The heavily ridged metal tracks chewed into Rusanesti's dirt road.

Standing in the open hatch of each tank were two uniformed men who waved to the children and threw candy. Cornel beat out many of the scrambling children to get a handful of sweets. He gave a piece to Georgica before making sure all the other children ended up with at least one treat.

One tank stopped to avoid running over a cow in the road. Cornel decided to go for a ride and scrambled up the side. Three other children climbed aboard after him. Through smiles, dust coated their teeth as they held on for a two-block ride before the tank came to a halt.

The soldiers waved their arms and shouted at them in a language the children didn't comprehend, but they understood the soldiers wanted them to get off the tank. The disappointed boys jumped down and ran alongside the procession to see if others would stop and pick them up. None did, but the children were delighted when more candy rained down on them.

As parents showed up, they frantically tried to round up their children.

The adults did not need to be told the soldiers were German. The appearance of so many tanks could mean only one thing—the war was getting closer to their village.

Cornel spotted his mother standing with his sister.

"I rode on one and got candy!" he shouted as he ran to them.

"You come here and stay with me." Oprita had to yell over the loud rumbling noise. Cornel could hear her well enough to pick up on his mother's angry tone. He tried to dodge her outstretched arm, but didn't succeed. She yanked him to her side and spanked him.

Everyone stood in the street until the last tank disappeared over the horizon.

Chapter 2

August 1, 1943

OPRITA TOOK A BREAK from her housework and leaned against the back door of their home. She counted her blessings as she watched her children pick tomatoes and pull weeds. Her two older sons were too young for the army but big enough to help. She knew other families were less fortunate.

Clanging of metal interrupted her peaceful moment. A chill ran down her spine when she realized it was the bells of the church ringing out a warning.

Oprita ran to the garden and grabbed Georgica's hand. Cornel grasped her long black skirt while the three older children just seemed to materialize at her side.

"Do you hear that?" John asked as a thundering sound intensified.

"Yes, please hurry," Oprita said. "The trench is just ahead."

They set off, anxiously running toward one of the six-foot-deep ditches dug in zigzag patterns on the outskirts of Rusanesti.

At the edge of the dugout, Oprita thrust Georgica into the arms of others who had already taken shelter. She herded John, Florica, and Aristotel into the trench. Amidst the scrambling, she realized Cornel wasn't with her. She spun around to see him standing yards behind her, his head thrown back, eyes fixed on a large plane and its four propellers that seemed to zero-in on him as he stood frozen to the ground. Cornel's eyes grew wider as a large formation came in at treetop level and bore down on their little village. Oprita lunged for Cornel and yanked him to her.

"They're American!" someone yelled.

Talk began to spread among the few men left in Rusanesti. These older men had served in the Romanian army and understood the significance of what was taking place.

"Looks like they're headed to the Ploiesti oil fields," one man said.

"We knew this day would come!" another man responded.

The mood shifted into quiet tension when they saw German and Romanian fighter planes engage the American bombers.

A bomb exploded in the distance. Screams broke out and Cornel wondered why everyone had their heads tucked to the ground. He wanted to see what was going on. Uncurling his body to look up, he saw only patches of sky through the mass of planes. He liked the noise and the unfamiliar yet interesting throb he could feel in his chest.

Cornel and Georgica jumped up to join others their ages who had dug their bare toes into the dirt, so they could be high enough to watch the drama unfold.

"Cornica! Georgica! Get down from there. You'll get your head blown off," Oprita said firmly as she reached up and grabbed the long shirts of the two boys. Georgica was glad to get down; he was scared to death. Oprita placed Georgica in her lap, and Cornel sat beside them, their backs against the cold dirt wall.

The ground shook as another bomb exploded. Georgica started to sob. Oprita tightened her hold on her youngest son and glanced down a few yards to see John and Aristotel comforting their sister.

13

"It's all right, shush now," Oprita tried to reassure little Georgica.

While his mother was distracted, Cornel climbed out of the hole. A screaming noise made him turn. His feet froze to the ground as a low flying fighter headed directly toward him. Cornel didn't know the frightening sound was a device on the aircraft that was meant to trigger paralyzing fear. It worked well on Cornel who tried to yell, but no sound came out of his mouth.

The German fighter pulled up just before reaching him. He leaned his head back to see the plane swoop up and fire at one of the American bombers. Another fighter joined in, and the bomber's wing started smoking. Fire erupted. The pilot tried to bring his stricken plane in for a landing, but it blew up when it struck the ground. Pieces of the plane flew in all directions.

Cornel thought he could reach the crash site and ran as fast as his five-year-old legs would take him. When Cornel left, other children followed to get a closer look at the wreckage.

Cornel got about a hundred yards away when something stopped his momentum. Oprita grabbed his arm and then his ear as she led him back.

"What's gotten into you? Do you want to get killed?"

He sat quietly and heard the approach of another wave of planes. He looked up and watched them pass as he thought about the temporary German camp outside their village. Daily, Cornel had been sneaking over to the camp with his best friend, Mozoc, one of Dolana's three dogs.

As he sat reflecting, he hoped the American bombers didn't notice the German camp as they flew by; if they missed their aim, the bombs could hit Rusanesti and kill their dogs that they left at the house.

14

The trench shook from a close explosion. Cornel couldn't take sitting still any longer and climbed up to watch.

"I'm going to fly planes one day," Cornel proclaimed to those around him. It didn't bother him that no one seemed to be listening. "I'm going to fly planes like those; I'll fly high in the sky." He didn't want to fly so he could visit other places; Cornel had never visited a city, nor did he dream of venturing into such a world. His world began and ended in Rusanesti. He just wanted flying to be part of it.

Bombers continued to roll in overhead.

That day villagers were witnesses to one of the longest American air missions of the war. Known as Operation Tidal Wave, Americans had deployed 178 B-24 bombers from a base in North Africa to destroy oil depots critical to Hitler's war.

CHAPTER 3

Fall 1943 – August 1944

N O ONE IN CORNEL'S VILLAGE died in the bombings, but life in Rusanesti was never the same. Villagers remained on edge, and their fear was justified. The bombings killed 120 Romanians and wounded 335 more.

The Americans only destroyed 45 percent of the oil production, so eight months later, in April 1944, they returned to Ploiesti to hit the oil fields again. This time the bombers of the U.S. Fifteenth Air Force, operating from a base in Foggia, Italy, received protection from the Air Force's African-American Tuskegee Fighters.

The younger children of Rusanesti liked the excitement, but for their older siblings and parents, the second raid was just as frightening as the first. For Cornel, it was another chance to study the planes he hoped to one day fly.

The second attack further slowed but did not stop oil production at Ploiesti. Throughout the summer of 1944, the people of Rusanesti sought safety at least twice a month.

Between attacks, the people of Rusanesti tried to get back to a normal life. For Cornel that meant doing his chores on the acre of land around their home and helping in the family's fields that were located a few miles outside the village.

Cornel looked up from pulling weeds in their garden when

he heard cries from women and the sad music of a clarinet, tuba, trumpet and big bass drum. He looked through the opening in the fence and saw his priest and a mother and her daughter leading a funeral procession. He recognized the girl from his class and remembered hearing that her father had been killed in the war.

Cornel thought about his own father and prayed that he was okay. He glanced at his mother whose gaze was fixed toward the melancholy sound. Her fingers covered her cracked lips that seemed to contain her worried thoughts. The deep vibrations of the bass drum kept the slow pace of the funeral procession as it continued toward the cemetery just up the street. Oprita stayed transfixed in her daydream state.

A few days after the funeral, the clanging bells resounded through Rusanesti. It was August 19, 1944. Oprita gathered her family and ran for safety. Even Cornel hoped this raid wouldn't last long. The dugouts now smelled like their outdoor toilet. People couldn't leave, so they urinated and defecated in the trenches. Walking barefoot through the filth was worse than the smell. Cornel kept his head and nose as high as possible. Besides, that's how he could best watch the planes as they zipped in and around trying to shoot one another down.

Cornel still didn't understand the significance of all that was happening. He listened to older men discuss the situation when there was a break in the action. He heard them talk about the implications of the Battle of Stalingrad. They said it was one of the bloodiest battles in history and a turning point in the war.

Oprita had told Cornel about his uncles who fought in the Battle of Stalingrad. His uncle Constantin Ciobanu died there, not from a bullet, but from the freezing temperatures. Constantin's brother, Ion, was part of a cavalry unit. He survived, but his prized

17

white horse was shot and killed. Ion was still fighting somewhere in the Soviet Union.

The older men said that Germany was weakening, and the Soviets were advancing toward Romania.

Cornel wondered what all this meant for his father coming home from the war.

The ground shook when a plane exploded in the distance. Cornel peeked over the edge to watch the smoke billow into the sky.

This was the United States Air Force's final raid on Ploiesti.

September 1944

NEWS HAD NOT YET TRAVELED to Rusanesti regarding the coup that had taken place on August 23, 1944. Twenty-two-year-old King Michael had arrested Romania's military leader, Marshal Ion Antonescu, in order to break ties with Hitler. The young king's intentions were to save the country from destruction and prevent the Soviets from seizing power. By proclaiming his loyalty to the United States, Great Britain, and the Soviet Union, the young king hoped the Soviets wouldn't invade Romania. Despite his efforts, Soviet troops moved into Bucharest and then to other parts of Romania.

Returning from the fields one afternoon with her children and a wagon of just-harvested corn, Oprita sensed something was wrong. As they entered Rusanesti, their horse-drawn cart was the only one in sight. Children weren't playing in the streets, and sobs could be heard coming from the houses they passed.

Oprita, Cornel, Florica, and Georgica unloaded supplies while Aristotel drew water from the well and John took care of the horse. Oprita decided the corn could wait until tomorrow.

"Cornel, please start a fire so we can have something warm for supper," Oprita said.

"Okay, Mama."

Cornel gathered wood and had only a small flame started when he heard someone at the door.

"Come in and rest," Cornel heard his brother John say. Cornel turned to see John's girlfriend, Florina, coming through the door.

As Florina spoke, fresh tears flowed from her swollen eyes. "The Soviet trucks and tanks came through while you were away. We ran home, and Mama and I hid in the attic. We heard girls screaming and crying from homes near us.

"Mama put her hand over my mouth to make sure I didn't scream when they knocked down our door. I knew better than to utter a sound. We could hear them tear apart our house."

The fifteen-year-old girl sobbed. Florina's voice cracked as she tried to speak; rivers of tears rolled down her pretty face. She tried to start again but still couldn't get the words out. John reached for her hand. She closed her eyes and took a deep, ragged breath.

"We came out of the attic after all the noise stopped. Our house was ransacked. We went to our neighbors' homes, and my friends said soldiers knocked down doors to steal food, alcohol, and whatever else they could find.

"Some girls had run from their houses, but the soldiers caught them. They raped girls — and their mothers!"

John took her in his arms and let her cry on his shoulder. After a few minutes, she sat back and said, "Everyone is afraid to tell what happened, but I can tell who was raped just by looking at their faces."

The Soviets hadn't touched the Dolana house, probably because it was far enough off the main street. Still, the Dolana family felt devastated for those whose lives had been irrevocably changed.

Oprita put her arm around Florina and pulled her close while she wondered what other tragic events might lay ahead.

PART II

Soviets Introduce Communism

CHAPTER 4

May 1945 – December 30, 1947

WORLD WAR II OFFICIALLY ENDED for Romania in May 1945. Husbands and sons who survived battles and extreme weather conditions returned to their families. Marin came home from the war to an emotional reunion with his family. Oprita felt the worry begin to lift from her shoulders. Marin was just as relieved; he had spent many anxious hours wondering if his family had survived the bombings.

Now Marin worried what influence the Soviet Union would have on their lives. For Eastern Europe, it was a time of uncertainty and turmoil.

Radio and newspapers didn't reach their village. To learn what was happening, Marin occasionally took a train to Bucharest and visited with Marin Popescu, Oprita's first cousin who worked closely with King Michael in the palace. When Marin Dolana returned to Rusanesti, he would share the information with Oprita and his trusted friends.

Marin learned that soon after the war, Joseph Stalin announced to the Allied countries that he was going to restore a democratic state to Eastern Europe. Romanian King Michael knew this wasn't the true objective. He sent a pleading request to General Dwight Eisenhower for the Americans and the British to occupy Romania.

Eisenhower sent the message to President Franklin Roosevelt and British Prime Minster Winston Churchill. The two leaders declined to help.

On another trip to visit Bucharest, Marin discovered that Soviet troops had surrounded the palace on December 20, 1947. Communist leaders Petru Groza and Gheorghe Gheorghiu-Dej asked King Michael to sign an abdication statement. King Michael refused. Groza encouraged him to reconsider and told the king if he didn't sign, they would shoot one thousand students currently under arrest. King Michael gave in to avoid more bloodshed. Thus, the Romanian kingdom ended, and communists took over the government, calling it the Romanian People's Republic.

Fall 1948

RUSANESTI HAD YET TO FEEL the impact of the new government. The Dolanas continued to live as peasants. Georgica was now nine, and Cornel was ten. Seventeen-year-old Aristotel was in Ramnicu Valcea (Rm. Valcea) studying theology at an Orthodox seminary and following in the footsteps of his grandfather and great grandfather who were respected priests. Florica had grown into a beautiful, tall, slender, dark haired woman of twenty. John, a handsome young man of twenty-two, had married Florina and had his own home.

Every Sunday, the Dolana family attended the Romanian Orthodox Church, the only place of worship in Rusanesti. The sparse structure was embellished by a detailed, colorful painting on the exterior stucco above the church's large, open windows.

The church was a source of comfort to the villagers — although the service itself could be trying, especially for the little ones. There were no chairs or pews, so everyone stood for the hour-and-a-half service.

One Sunday in the fall of 1948, the Dolanas visited with their friends after they filed out the church entranceway. Normally, Cornel tried slipping away immediately after the last "Amen" because his parents always had chores for him. This morning he decided he wouldn't wander too far because if he misbehaved, he'd miss out on the scrumptious sweet cake his mother made only on rare occasions.

Oprita sent Cornel home ahead of the family to catch their lunch — one of the chickens in their yard. The Dolanas lived next door to the church, so Cornel didn't have far to go. He chose one of the older chickens. He tried sneaking up on the brown bird, but it flew away.

He caught the eye of the meanest of their roosters and wished he could kill him, but he knew that wasn't allowed. This bird seemed to enjoy attacking Cornel, and this day was no different. The rooster flew up and attached its feet to Cornel's arm. The bird flapped its wings and pecked at Cornel's back while he ran around the yard trying to rid himself of the assailant. The bird finally relinquished its prey and flew back to its favorite perch by the door, the same spot from which it crowed an ear-splitting wake-up call every morning.

Steering clear of the rooster, Cornel spotted another chicken in a corner. This time he got a good hold of it and clutched it in his arms as he ran into the house to get a knife. He went back into the yard, stepped on the chicken's feet and held its head up. With a snap of the knife, he sliced through the neck.

"Did you kill the chicken, Cornica?" Oprita asked when she returned.

"Yes, Mama, it's inside the kitchen door." Cornel had learned the hard way not to leave the chicken outside where their dogs — Mozoc, Grivei, and Pasalica — would help themselves to a tasty meal.

"Bring in some wood for the fire," Oprita yelled out the door. Cornel obeyed and laid kindling over the pile of cold ashes. The cooking fire was built directly on the dirt floor, offset about three feet from a corner where the brick wall was blackened by years of smoke. His mother stacked a few pieces of wood on the kindling, struck a match to light the smaller twigs, and then blew at the base until the larger wood caught. The smoke rose through a hole in the ceiling, but without a chimney to lead it, some of the smoke lingered in the room.

The flames soon licked the bottom of a water-filled cast-iron pot suspended by a chain over the fire. When the water came to a full boil, Oprita dunked the chicken by its feet. After about ten minutes, she pulled the bird from the pot and took it outside. The family's cats and dogs, which had learned that Oprita with a chicken meant a handout of intestines, ran to her side. Their eyes followed her every movement as she plucked the feathers and split the chicken open.

Oprita filled a small pot with fresh water from the well and tossed in the chicken's head, feet, heart, and gizzard. She hung the pot over the fire to boil and arranged the split chicken on a steel grill that rested on top of the hot coals. She swatted at the flies that swarmed to the food.

The dogs kept a vigil just outside the open door. The cooking bird's aroma drew Cornel from the next room to see if the meal would be ready soon. Oprita took one look at her son and began to scold him.

"Cornica! Look at that shirt. The first day and you're already covered with mud!"

Oprita handed out clean clothes on Sunday mornings so her family would be presentable for church services. Once a week she and Florica carried dirty clothes to the Olt River. Kneeling down at water's edge, they rubbed the clothes against wet rocks and swished them around in the water until the dirt floated away in the current. Oprita and Florica lugged the heavy, wet clothes home and slung them over the clothesline in the yard. When the garments were dry, Oprita hung them on hooks in the bedroom. With only two outfits per person, they didn't need a closet.

"I'm sorry, Mama." Contrite about the dirty shirt, Cornel decided to show his mother he was responsible. He called to Florica to help him move the table that had been pushed against the wall. The children lifted the table and set it alongside the one bed in the room making sure it was positioned evenly on the bright orange woven rug. They each carried a chair to the table. Then Florica placed a clay bowl and plate and wooden spoon at everyone's place.

"Marin, I need a bucket of water," Oprita called as she leaned out the kitchen door.

Cornel ran outside to help his father and found him talking with the priest, Father Manoila.

Marin appeared in the doorway with the water and announced, "We have one more for lunch."

Oprita served a salad followed with soup. Out of respect for their guest, she placed the coveted chicken head in the priest's bowl. He was pleased. Oprita allotted Cornel his favorite part, the gizzard. His father and brother each got one of the feet. Oprita put the heart in her bowl and then served the meat. No one talked during the meal. They were too intent on dipping each piece of chicken into the garlic paste and relishing every bite of the feast.

Cornel finished first and hoped everyone else would hurry so his mother would serve the sweet cake she had made the night before. He scratched at the bedbug bites on his arms and legs and squirmed in his seat until his mother placed a piece of cake on his plate. He savored every bite; each morsel provided him a moment of serenity.

The meal finished, Father Manoila rose from his seat, thanked the family, and turned to leave. Marin pushed back from the table and walked his guest to the door where the two men exchanged a few quiet words. Cornel and Georgica stopped their chatter to try to hear what was being said. The men noticed the boys listening and stepped outside. Every few minutes, other men, mainly relatives of the Dolanas, showed up and joined in the conversation. After a while, the men moved inside to the guest room.

In addition to the small kitchen, the Dolana home had three rooms, and each served several purposes. All rooms had at least one bed with a straw mattress, a table, and two chairs. The center room served as both the dining room and a bedroom. The Dolanas primarily slept in the main bedroom to the left of the center room where the family shared two beds. The guest room, on the other side, hosted visitors and served as the gathering spot for Marin's friends.

Cornel watched from the doorway as each man took a seat in a chair or on the bed. Marin served the men a glass of *tuica* (homemade liquor) from a batch he had just finished distilling.

Cornel and Georgica weren't invited into the guest room. They hovered in the doorway as the men sipped their liquor. Marin noticed his sons and rose to shut the door. Sensing something was up, Cornel and his brother sat against the wall in the adjoining room. They knew their father would be angry if he discovered them eavesdropping, but they couldn't help being curious.

"I just got back from Bucharest and have some disturbing news."

Cornel recognized the voice of Ion, an uncle who lived in the neighboring village of Cilieni.

"Gheorghiu-Dej was elected secretary general of the Romanian Workers Party and is rounding up the Iron Guard and others who oppose communism."

Several men grumbled and spoke at the same time. Cornel couldn't make out what was being said until he heard Pericle, Oprita's cousin, speak above the voices. "They're making major changes all over."

"It's terrible," said Marin's brother Costica. "I don't like them replacing our *politia* (police) with their *militia*."

"They want us to live by their new rules, and they want their own in power to enforce them," Marin said.

"Have you come across the *militianu* (communist policeman) they brought in to rule Rusanesti? Comrade Argesanu has lost no time in showing us how strict and unreasonable he is," Costica said.

"We can't go anywhere without telling him," Marin said. "I had to report to Comrade Argesanu before I left for Bucharest and then report to him when I got back."

"*Militieni* (communist policemen) are bad, but the *Securitate* (secret service of communist Romania) are even worse," cautioned Stefan, another of Marin's brothers.

"I've heard you're in real trouble if they get involved," said Father Manoila.

The men chatted with each other until Ion interrupted.

"I've been holding off the worst news. I was told they plan to take away our land and make us work in collective farms."

"No," Costica blurted out.

"What happens if we all refuse?" Pericle asked.

"We can't give in to them," Cornel heard his father state in a very determined voice.

The men discussed and debated the troubling developments late into the afternoon. Cornel and Georgica stuck by the door, listening as the men clinked their glasses and pledged to stick together against the communists — and out of the way of Comrade Argesanu. Finally the men began to say their good-byes. The boys unfolded their stiff legs and scattered.

The visitors left the house and walked to the gate where the Dolanas' animals — cows, geese, turkeys, horses, and oxen — were waiting to be let in. One family member would lead the animals to the community pasture each morning and turn them loose to graze all day alongside the other people's animals. No one had to bring the animals home; each creature, on its own, meandered back to its respective home at day's end.

Marin opened the gate and the men filed out. Once everyone threaded their way through the animals and said their goodbyes, Father Manoila said, "God help us."

CHAPTER 5

THE NEXT DAY CORNEL AND GEORGICA set out for school, keeping together for the one-mile walk. Usually they dawdled, not eager to begin another week cooped up in the two-room schoolhouse. Although they enjoyed getting away from their chores and even liked the schoolwork, it was all too easy to get on the wrong side of their strict teachers.

To the boys, Father Manoila was just as bad. The priest taught religion, and if students had not memorized their prayer or scripture for the day, he would twist the children's ears and put them in the corner of the classroom where they were forced to kneel on pebbles or stand on one leg with hands in the air. If they put the other leg down, they'd be told to balance on one leg even longer. When students got out of line, Professor Voinea would smack them on their hands until blisters rose. Heaven forbid if their parents found out, for they would punish their children with a strap across their bare behinds.

The Friday before, Cornel had been punished by his parents and Father Manoila for not reciting his assigned prayer exactly. The priest had said, "If you don't learn your prayers by Monday, you'll be punished again." Cornel, taking the threat seriously, had hidden in the attic most of Saturday and memorized his lessons.

That Monday morning, Cornel hurried his brother along, eager for Father Manoila's praise. The school bell rang as they arrived. Cornel and Georgica rushed inside and waved as they split to enter different rooms. Cornel scrambled with the other students to take a seat on one of the benches. As he rested his elbows on the table he looked up and saw a man standing at the front of the room. The man was wearing a uniform. Cornel looked around the classroom for Father Manoila; he wasn't there.

Professor Voinea stepped to the front of the class. He said, "I want to introduce you to Lieutenant Ariciu. He is with the Securitate of the Communist Party."

Cornel thought the teacher seemed nervous. He had heard the word "Securitate" only the day before when the men had visited his home. Cornel remembered how Stefan had spit out the word. He decided he had better be on his best behavior.

Lieutenant Ariciu took two purposeful steps to the front of the classroom. Professor Voinea stepped aside. Lieutenant Ariciu stared at the students until they sat up straight and every eye focused on him.

"Take out your history books!" Lieutenant Ariciu commanded.

He yelled out a number, and each student nervously flipped to the designated page. Cornel looked down to avoid being noticed by the man in the uniform. Cornel did not want to be called on to read. The information was about Romanian kings, which Professor Voinea had covered weeks ago.

"Rip it out!" Lieutenant Ariciu ordered.

Astonished, Cornel jerked up his head to determine if the man was trying to trick him into getting into trouble again.

"I said rip out the page!"

The man's harsh voice assured Cornel that he was meant to do as told. Cornel slowly pulled on the page, watching as the paper came away from the center of the book. Toward the bottom, the tear jumped off track, leaving jagged halves of words along the book's gutter.

"Now, pages twenty-four through twenty-seven. Rip them out!"

Cornel flipped as instructed and recognized the material as a history of the Orthodox religion — a lesson he detested — and he could not remember much about it. Cornel grabbed the pages two at a time and drew them down firmly, each time jerking the paper the last two inches to be sure he did not leave fragments. He was getting the hang of it now and felt smug to see the hated lesson disappear from his book. He smiled as he thought that no one would be asking him to recite that lesson again.

Lieutenant Ariciu led the class through a list of page numbers, each time telling the children to remove them. It was as if the printed paper had offended the man in uniform.

When Lieutenant Ariciu called out the last page number, Cornel realized half his book was gone. The students had stacked so many loose pages on the table that some had floated to the floor. The boy and girl beside Cornel pushed the paper at each other with their toes. Neither Lieutenant Ariciu nor Professor Voinea said a word about the mess.

"You will not have to study scriptures or say prayers any longer. In fact, you won't have to attend church either," stated Lieutenant Ariciu.

This was a bigger surprise to Cornel than the book-tearing exercise. He felt relieved at the thought of not having to memorize scriptures and prayers, which would mean no more painful punishments — but to not go to church on Sundays? He liked walking into the church with his family and coming home for a Sunday feast. One positive thought crossed his mind: *I won't have to go to confession.* He didn't like confession because Father Manoila told his parents what he'd said, and Cornel often ended up getting the strap again.

Lieutenant Ariciu, his back ramrod-straight, marched from the room. The students followed him with their eyes as if they'd been ordered to do so. Professor Voinea brought their attention back to the classroom.

"Now we're going to the pasture for a celebration on communism. Your parents have been told to be there as well," the teacher said.

The students were quiet as they left the school. Georgica's class followed them. Then the children whispered excitedly among themselves as they followed their teachers for this unexpected break from lessons. As they reached the field, Cornel and Georgica spotted their parents, waved to them, then made themselves comfortable on the grass.

Lieutenant Ariciu stepped on the makeshift stage of a few raised boards.

"Your country is now under communism," he announced. "You are going to have a better life. We have come to improve your lives. Your old government was exploiting you, but with the new communist government, you will be free, and your village and country will prosper. Romania will be greater than America. Everyone's lives will benefit once the communist way of life becomes yours."

Lieutenant Ariciu continued with his speech. The young students squirmed as boredom set in; they couldn't comprehend most of what was being said. Cornel was thankful when the man finally finished.

Professor Voinea motioned for all students to follow him to

the side of the six-inch-high wooden platform. Lieutenant Ariciu called students to the platform one by one. He announced each student's name while Comrade Argesanu tied a red scarf around the slender neck of each boy and girl. The children beamed excitedly and stood tall as they were recognized in front of the entire village.

"You are now Pioneers," Lieutenant Ariciu said. "You must wear these scarves at all times. You'll not be allowed to join the Communist Party until you are older, but we will be helping you study communism and the Russian language."

Lieutenant Ariciu welcomed all the adults who were qualified to join the Communist Party. Then he began to extol the virtues of collective farms.

"From now on, everyone will work the same and split equally in the harvest. You will have more than you've had before."

Just before concluding, Lieutenant Ariciu said, "Everyone is to gather this evening at the primary school where we will show a film."

Then Lieutenant Ariciu dismissed everyone. The children chatted, happy to hear they didn't have to go back to school.

"A movie!" the children shouted. "We get to see a movie." They had heard of movies but had never seen one.

Cornel and Georgica were so excited about seeing a movie that they could hardly eat. Oprita urged them to finish the cabbage rolls she had stuffed that afternoon. She told the boys they didn't have to do chores and gave them permission to leave immediately for the schoolhouse.

"Your father and I will be along soon," she said as she shooed them out the door. Cornel and Georgica met their cousins in the street and then ran to the school.

They saw a truck over by the schoolhouse. It had been parked with the rear aimed at the center of the wall. The boys studied the two machines in the truck's bed.

"Look, a generator, just like they use at the carnival in the fall," said one of Cornel's friends.

"Oh, the carnival…I wish it was tomorrow. It's my favorite!" said Cornel. All the children nodded in agreement. The carnival was the one time of year when villagers could buy or barter for animals and household items they couldn't make or grow themselves. To the children, the carnival meant candy and riding on the one ride operated by a generator.

The smaller boys tried to pull themselves up over the side of the truck for a better look at the other machine.

"This thing will shine the movie to that wall." said an older boy who appeared behind the curious children.

Assured he was in the right spot for the big event, Cornel staked out a few feet of ground in front of the school wall, not far from the truck. Georgica and the others followed his lead.

Florica, Florina, and John showed up not long after the boys. Oprita and Marin appeared at exactly the designated time.

The recent rains had turned the school ground to mud, so most people didn't sit. They stood talking, most wondering how the changes would affect them. Some argued that their lives might improve, like Lieutenant Ariciu had said. Others questioned the effects communism would eventually have on their lives. A few people said they had been approached about joining the Communist Party.

Lieutenant Ariciu climbed into the truck bed and stood facing the crowd. "We have a film to show you. If you cooperate, you too can have this kind of wonderful life."

Cornel watched Lieutenant Ariciu simply touch the machine

and make light burst from a hole in its front. Romanian folk music filled the air. The side of the building suddenly came alive with beautiful wheat fields. Cornel's eyes grew wider as people appeared on the wall. They looked like a family of peasants, but these peasants sang while harvesting wheat. Then the happy family on the screen seemed to turn to Cornel and talk to him alone.

"Hail to Secretary General Gheorghiu-Dej of the Communist Party of Romania who is the greatest person in the world. Because of him, we have so much. It is so great to be part of the Communist Party. Thank you to the Leader of the Soviet Union Joseph Stalin for liberating us, getting us out of misery, and giving us more than we've had before. In five years, we are going to surpass the Americans."

The film continued with scenes of government trucks picking up riders. The people sang as they rode in the back, the communist flag waving in the wind. The trucks stopped at vibrant fields of wheat, and the happy people jumped down and went to work. The movie family again talked about how delighted everyone was with the collective farms. The children and adults sang and danced.

The scene on the wall changed to train cars being filled with wheat. Then the train started down the track. It gained speed and rapidly headed toward the front of the picture.

"It's going to run us over!" someone yelled. All the children screamed and instinctively jumped backward to get out of the way of the train. When they did so, they fell into a mud hole behind them. The parents laughed as the children emerged with mud-smeared shirts and dark faces.

When the film ended, Lieutenant Ariciu stood and again addressed the people of Rusanesti. "We'll be expecting you to sign up for the Communist Party and the collective farms."

In the months to come, the day's strange occurrences in Rusanesti were to be repeated in small villages all across Romania.

CHAPTER 6

Late Fall 1948 – Summer 1949

THE POOR AND LESS EDUCATED were asked to join the Communist Party first and were given jobs as tax collectors. Securitate Lieutenant Ariciu gave recruits authority to beat their fellow citizens if they didn't pay their taxes or if they failed to follow other communist dictates.

Lieutenant Ariciu placed Marin Dolana in the category of *chiabur*, people of middle class who could never join the Communist Party. Marin had graduated from high school and owned one hundred acres of land, which was reason enough for his exclusion from the Communist Party. The authorities needn't have bothered to exclude Marin. He had already made his decision never to succumb to totalitarian ways. He was among the villagers who banded together to defy the communists' initial push for collective farms. Independence was not something to be sacrificed easily.

Some villagers believed the communist propaganda. They lived by a river where people had become accustomed to going with the flow and adjusting to droughts, floods and other weather-related challenges. The government made promises and compromises that seemed decent at first. The strategies worked on villagers who could not see behind the tactics, and they myopically fell into the communist way of life.

Marin could see through the communist scheme. One compromise, which he expressed as a trap, was to allow peasants to participate in cooperative farms rather than collective farms. Instead of having to give up their land, people would work all lands together. Many people gave in to this ploy, but Marin remained unwilling to go along.

Lieutenant Ariciu selected George Dudescu, a well-respected man from Rusanesti, to be mayor. With Dudescu as the titular leader of Rusanesti, Lieutenant Ariciu hoped to lure the people willingly into the communist way. In his heart, Mayor Dudescu wasn't a communist, but he agreed to become mayor because he hoped the position would enable him to help the village.

Lieutenant Ariciu asked Mayor Dudescu to call a meeting. Everyone came, knowing they would be persecuted otherwise.

Securitate agents were brought in from other regions. The lineup, which also included Comrade Argesanu, was intended to intimidate. Lieutenant Ariciu walked commandingly to the front of the platform.

"There are those among you who are exploiting you and causing you to suffer," he announced.

"Down with capitalism!" yelled Constantin Ghigeanu, a poor village resident. Ten others joined in.

Marin Dolana and other neighbors were shocked and surprised to hear Rusanesti villagers speak up for communism. They did not realize these neighbors had been selected and paid by Lieutenant Ariciu to be vocal during meetings. The men selected had fourth-grade educations and little land, so they believed they had little to lose.

Lieutenant Ariciu continued his speech.

"The *chiaburi* and *burghezi* of your village are taking advantage of you. They don't pay you enough for the work you do, and they don't share their wealth with you."

"Down with the chiaburi and burghezi!" the shills yelled. The rest of the villagers again exchanged bewildered glances.

Two Securitate agents ushered a man onto the stage. Oprita's heart stopped. The handcuffed man was her cousin Mitruna who owned two hundred acres of land, twice the amount owned by the Dolanas.

"This man has refused to give up his land for the benefit of all of you. He is a traitor, and we find him guilty," said Lieutenant Ariciu.

"Give him the death penalty," Constantin yelled as if on cue.

The crowd let out an involuntary gasp, an indication that the incident had accomplished the shock value Ariciu intended.

The Dolanas knew the Ghigeanu family that lived in one of the mud homes on the other side of the village. One of the family's sons, Dumitru, was in the same class at school as Cornel. The Dolanas had tried to help the Ghigeanus many times in the past. They invited the family to dinner when they knew they didn't have enough to eat. On occasion, Marin hired Constantin to work in the fields and paid him a percentage of the harvest. Now Constantin stood proposing the death penalty for their relative.

Lieutenant Ariciu continued.

"He is condemned to prison and hard labor at the Danube-Black Sea Labor Camp. Those of you who do not cooperate are doomed to the same fate."

Marin had heard that prisoners at this labor camp were fed little and forced to dig deep canals with hand shovels. Inmates were often buried alive when unsecured walls collapsed on them. Marin feared he would be next on the Securitate list. It was the impact the arrest and sentence was intended to achieve.

During the next couple of months at village meetings, Securitate continued to bring people who owned the most land, one or two at a time, up on stage and announce their fate. Marin heard rumors that across Romania highly educated people were also being put in jail or executed. These groups, Marin figured, were feared by the new leaders.

Those who gave up their land voluntarily were honored. Lieutenant Ariciu would call a meeting, and everyone would gather at the village hall as required. Mayor Dudescu would usher onto stage people who had joined collective farms.

Lieutenant Ariciu would then announce, "We want to recognize those who have accepted the way of the future. You should thank these individuals, for they are helping to make a good life for this country and this village. Those of you who join the collective farms will have a better life."

At one meeting Lieutenant Ariciu announced, "Those of you who have not joined the collective farms are being asked to give a quota of last year's harvest to the government." Dismay spread among the people who had not yet given up their fields. The harvest not consumed by families and their animals was used to barter for other supplies.

Ariciu waited for the people to settle and announced a second requirement. "When you bring your quota of harvest, you also are requested to turn in any firearms."

The people were shocked. They could not understand why they had to give up their firearms, a means to important food sources.

Marin was among those who went home, selected a few bags of wheat and corn, and brought them back to the village hall. He sullenly turned in his double-barreled shotgun. Cornel was wistful when he saw his father surrender the shotgun. It meant the loss of special times hunting with his father and no more rabbit suppers.

No one wanted to give precious food to the government. Many peasants including the Dolanas removed some of their supplies from the storage bins and hid them in hay bales.

One morning as Marin worked by the river, he envisioned the entire village caught in a swift current and sucked into a whirlpool. Marin suspected that the communists would never let go of his village even if everyone relaxed and gave into their ways.

Marin remained unwilling to compromise on the collective farms. Each day he grew more guarded and less willing to discuss his views. He knew his neighbors felt the same way.

Late Summer 1949

WALKING HOME ONE MORNING from his task to return a borrowed needle for his mother, Cornel saw people gathered in front of his friend's house. He stopped to watch.

The people stepped back to make way for Popa Costica who was being led away by militieni. Cornel spotted the man's sons as they followed their father to the street.

"What is happening?" Cornel asked Daniel and Dan Costica.

"My tata, my tata," Daniel moaned. "The informers told on him. They are taking him and our grain."

Cornel ran home in a surge of panic.

Whipping around the corner and into the kitchen, Cornel came to a panting halt in front of his parents.

"They're coming down our street. Militia are going to find our hidden bags," Cornel yelled.

"Quiet. Be quiet now," said Marin. "It's too late to do anything. They'd see us if we tried to move our wheat and corn now. Go to the garden and do your chores. We will be right here."

Cornel obeyed. Pretending to work in the garden, he peered through the open spaces between slats of the five-foot-tall wood fence surrounding the Dolana house. *Maybe they won't stop here today*, he prayed.

The three Dolana dogs charged the fence, slamming into it as they snarled and barked. *They've come*, he thought. Cornel hid behind the barn. He hoped the dogs would keep the men away.

"Come out! Call off your dogs!" A voice yelled from the street.

Nothing happened. The voice shouted through the fence again.

"Marin Dolana, tie up these dogs now! You know what will happen. Come out now, or I'll lock you up in prison immediately."

Cornel peered around the corner of the barn and saw his father step from the back door. Cornel ran to help tie the dogs to a tree. Marin opened the gate to Comrade Argesanu and two villagers who were known informers paid by the communists. The informers held long sticks.

The two villagers headed to the large piles of hay and corn and wheat stalks. They began to stab at the stacks with their sticks. Argesanu looked on, tapping a hard rubber baton on his leg. The men repeatedly jabbed forward, then hauled the sticks back out. Cornel watched his father's face and tried to duplicate Marin's stony expression. But neither father nor son could help but flinch when one man's stick did not penetrate the haystack as deeply. The man buried his shoulder as he groped deeply in the hay, finally emerging with his prize, a plump bag.

Argesanu raised his baton and shook it at Marin. "You know this is not allowed."

It was not a question, so Marin remained silent.

Oprita appeared in the kitchen door with little Georgica beside her.

"We will have nothing to eat," she said loud enough to make sure Argesanu heard. "And what did you get for informing on us?" This she yelled at the searchers.

"Shut up!" Argesanu told her.

Georgica, scared and worried about his mother, grabbed her skirt and cried.

The informers continued their search. After they turned up ten bags, they dragged them to Argesanu's feet. Marin looked up at Argesanu, worried he would be sent to the canals.

"You're coming with us!" Argesanu said.

"Where are you taking him?" Oprita asked, trying not to sound as if she were begging.

"If you don't shut up, I'll take you in too," Argesanu said.

Cornel followed as Comrade Argesanu led his father down the street.

"Tata!"

"Go home, Cornica. Go to your mother," his father said.

Cornel ran to the house.

"Mama. Where are they taking Tata?" Cornel screamed. Oprita welcomed Cornel in her arms. She reached around and pulled Georgica into the embrace. The three wept.

"That's enough." Oprita drew away from her children. "We have to put everything back in piles before it gets ruined."

A few hours later, their barking dogs let them know someone

was at the gate. The boys rushed outside as their father came into the yard.

Marin wrapped his arms around his sons and walked toward the house. Oprita ran to her husband and pulled him into a squeezing embrace

He explained that Mayor Dudescu, whom he had known all his life, had stepped in to rescue him. Dudescu had pleaded with Marin to cooperate with the communists.

"He told me that for old time's sake he could overlook the hidden grain," Marin relayed. "He made it clear he couldn't help us again."

With less grain, Oprita cut back on food she prepared for the family. There was still grain in the storage bins, but if they ate it, there would be no seed to plant next year's crop.

The following Saturday evening, Cornel's two uncles came to the Dolana home. Father Manoila and four men from surrounding villages joined them. The men assembled in the guest room. One man was a stranger to Cornel.

The Dolana home had become a favored meeting place because it was off the main street. The men could walk through the forest or along the river so they wouldn't be detected as they made their way. Marin or one of the Dolanas would have to meet them at the back gate to keep the dogs from attacking them. On occasion, men who lived long distances away would spend the night. Marin shared his tuica, and everyone shared news they'd heard from Bucharest.

Cornel hung outside the door, hoping to find out what was going on. Once the tuica started flowing, he knew the voices would grow loud enough for him to hear.

The men talked about whether the Americans were going to

liberate them from communism. Marin shared his story of the close run-in with the authorities. Others shared similar stories and told of some men who were taken to jail.

Cornel recognized the voice of a man from Cilieni.

"We have a large group of resisters, and we've banded together," the man said. "We're not going to let them take our land."

"We can't," the other men vowed.

The Cilieni man continued, "I want to introduce all of you to Ion. He has been helping villages like ours to resist."

Everyone welcomed Ion and thanked him for his efforts.

"Marin, I need to ask you a big favor," the Cilieni man said. "We need a place for Ion to hide. Can he stay with your family?"

"I don't think we're being watched any more closely than other villagers. We'd be honored to have him."

All the men but one dispersed. Marin escorted Ion into the kitchen. Cornel followed, peering at the stranger who was a little shorter and heavier than his father.

"Oprita. We're going to have a visitor for a while. His name is Ion Popescu. Please prepare the guest bed for him," Marin announced.

Ion stayed for a few days, and then the mysterious man left.

Chapter 7

Fall 1949

WITH THE END OF SUMMER, the children returned to school. This was a particularly beautiful fall day. Professor Voinea granted his students a fifteen-minute recess after a morning spent conducting lessons in Russian grammar.

The boys ran outside to grab the three-foot swords of wood they'd left propped against a tree. The boys took sides, six on each, and began their mock battle. Dumitru Ghigeanu swung his sword at Cornel who blocked the blow. Their swords clunked heavily against each other. Cornel gained the upper hand.

Frustrated, Dumitru threw his sword to the side and dove at Cornel. Cornel bent forward, and Dumitru went tumbling over Cornel's back. Dumitru yelled in pain.

The teacher sent a student running to tell Dumitru's father. Constantin Ghigeanu checked on his son and then stormed into the classroom. He zeroed in on Cornel and swore and yelled at him.

"You worthless, horrible boy! You broke my son's leg. You don't deserve to live. You and your chiabur family are destroying this village."

Cornel trembled in his seat, tears dropping from the corner of his eyes. He had wanted to defend himself, but Dumitru's father wouldn't give him the chance.

"I'm going to have you thrown out of school. Comrade Argesanu will hear about this."

Constantin carried his son home.

When Cornel saw Argesanu enter the classroom the following day, the boy froze in place. He wished he could disappear. What had Dumitru's father said? Was Argesanu going to arrest him? Was he going to be sent to jail? Cornel's eyes grew wide when Argesanu looked right at him.

"You are not worthy of being a communist and neither are your friends," said Comrade Argesanu. He called each one by name. "All of you come to the front of the class." Each shook with fear as Cornel and his fellow sword fighters rose and walked to the front of the class.

"You are being stripped of your Pioneer status," Argesanu said as if they were criminals. He removed the scarves each student had been required to wear to school since they had been issued at the initial ceremony. "You will never be allowed to join the Communist Party."

Argesanu left the school. The boys returned to their seats with great sighs of relief. After school let out, Cornel saw that Georgica's scarf was also gone.

A few days later, Grivei, Pasalica, and Mozoc notified the Dolanas that people were near their home. Two uniformed men entered through the front gate to avoid the dogs and walked up to Marin who was standing near the front door.

"We need to meet with you," Lieutenant Ariciu insisted. Comrade Argesanu stood beside him with a glaring look. The two men proceeded into the house past a startled Oprita. In the middle room, they pushed the table over to the bed to make room for three and motioned for Marin to sit.

Ion Popescu, who had returned a few days before to take refuge at the Dolanas, heard the men come into the adjacent room. The guest room provided no means of escape because bars covered the two windows. The door to his room was locked. He hid himself between the bed and wall and hoped they wouldn't search the house.

"We have decided to give you a choice," Lieutenant Ariciu told Marin. "You can choose to join the collective farms like many of your neighbors. Or, you can accept a different one hundred acres of land, and you and your family can continue to farm independently."

"If you decide to take the one hundred acres," Comrade Argesanu interjected, "you will be required to give 85 percent of your harvest to the government. If you don't give it to us willingly, we will come and take it forcefully."

"Why not let me keep the land I own now?" Marin asked.

"Your land is closer and much better-suited for the collective farms than the land that we would trade you," Lieutenant Ariciu stated.

"Where is this land?"

"You can come by the village hall, and we will show you on the map," Lieutenant Ariciu stated. "You'll need to go to Rosiorii de Vede and Vedele, the closest villages to where the land is located, and register your ownership."

"How can I work there? Do you realize how long it would take to get to the fields? It would take me more than a day."

"We recognize it would be a hardship. That is why you are

given the choice of joining the collective farms. You know it would be better for your family and better for your community."

Marin did not buy what the lieutenant was selling. His family had worked hard for many generations to acquire land, and he didn't want to be the one who lost any of it. He felt trapped; if he tried to hold on to his original acreage, he would go to jail, and the family would lose everything. The alternative acreage was better than joining the collective farms.

"Our own land is important to our family," Marin stated with pride. "We will accept the trade."

The men left without searching the house.

Later that week, as the family gathered around the dinner table, Marin showed the family his plans for building a false wall in the kitchen.

"First we need to make some bricks. Then we will work from the inside, and no one but us will know. If we don't do this, we will be left with only 15 percent of our harvest. You know that would not be enough to live on."

Marin explained that they would access the hidden space through the attic. The hole would be large enough for many bags of cornmeal and wheat flour as well as bags of wheat and corn seed.

As they went about their chores, the family began work on the bricks for the wall. They mixed mud, cow dung, and hay and pressed the mixture into a wooden form. They dumped out the formed mixture and let it dry for a week. Marin cautioned everyone daily to never even hint about their false wall to anyone, even their closest friends. Now that many of their friends and neighbors had joined the Communist Party, the Dolanas couldn't trust anyone.

Once they finished making the bricks, they moved them into the kitchen and built the wall.

Early Spring 1950

SPRING TEMPERATURES SOON melted the snow and Marin announced they would begin going to their new fields. "Cornel, until school is over for the summer, you're going to be responsible for looking after Georgica and everything at the house."

Oprita made bread and cheese for the two boys and packed up similar food for Marin, John, Florica, and herself. John and Marin loaded supplies and farming tools into their wooden wagon and hitched the horse. Cornel and Georgica, now twelve and eleven years old, waved good-bye as the wagon pulled away.

Before they left the house for school, Cornel and Georgica ate the bread and cheese. The two dogs that remained at home tried to squeeze between the boys' legs as they went through the gate. The brothers patted the dogs on the head and told them they had to guard the house.

Spring rains fell as the boys returned home. They enjoyed the feel of mud easing through their toes as they walked through the streets. A block before they reached their house, Cornel whistled to the dogs.

"Grivei, Mozoc," Cornel yelled. The dogs yelped and barked in delight.

Georgica opened the gate, and the dogs jumped up on them with muddy paws and licked their faces. Cornel petted Mozoc while Georgica played with Grivei. Cornel felt safe at home with the dogs there to help protect them.

The rain meant fewer chores, for which the boys were thankful.

They still had to feed the animals, but they could wait a day or two to turn the soil in the garden. Their parents had instructed them to plant onions, lettuce, carrots, peppers, and tomato seeds. After feeding the animals, Cornel and Georgica each cut their own bread, cheese, and onion for supper.

When they finished their meal, they walked next door to their Aunt Marita's house. There they drew a bucket of water and hauled firewood to her kitchen. The boys took after their parents who were always willing to help others. Georgica was growing up to be a hard-working, quiet and polite boy who was always respectful of others. Cornel appreciated the fact that Georgica respected him.

By the time they got around to studying their lessons, it was too dark to see. Cornel lit the kerosene lamps so they could do their homework.

The family returned a week later. The grueling forty-mile trip and long days working the fields had taken its toll on them. Cornel had never seen them so exhausted, yet they had no time for rest. They loaded more supplies and returned to the fields.

Each time his parents returned to Rusanesti, they were more fatigued than they'd been the week before. Cornel worried about their physical deterioration. For the first time in his life, Cornel was not looking forward to summer recess.

Chapter 8

Spring-Fall 1950

T HE DREADED LAST DAY OF SCHOOL CAME, and Cornel tried to resign himself to the months of field work ahead of him.

Cornel and Georgica took their time walking home from school as if that would delay the inevitable. They petted the dogs when they came through the gate and looked to see signs of their family. The horses and wagon weren't in the yard.

"Cornel! Georgica!" someone yelled from the house.

The two boys stopped playing with the dogs and looked up to see that it was their brother Aristotel.

"You're home!" yelled Cornel. They ran to each other with open arms. Cornel and Georgica were happy to see their brother, to learn of his adventures, and to have help with chores around the house.

Aristotel had traveled from Resita, where he was attending a trade school to learn how to be a mechanic. It was a far cry from Aristotel's dream to be a priest. Cornel had witnessed his brother's disappointment two years earlier when the communists had forced the closure of many churches, and being a priest was no longer a career choice for a young man.

The rest of the family returned to Rusanesti the next day. They took only a few moments to catch up with Aristotel, knowing there was much to prepare for their coming week away from home. They would have hours to talk with Aristotel on the long trip to the field. Oprita did take the time to comment on how Aristotel had grown much taller than the rest of the family.

They prepared enough supplies for a week. Oprita and Florica baked several loaves of bread, fried a chicken, and boxed up onions and cheese. Georgica caught and tied up a chicken that would be kept alive until later in the week. Marin, John, Aristotel, and Cornel loaded corn seed and hay into the wagon and then placed the blankets and tools on top.

Their plan had been to leave one family member at home, but Marin decided everyone was needed in the fields. Oprita asked one of her cousins to look after their animals and garden.

By midnight they were ready to leave. The horses were hitched to the wagon and everyone but Marin crawled in and snuggled between the blankets.

Marin brought the horses to a stop when they reached the Olt River shoreline. This particular day, he thought the river was low enough to cross about a mile north without spending extra time going south to Cilieni to take the ferry across the river. They all crawled off of the wagon to lessen the weight.

A three-quarters moon provided light as Marin and John each guided a horse by holding its leather harness. They hit the horses with a stick to force them to move at a faster pace as the four other family members pushed on the back of the wagon. If the wagon slowed or stopped for a second, the wheels would sink and get stuck in the riverbed sand. The wagon swayed in the current. Cornel and Georgica held on tight as the water reached their chests. They could feel the wheels start to settle in the sand at one point. Marin and John hit the horses harder and yelled, "Hey, hey, keep moving," while Oprita, Florica, and Aristotel pushed the wagon with all their strength. The wheels finally rolled onto dry ground.

"Whoa, whoa," Marin yelled at the horses when they reached flat ground. He was greeted by Pasalica and Mozoc. The dogs had swum across the river and were waiting patiently on the far bank for the wagon to catch up.

"Okay, we made it," Marin called to his family behind him. "We'll let the horses rest here for a while. Everyone can get back in the wagon and get some rest, and when the horses are ready, I'll take us from here."

They couldn't stop long or they wouldn't have time to work the field and plant all the corn. Cornel and Georgica immediately fell back to sleep. John closed his eyes knowing he would get the next shift. Florica and Aristotel climbed aboard and tried to get comfortable. Oprita stayed by her husband until they were ready to go.

Marin decided the horses had rested enough. He grabbed one of them by the handmade halter and led the team down the path. He turned the horses to the left when they reached the main dirt road, then scrambled aboard the wagon. Marin did not own reins, but he didn't need them. The horses would continue down the road if he occasionally clicked his tongue.

Sleep didn't come easily to those trying to rest. The wagon jumped and jarred as the wheels hit holes and ruts in the dirt road. In one area where it had rained, the wagon wheels got stuck. The older children helped push the wagon while Marin pulled the horses forward until the wheels moved freely.

Marin again rested the horses halfway into the trip, when they reached Turk's Well, a place named after the Turks who fought battles and occupied the area in the 1400s. To allow his father some much-needed rest, John watched the horses during the break and then led the animals along the path.

Marin awoke after a short sleep. Cornel woke when he heard his father stir.

"How much farther, Tata?"

"Very soon, very soon."

John grabbed the halter of one horse to stop the wagon at the field. Work began immediately and continued until dark. Most evenings everyone was so exhausted that they'd eat, then spread their blankets on the ground and fall asleep immediately. The first several days they could sleep on hay, but by the end of the week, the horses had consumed it all. Seven nights of living outdoors and working hard all day on only four or five hours of sleep was an exhausting routine.

Marin tried to lift their spirits by telling stories. The family favorite was Marin's version of Dracula. The children had heard it many times, but welcomed the distraction.

"Prince Dracula was a great warrior from Wallachia," Marin began. "After Dracula beat the Turks in a battle, the Turks regrouped with a bigger army and sent a commando to kill Dracula. Dracula figured they wanted to kill him, and so he asked someone who looked like him to sleep in his tent while he slept with the soldiers. A Turk quietly slipped into Dracula's tent."

Marin acted out sneaking into the tent with a knife. "He killed the man sleeping there. The commando returned to the Turkish army leader and told him he had stabbed Dracula to death with his knife.

"To revenge the killing of his double, Dracula gathered dead Turks from the next battle and impaled each with a stick through their bodies and displayed them around the battlefield." Marin jumped around pretending to jam a stick through bodies.

"The Turks returned and were shocked by the dead bodies standing up on sticks. When they saw Dracula riding around on his horse, they thought it was his ghost that had been brought back from the dead. They were so scared they rode away in fear." Pretending he was Dracula, Marin raised his arm and claimed victory to his army. The family cheered.

The children finally settled down and spread their bedding on the ground around the fire. They cuddled into their mother's handmade blankets, which they topped with their coats Oprita had made out of wool from their own sheep. Mozoc snuggled close to Cornel. Pasalica lay by Georgica. It didn't take long for the young boys to fall asleep. No one tended the fire through the night. As temperatures dropped, Cornel pulled his wraps over his head.

Two more long days of hard work extended past dark. Cornel was exhausted. He knew it wouldn't do any good to complain. His father and mother, obviously fatigued, were doing their best to keep everyone motivated.

They finally started the long journey home. When they ran into hard rains, the roads turned to mud, slowing their progress. A few times along the forty-mile journey, the wheels sank deeply into the mud. They lost precious time and energy freeing the wagon.

Marin knew they could not ford the Olt River that day. They would lose two more hours by going to the ferry, but that was better than losing their wagon, horses or endangering his family. As they waited for the ferry, the Dolanas washed the mud from their bodies and clothes at the river's edge. They tracked the ferry's progress to their side of the river, the children fascinated by the pulley system of a chain that spanned the width of the river. Two other wagons arrived. The ferry anchored to shore. Each family led their horses and wagon onto the flat wooden surface and waited patiently for the twenty-minute ride to the other side. Seeing the swollen river and velocity of the current, Marin was thankful he'd made the decision to take the safer route.

When they finally reached home, Cornel did his chores and went to bed.

Cornel wondered whether his mother had slept at all when she woke him for breakfast. "After you eat, we need to finish planting the garden," said Oprita.

In between trips to the fields, the Dolanas tended to their garden, which the communists allowed. Thankfully, they did not have to turn over 85 percent of their garden produce to the communists. Oprita canned what they did not eat to help them get through the winter.

The family kept working and traveling the long distance each week to work the fields. Their bodies grew increasingly exhausted.

When they harvested the wheat, they tried to time their arrival to their home in the middle of the night so they could put a portion of their crop behind the false wall before turning over 85 percent of it to the government.

Next they harvested canepa, planted to provide fibers for clothing, blankets, rugs, and rope. *Canepa* was tied together in a bunch and left submerged in a protected cove of the Olt River. After the water softened the stalks, the family worked to remove the outer stalk by first smashing it with a club and then hitting it against a tree to retrieve the inner fibers of the plant.

In August and September, the Dolanas harvested corn and sunflowers, followed by the most demanding work of picking cotton. Cornel hated picking cotton because the sharp pods would puncture his hands and fingers. In the past, his mother only weaved cotton garments for herself and Florica. Cornel and his brothers' clothes were made from the scratchy canepa. This year they'd have to give the majority of the cotton to the government so each time the pods pricked his hands, he felt as if he were being punished by Lieutenant Ariciu and Comrade Argesanu.

In the fall Aristotel returned to Resita, and the young boys started school. But Marin, Oprita, Florica, and John worked on. It was the only way to keep from losing their land.

PART III

Impact of Resisting

CHAPTER 9

Late Fall 1950

Oprita's cousin Marin Popa, from the neighboring village of Cilieni, walked into the Dolana home just before dawn, startling Oprita.

"Well, good morning. Are you going fishing this morning? Marin didn't mention preparing breakfast for you."

"I have news for Marin," Marin Popa said, his voice cracking. Oprita saw the gravity of the situation in his eyes.

Cornel had finished collecting eggs when he saw his cousin arrive. He knew something was wrong by the way he walked down the path. He stood by the kitchen door to listen.

Cornel's father came into the room and asked, "What's going on?"

"A group of resisters from Cilieni revolted last night against all communists who worked at the village hall," said Marin Popa. "Without guns, the resisters were armed only with knives and axes. They killed the mayor, the mayor's assistant, and some militieni and Securitate."

"Unbelievable," Marin said.

Marin Popa continued, "Unfortunately, there were too many Securitate agents who intervened and arrested some of the leaders of the revolt. Ion escaped. If it's okay, he's going to need to hide out here for a while."

63

"He's welcome here anytime," Marin replied, knowing the risk.

"Lieutenant Ariciu of the Securitate is asking questions of every-one in Cilieni to find out who was involved," said Marin Popa.

Cornel couldn't tell from the conversation whether his cousin had been involved in the attack on the communists, but he figured that Ion had participated. He was glad to hear Ion was coming back. An intelligent man schooled in engineering, Ion never told stories of his anti-communist activities to Cornel. They spent their time together on lessons. Thanks to Ion's tutoring, Cornel's grades, particularly in math, were improving.

"Will you stay for breakfast?" asked Oprita.

Marin Popa nodded, and Oprita set the table for one more.

"Did you hear they dismissed Mayor Dudescu?" Marin asked their guest.

"Yes, I heard," Marin Popa replied.

"Lieutenant Ariciu thought he was too soft," Marin Dolana continued. "They wanted someone in that office who would make people obey the communist rules."

"I'm beginning to think it's hopeless," Marin Popa said. "Too many people are scared and giving in to the communists. The Securitate is too strong. They'll never give up until they've taken everything away from us."

For the next month, Marin Popa kept the Dolanas informed of the government's actions. In Cilieni, the Securitate, led by Lieutenant Ariciu, continued their search for information. They interviewed everyone and beat people harshly if they didn't get the answers they wanted. They arrested all the resisters they could identify and hauled them away in small, motorized security wagons. Then Lieutenant Ariciu began expanding his investigation to outlying villages.

Snow came early and took its toll on the region. The people

who had not joined the collective farms had less to eat, just when they most needed nourishment against the bitter temperatures.

Early Winter 1950

CORNEL STEPPED BAREFOOT out of the elementary school into a foot of freshly fallen snow. Georgica followed close behind; Cornel knew he'd have to keep an eye on him. They usually looked forward to snow, but temperatures had dropped drastically. The wind cut sharply through their thin shirts and long underwear that covered their legs.

Cornel's bare toes felt the cold, and he wished he and Georgica had thought to bring their heavy wool socks which were their only defense against freezing temperatures. This morning they thought they could make do without their socks and their wool coats. Cornel took Georgica's hand to help him through the deep drifts.

When they arrived home, their mother greeted them with the socks she had sitting by the fire, so the boy's feet felt better as soon as they put them on. The boys then stood by fire in the kitchen to warm the rest of their bodies.

The foot-and-a-half-thick walls of their stucco-brick home provided some insulation against the cold. Nevertheless, the crooked doors and windows allowed the wind to whip through the house. Each room in the house had its own heating source. The open fire in the kitchen was built on the dirt floor, but the other three rooms of the house had a heating stove made of brick, which was cemented over for a smooth surface before being whitewashed. Still, on cold, windy nights, the home was far from comfortable. The family slept in one room to save wood and to take advantage of each other's body heat.

When the chill wore off, Cornel helped gather firewood for the kitchen and stacked wood in the bedroom where the family slept together in the winter.

Ion was staying the night in the guest bedroom with the door locked. Not willing to risk capture and to minimize putting the Dolanas in danger, Ion would not leave or return to the house unless it was in the middle of the night.

The guest room was the most ornate and had more amenities than the other rooms of the house. Rust-colored ceramic tiles covered the entire stove heater and pipe from floor to ceiling. When the light was shining on the tiles, a beautiful glow illuminated the room. Oprita's most valued woven rug hung beside the bed. The product of many hours of hand-woven work with canepa fibers, the rug was a profusion of red and burgundy flowers against a black background. Another prized hand-woven rug, this one a red-and-black pattern, lay on the ground in front of the bed. It provided some warmth against the cold dirt floor.

White curtains hung over the windows and covered the vertical bars. During these times of rationing, it was not uncommon for the desperate to steal. To survive, people often took from others, and Gypsies regularly robbed homes as they passed through villages.

Cornel knocked on the guest room door to deliver wood. Ion unlocked the door and smiled in appreciation. Cornel opened the stove's solid door, which was four feet up from the floor. He placed wood into the opening, then closed and latched it.

"Could you use help with your homework tonight?" Ion asked.

"Yes! Thank you!" Cornel said without hesitation. "I do have to finish my chores first."

"I'll see you in a little while."

After he completed his chores, Cornel grabbed his books and more firewood. He knocked as he entered Ion's room.

Cornel sat on the bed and ran his hand over the red-and-black comforter filled with horse hair. Ion pulled up a chair and looked at Cornel's math assignment. When Cornel struggled, Ion helped him to understand how to work through the problem to come up with the correct answer. Cornel caught on quickly and answered many without additional help.

"Supper!" Oprita yelled.

Ion and Cornel joined the family. Cornel was pleased to see his older brother John at the supper table. He liked it when one of his older brothers visited because they always helped around the house. He seldom saw Aristotel who was living in Resita. After John married Florina and moved over a mile and a half away, he wasn't around all the time. Cornel guessed his brother would stay the night instead of walking through the frigid night air.

After supper, Ion thanked Oprita for dinner and the extra blankets she had offered to him. He returned to the guest room and instinctively locked the door.

The family moved to the main bedroom, where the fire brought the room to fifty-five degrees Fahrenheit. Marin removed bricks from beside the stove and put them under the covers of both beds to warm them. Cornel, John, and Marin crawled under the wool blankets in one bed; Oprita, Florica, and Georgica slept in the other. When the fire went out, the room temperature dropped to forty-five degrees. Cornel, feeling the chill, pulled up the extra blankets at the foot of the bed. Soon everyone was asleep.

A pounding on their front door startled everyone out of their deep sleep. John and Florica jumped out of bed and made their way through the darkness. The dogs were barking ferociously in the backyard. John and Florica saw lights from a car shining through the front door's window and knew it had to be the Securitate, because they were the only ones with vehicles.

"Open the door," Lieutenant Ariciu yelled.

John and Florica stood still, hoping they would go away.

All of a sudden, the window shattered, the lock gave way, and the door swung open and struck Florica. She stumbled backward, hit the side of the bed, and fell to the floor. Ten Securitate agents charged through the opening. Before John could react, four men pinned him to the floor. They beat him with the butts of their guns and kicked his body.

Horrified, Florica screamed. She scooted toward the bed, put her back against the bed frame, and sat on the dirt floor. She wrapped her arms across her chest in a defensive position. In between her high pitched terrifying screams, she yelled at the men who were beating her brother, "Stop, please stop, don't kill him. No, no, no, please don't."

She wondered why her father or brothers did not come to help her and John, but she could not hear their screams over hers.

Four men had charged the main bedroom. One had a flashlight, which provided a clear view. One man grabbed Marin by the collar and held him while the other men slammed him with the butts of their guns.

Cornel tried to grab his father's shirt and yelled out, "Tata, Tata," but the men knocked him away and then dragged Marin to the floor.

Marin put his hand up to his head just as a rifle stock jarred his skull. He convulsed with each punch and kick that met his body.

"Please stop! Please have mercy!" Oprita screamed. She and Georgica had gotten out of the bed and went to the corner of the room. Oprita trembled with remorse that she couldn't save her husband or find out what was happening to her son and daughter in the other room. Tears of helplessness and fear flowed steadily from her eyes.

In the center room, Lieutenant Ariciu stood erect, a flashlight shining on his men beating the young man. He watched until he was sure his men had accomplished their first task satisfactorily. John lay unconscious on the floor. Florica's tears flowed, and her screaming continued. Lieutenant Ariciu looked at her in disgust as he turned to enter the bedroom.

"Please stop! Please stop!" Oprita continued to scream to the men beating her husband. When she saw Lieutenant Ariciu enter the room, her terror intensified.

The men beat Marin while they swore and yelled, "Traitor, capitalist, chiabur."

Too scared and stunned to react, Cornel and Georgica stared at the horror unfolding before them.

Lieutenant Ariciu stood by the door. His normally stoic face took on a sinister grin as if he were thoroughly enjoying every blow Marin received.

After they tied Marin up, they pushed Cornel off the bed, and he landed on the floor between the two beds. Ariciu lifted the pillows and discovered Marin's Beretta semi-automatic pistol. Finding such a weapon infuriated Ariciu. This was a gun that long ago should have been turned over to him. He looked at his men, and twitched his head toward Marin. The men took this as a signal to resume the beating with intensity.

"Do you have more guns? Tell us where they are!" Lieutenant Ariciu demanded after his men had beaten Marin to his satisfaction.

"I have no more," Marin struggled to say.

Hitting him across the face, Ariciu said, "Tell us the truth."

"I'm telling the truth."

The Securitate agents tore the blankets off the beds one by one. They felt the straw mattresses. They bent to search under the beds.

One man grabbed Cornel and shoved him into the corner where Georgica was already huddled. Cornel held on to his brother, both paralyzed with fright from not only what they were witnessing with their eyes, but what they were hearing with their ears. They could not hear their brother. Florica's screams had turned to sobs.

The two remaining Securitate agents searched the rest of the house and found a locked door. Cornel heard the door crash in and knew it had to be Ion's room — the one with bars on the windows. Ion had no way to escape. Cornel could hear moans as they beat him.

Lieutenant Ariciu returned to the center room and looked harshly at Florica who had not moved from the floor. She started screaming again. He demanded she be quiet. She tried to strike him when he came within range, but she couldn't stop his approach. He slapped her hard across the face and kicked her. She screamed even louder.

They finally stopped beating Marin, but the beating of Ion went on.

Lieutenant Ariciu came back into the bedroom and grabbed Oprita.

Cornel and Georgica screamed, "Mama, Mama, Mama," as the men forcefully led her out the bedroom door and into the kitchen.

"Why were you hiding this man in your house?"

"He was just a guest."

"Have your husband and Ion helped to turn people against communism?"

"My husband's a good man. All we ever wanted to do was to take care of ourselves and our land. We have no interest in politics or conspiracy. We mean no harm."

Lieutenant Ariciu slapped her hard across her face.

"We want the truth! How long have you been hiding Ion in your home?"

Oprita cried. He continued to drill her. But she didn't say another word. She just cried and covered her face with her hands. He finally let her be and turned his attention back to Marin.

"Get up!" Lieutenant Ariciu yelled at Marin. Marin tried, but with broken bones and tied hands, he didn't have the leverage to rise. Two men grabbed Marin's arms and dragged him through the house, out the door, and down the long icy path where a military vehicle awaited them. The men shoved Marin into the side door.

Ion's cries finally stopped. Lieutenant Ariciu supervised as two other men dragged Ion's body through the house and outside to the street. Three men threw Ion into their vehicle.

Oprita heard vehicles move down the street. Still crying, she ran to her eldest son. He was conscious, bloody, and moaning.

"Oh, my God, what have they done to you? What will they do to your father? What will we do without him?"

Oprita lit the kerosene lamp so she could see to tend to John. Florica draped a rug over the front door window to keep out the cold and wind, which had stolen the heat from the house. They all helped John into the family bedroom and onto the mattress where they covered him with blankets.

Cornel and Georgica put more logs in the bedroom stove.

Then they started a fire in the kitchen to warm a bucket of water that had frozen overnight.

Through tears, Oprita and Florica tended to John all night. With no doctor, they did what they could, staunching the blood, cleaning his wounds and keeping him warm. The boys couldn't sleep and continually prayed that their brother would survive.

Oprita made breakfast when sunlight finally helped to fade the darkness of the night. John struggled but was able to eat a little.

After Cornel and Georgica completed their chores, Oprita asked Cornel to walk to John's home and tell his wife, Florina, what had happened. John told Cornel not to bring her back. He did not want her to see his battered body.

Oprita could see that Cornel was apprehensive about leaving.

"Don't talk to anyone, don't say what happened," Oprita cautioned.

People stared at Cornel as he made his way through the streets. He heard people talking about others who were arrested and how Securitate had searched every village in that region. Word somehow spread about his father, and Cornel could hear people whisper about Marin and the anti-communist he had been hiding. Villagers seemed surprised; they had not known Marin had taken in an important stranger.

The biggest topic of discussion in the village was that the priest had been arrested. They had confiscated Father Manoila's house a year earlier, turning it into the village hall, but had allowed him and his family to live in a tiny room in the back of the house. Now he was in prison.

Cornel sensed gripping fear in the village. *Who would be tortured next?*

CHAPTER 10

December 1950 – April 1951

OPRITA CRIED WHEN SHE WAS ALONE. The longing for her husband and despair over the changing world was almost more than she could bear. She forced herself to remain strong for her family. Her children were worried they might never see their father again.

"If only they'd tell us where he's been taken," Oprita said, implying her slight hope that he'd been imprisoned and not killed.

John's wounds slowly healed, and the family took solace in the fact that he survived. If they had lost John too, the family would have had a hard time holding on to any hope.

Cornel missed his father. His mother and John discussed his father's possible fate, but they always brushed a sheen of optimism over their conversations in case the younger children were listening. Hearing his mother cry when she was in another room, Cornel cried for both parents. He made a promise to himself that somehow he would get back at Lieutenant Ariciu, the man who had brought harsh conditions and tragedy to their family.

Cornel also missed Ion and his tutoring. The family never mentioned Ion's name or discussed his potential fate. They trusted no one, and one innocent word would be risking further reprimand from the Securitate.

The harsh winter, with snowfall exceeding the height of their windows, added a new element to the endurance test. Animals still needed to be fed and watered. They prayed that the wood they had chopped and stacked in the fall would last until the thaw; if it did not, the family might freeze.

Harsh weather didn't provide the young ones a break from school. Teachers expected students to attend even on the most extreme weather days. Cornel and Georgica never missed a day. Oprita stressed the importance of education. An intelligent and educated woman, she taught her children how to speak French. No one else in their village knew French, but it was her favorite language, and she wanted her children to love it like she did.

Oprita also enjoyed reading, but she had no time for books now. Oprita and Florica worked day and night, partially to beat back their anxiety but also out of necessity.

As John healed, he tried to help as much as possible, but he had to care for his own house and animals. Cornel and Georgica helped when they could. They were on their best behavior and completed their chores before they were asked to do them.

Spring brought added stress. They had managed when Marin was away at war, but the world was much different now and their fields were farther away. The Dolanas were relieved that Aristotel traveled to Rusanesti from Resita to help work the distant fields. The entire family worked twenty hours a day to put in the seed, even while knowing they'd have to turn over most of the yield. If they were to eat, they had no choice but to keep farming.

Late Spring – Summer 1951

SIX MONTHS AFTER MARIN AND ION were dragged from the house, the Dolanas learned by word of mouth that Marin was in a prison in Craiova and was going to trial. Hope crept back into the Dolana home. All of this time, they had not known his fate.

Oprita, John, and Aristotel reported to Comrade Argesanu to receive permission to leave Rusanesti to attend the trial in Craiova. Then the three walked eight hours to the train station in Caracal. They could have walked four hours to the station in Studina, but the wait to change trains in Caracal would have been longer than the extra time to walk. They took the hour and a half train ride to Craiova.

They reached the courthouse before the military tribunal began. John saw Marin through the gate.

"Tata, we're here. Tata," John screamed.

"Marin!" Oprita cried.

Marin looked up, and his drained soul brightened for an instant. His hands and feet were in shackles and his body was emaciated.

"Don't talk to this man. Leave!" yelled the guard as he hit Marin across the back to make him turn away.

Oprita and her two sons saw Marin again as the guard brought him to the door of the courtroom. The Dolana family was not allowed to enter and waited outside for the news.

Inside, the military trial began. The prosecutors stated that Marin was accused of conspiracy against the state. Marin was not allowed to defend himself, and no lawyer was appointed to him. Only the prosecutor spoke. After hearing the charges and without any discussion, the judge declared Marin guilty.

Oprita, John, and Aristotel watched the courtroom door intently as they waited for Marin to exit. The doors opened and Marin was led out, still in shackles and chains.

"Marin!" Oprita yelled.

He turned his head to see his family, but guards hit him across the back of his head, thrust him forward, and took him away.

John left his mother and brother to discover how they could learn Marin's fate. He returned with bad news.

"We won't be able to find out father's sentence until tomorrow," John told them.

They spent the night on the courthouse steps. People filed past them in the morning. They kept their eyes peeled to the door where announcements were posted. Finally, a man came and attached a piece of paper. As John read through the list, he found his father's name.

Oprita looked at John and knew the news was not good.

"They've sentenced him to three more years," John said. Oprita's knees collapsed, but John and Aristotel caught her as she fell. Tears erupted.

Oprita had prayed daily for her husband's release, once she learned he was alive. Even though her prayers weren't answered, her faith in God didn't waiver. Her prayers beseeched God to allow her husband to survive. In her brief glimpse of him at the courthouse, she had not missed the bruises that covered his face and arms; what was covered by his clothing? He had lost weight and appeared weak. What had he endured and could he survive three more years in prison? Now that he had been sentenced, would the torture continue? Oprita had every reason to be concerned.

At home, Florica, Cornel, and Georgica waited and prayed that their father would be with their mother and brothers when they returned to Rusanesti. When they heard voices, they ran outside, hoping to see their father.

"Father won't be coming home," John said.

Oprita hugged her youngest. She couldn't hold back the tears as she offered what comfort she had to give. "We're doing okay, and we have to continue to do well for your father."

The Dolanas worked ceaselessly and managed to farm all one-hundred acres. They even harvested corn from the field forty miles away, only to receive three bags as their portion. Oprita resolved that three bags were not enough to justify the damage to her family. She decided they would not farm that field next season even though Lieutenant Ariciu would reclaim the land. She hated to let Marin down and lose the acreage, but she decided her energy should go toward doing what she could to keep the rest of the land.

Summer 1952

MIDWAY THROUGH THE SUMMER, Grivei, Pasalica, and Mozoc sent out a warning that unwelcome visitors were again at their back gate. Cornel looked out the window at a truck coming to a halt outside his gate. He recognized two of the men riding up front.

"Mama, the Securitate are here!" Cornel yelled in a panic, but he raised enough courage to follow Oprita out into the yard.

The three dogs barked and then shifted into low growls, baring their teeth as several men jumped off the truck.

Oprita didn't say anything, waiting to hear what they wanted. Grivei, Pasalica, and Mozoc continued to bristle and growl.

"Calm your dogs," demanded Lieutenant Ariciu, Comrade Argesanu at his side.

Cornel tied up Grivei while Oprita corralled Pasalica. Cornel called to Mozoc as the men swung the gate open. One man slipped a noose around Mozoc's neck. The surprised dog turned and snapped at the man, who tightened the noose.

"What are you doing," yelled Cornel. "Don't hurt my dog."

"We are taking all dogs," Comrade Argesanu told Cornel and Oprita. Comrade Argesanu and Lieutenant Ariciu had come through the gate and stood watching as the men circled the tied-up animals.

"No, you can't. They're my friends," Cornel cried out.

He ran to Mozoc, grabbed his friend and dug in with his feet. He tried to work his bare toes into the hard dirt, but the man dragged both Cornel and Mozoc across the yard toward the gate. The dog jumped, twisted, and clawed to try to break free from the tightening rope. Cornel held on.

"Let go, you stupid child," the man snarled. He dragged Mozoc and Cornel several more yards. Comrade Argesanu stalked to the struggling mass of fur, boy, and man and pried Cornel off the dog. Twisting and screaming, Cornel couldn't work his way out of the man's grasp. Blood oozed out of the scratches on Cornel's skin made by the frightened canine.

Another man managed to slip a noose around Grivei and then one on Pasalica and untie them from the tree. Instantly the dogs resisted, becoming more frantic as the men tightened the nooses and dragged the dogs through the gate and into a big cage strapped in the back of the truck.

"Where are you taking my dogs?" Cornel yelled as the truck pulled away. Oprita didn't say a word, but she didn't attempt to make Cornel be quiet. Cornel ran after the truck, hollering and crying. "Don't take my dogs. Please don't take my dogs."

The truck stopped. Cornel ran to catch up. Lieutenant Ariciu stuck his head out the window, yelled obscenities at Cornel and ordered him to go home.

Cornel stopped in the street, but made one more try.

"Mozoc, Grivei, Pasalica come! Come here!" Hearing his voice, the dogs barked and scrabbled at the wire of the cage.

The truck went on to the neighbor's house. Cornel stood in the street, watching as the truck stopped at every house and brought more dogs to the cage. He listened to the cries of other children as their pets were taken away. Some joined Cornel in the street, tears falling uncontrollably down their faces as the truck disappeared around the corner. A while later, he spotted the truck turn onto the main road and head out of the village.

Cornel, driven to know where they were taking his dogs, walked in the direction the truck had taken. He lost sight of the vehicle, but a dust trail told him he was headed the right way. About a mile out of the village, he spotted a group of men in a field. They seemed to be standing in a circle, leaning on long sticks.

Cornel crept closer, headed for a tree near the field. He knew the men would see him if they happened to turn around and look up, but either they didn't detect him or didn't bother to ask what a boy was doing. He reached the tree and scrambled up to a limb that gave him a view.

What had looked like sticks were shovels, and the men heaving dirt into a large hole. The men turned toward the truck, drew heavy gloves over their hands, and gathered at the cage's door. One man stepped up, opened the cage and grabbed a dog by the scruff of the neck and hauled it down to the ground. He shoved the dog down and trapped it with his foot by jamming his boot into the dog's throat. Another man stepped forward, raised his shovel, and smashed the dog's skull.

Cornel almost vomited. The skill of the men in killing the dog showed they had repeated the process countless times.

They skinned the dog and threw the carcass into the hole. They worked their way through the cage of dogs. Cornel watched to see if Mozoc, Grivei or Pasalica would be next. All three dogs were among the final animals pulled from the cage. Cornel shut his eyes.

His father, Ion, his battered brother, and now his dogs. Cornel's head dropped from the weight of anger he felt towards Comrade Argesanu and Lieutenant Ariciu. The men had robbed his family and his friends of everything important to them.

When the truck and the men were gone, Cornel climbed down from his hiding spot and walked home. He curled up on his bed, wracked by intense emotional pain in every nerve of his body. He did not tell anyone what he'd seen, especially his mother, but she knew and left him to grieve.

He heard later that the dogs' skins were used to make shoes and boots. For days, the wind blew a horrific smell through Rusanesti.

A few weeks later, the men returned to the Dolana home. It was a day when Oprita and her children were home between trips to the fields. Every member of the family was busy with a task in preparation to leave again. Oprita was outside feeding their animals, so she was the first to see that the group included Comrade Argesanu, Lieutenant Ariciu, and the same informers.

No one spoke to her. The informers approached the Dolana's two horses, tied ropes around their necks, and led them through the back gate. Comrade Argesanu and Lieutenant Ariciu simply watched.

"What are you doing!" screamed Oprita. "Those are our

horses. You can't take them. We need them to farm! How do you expect us to bring back the harvest?"

"You have no choice." Lieutenant Ariciu said.

They took what they came for and led the horses toward the center of the village. Cornel followed them partway down his street crying and yelling at the men.

Lieutenant Ariciu yelled back, "To hell with you. Go back home now." Cornel finally obeyed.

The Dolanas found out later that all the horses from Rusanesti were taken away from their owners.

Peasants trained their oxen to pull the wagons to and from the fields, an added chore to their normal duty of pulling the plow. With the loss of the horses, Oprita decided to give up another forty acres of land, leaving them with only twenty to plant and harvest.

The family made it through another harvest season, giving most of their yield to the communists.

CHAPTER 11

Week of March 5, 1953

CORNEL AND GEORGICA WERE on their way to school when they noticed the flag was being lowered to half-staff. After the students had settled in their seats, Professor Voinea announced that Joseph Stalin, leader of the Soviet Union and Communist Party for nearly thirty years, had died March 5, 1953, at the age of 73 after suffering a cerebral hemorrhage.

"School will be closed for the week as the country mourns his death," announced Professor Voinea.

Students wanted to rejoice for the week off, but they knew it would not be appropriate to let their feelings show.

"We all need to report to the village hall," Voinea stated. The students jumped to their feet and followed their teacher. Their parents were already gathered; they were told they would not have to work the collective farms for a week so they could mourn for Stalin.

Lieutenant Ariciu gave a lengthy speech about the loss of their great leader. Upon the conclusion of his speech, he told them that they would participate in a parade to honor Stalin. Some people were asked to hold banners, while everyone else was given a flag. The Dolanas received flags.

Children and adults marched on the main street waving their

flags. When the peasants reached the last house on the street, they were asked to turn around and go back three miles to the other end of village. This went on several times, further weakening the already tired and starving residents. Finally they were released to go home. The overworked villagers welcomed the much-needed, week-long break.

Peasants hoped things would change for the better, and for a while they did. Comrade Argesanu seemed not to look for infractions. Fewer people were sent to jail, and tension in the village eased.

Spring – Early Summer 1953

ON A SUNDAY ABOUT A MONTH after Stalin died, the older Dolanas were home from working the fields. Cornel had finished his chores and was playing in the yard. He heard the gate squeak and looked up to see a skinny stranger with a beard and dirty clothes. When the man came closer, Cornel realized who it was. He couldn't believe his eyes.

"Tata, Tata!"

Marin caught Cornel in his arms.

"You're home! Tata!" Cornel hugged his father tightly.

In the kitchen, Georgica and Oprita heard Cornel call his father's name. Oprita's heart jumped and she couldn't breathe as she stood frozen in disbelief. Georgica ran outside and squeezed in between Cornel and Marin for his hug. "Tata, Tata," Georgica kept crying.

"How are my two sons?" Marin asked. Florica ran from the house to her father and joined in the hugs.

"My daughter, Florica."

Oprita got her breath back and ran through the house, slammed the door open and leaped to Marin, tears streaming down her face.

"Marin, you're home." Oprita could hardly speak. The two embraced for several minutes.

"I've missed all of you," Marin said with tears running down his face.

Everyone continued to cry with joy, taking turns to hug their father. Oprita suddenly realized how pale Marin looked.

"Let your father come in and rest."

Marin sunk into the mattress that served as a couch in the center room. Oprita served Marin cheese, bread, and water. Everyone gathered around him to hear his every word.

"You've lost so much weight," Oprita whined. Marin's body was down to skin and bones. The family could see the deep sores caused by the shackles, and the bruises from countless beatings were still visible as well.

"Looks like you and the family haven't had much to eat either," Marin responded.

"Life has been difficult since you left. Oh, Marin, I'm so sorry, but I had to give up most of our land. Without you, we couldn't keep up with it. Then Lieutenant Ariciu and Comrade Argesanu came and took our dogs and the horses." Oprita's tears flowed as she told Marin of the changes that had taken place.

"How did you get out? I mean, out early?" Oprita asked.

"I was one of the lucky ones. After Stalin's funeral, they commuted the sentences of a few of us. I guess it was supposed to be a gesture of good will."

"Cornica, while I'm cleaning up, please run and tell John and your uncles that I'm home."

Cornel couldn't wait to spread the good news and ran to tell everyone his father was home.

"Your clean pants and shirt are hanging in the bedroom," Oprita said.

Marin started with a pail of water and went to work on the crust of grime on his skin. He found a blade and shaved off his beard, but left a thin mustache. He ran his hand across the clean shirt and pants, savoring their freshness, and thought how lucky he was to be at home. He knew many equally innocent men who were still in prison. He slowly slipped into the clean clothes and kicked his dirty rags aside.

Marin walked with Oprita around their yard. He took note of the remnants of corn and straw, but said nothing to Oprita. She had done the best she could.

Neighbors dropped in to welcome Marin back home but didn't stay long. The house was already filled with the five sets of uncles and aunts plus all the cousins who came to celebrate the return.

Marin remained somewhat reserved. He watched and listened as the family told him what had transpired in his absence.

The men excused themselves to the bedroom after all the women and children had their chance to talk with Marin. Cornel was still not old enough to join the group, so he propped himself by the door.

Cornel heard the clink of glass against glass and assumed tuica was being offered around the room. Then he heard Stefan, his uncle, ask Marin if the prison conditions were as bad as everyone had heard.

"I'm one of the lucky ones to have survived my time. So many men died. Those men had not committed a crime and were just trying to stand up for their rights and Romania, no different than me."

Marin looked down at his hands and shook his head, not knowing how to tell of the horrors he had endured. No one spoke; everyone waited for Marin to break the silence.

"No man should be put through such brutality, such inhuman treatment. I almost froze in that tiny cell. There was no heat, and I did not have a blanket. It was dark all the time. They kept shackles around my ankles and hands. They beat all the prisoners constantly. We endured kicking, being hit with the butts of their rifles, and being thrown against the concrete walls — anything to keep us weak and on the floor. I could hear the screams of men as the guards went from cell to cell. When the screams were from the next cell over, then I knew I was next."

Marin closed his eyes and shook his head. The men's eyes were glued on Marin. A moment later Marin continued.

"My stomach and body ached from starvation. We were given a watery, buggy cup of soup twice a day. The first few days I refused to drink it. When I realized that was all we were ever going to get, I picked out the bugs and drank the horrible liquid. After a while, I drank it all." Marin didn't miss how everyone cringed at the thought of gladly eating bugs. "All of you look like you've been hungry, too."

One of his cousins responded, "Lieutenant Ariciu keeps taking more of the harvest, leaving very little to feed a family."

Tears ran down Cornel's cheeks as he listened to the suffering his father had endured for three years. But he was proud his father had been strong enough to survive. Cornel wondered if his father would have survived in prison much longer.

"You're very fortunate you were released." Marin's brother

Costica stated the obvious just to bring the talk back to something more positive than hunger.

"I couldn't believe it when they told me. I was afraid they might be joking. To be out of that hell and to see my family again." Tears welled up in Marin's eyes. "What of Father Manoila and Ion? Are they alive? What have you heard?"

"We don't know, we haven't been able to find out," Costica said.

Then it was Marin who decided to change the subject. "Oprita told me some of you were forced into the collective farms."

"I did everything I could to keep from joining, but they made it too tough on me. You can't believe how they make us farm," said Florea, Oprita's cousin.

"It's frustrating because government bureaucrats who know nothing about farming are making field decisions," said Pericle, another of Oprita's cousins. "Whoever is setting the planting and harvesting schedule in Bucharest is stupid."

"Last spring they forced people to plow when the soil was either too wet or too dry. They just didn't understand that soil like that is impossible to work into a good seed bed," said Stefan.

Florea chimed in. "Can you believe they made us waste precious seed by forcing us to plant in the drought? Only an idiot would expect the seed to germinate. Then they get upset with us because the crop doesn't grow. It doesn't make sense."

"Unbelievable," responded Marin.

"A few times they made people harvest the crop before it was ripe, just to meet a quota," added Oprita's cousin Nelu.

"Of course, it wasn't useable. A terrible waste!" Gica, another cousin of Oprita's, said. "We are all going hungry because of it."

Everyone had a story about how bad the conditions had become. Marin motioned to John to fill up everyone's glass again.

"Now that Stalin is dead, the Americans are coming to liberate us and give us back our freedom," said Florea.

"Next year we will be free," John added. Everyone cheered and raised their glasses.

For three days, the family did not go to their fields, and Cornel and Georgica were allowed to stay home from school. After the welcomed break, Cornel's mother, father, sister, and older brother went back to work, and Cornel and Georgica resumed their studies. His family wasn't as exhausted when they returned home because they had fewer acres to farm. For a while, Cornel's life seemed whole again.

One day, when everyone was home, Lieutenant Ariciu and Comrade Argesanu returned with their informants. Marin saw them coming through the gate, and his heart raced.

The men didn't say anything to Marin as they approached the two oxen and two buffalo. They put ropes around the beasts' necks and led them away. Marin couldn't help himself and spoke up, "You can't take our oxen. You've already taken our horses." They swore at Marin, took the animals and left.

Marin saw through the ploy: The animals were gone, so he couldn't farm. If he couldn't farm, he'd have to give up his remaining land and join the collective farms.

A week after they lost their animals, the family waited at the village hall for a wagon to take them to the fields. They were promised a portion of grain for their labor.

Oprita and Marin had hoped to get relief after they succumbed to the collective farms, but Lieutenant Ariciu and Comrade Argesanu demanded long workdays.

Cornel and Georgica dreaded the day school ended. Along with the rest of their family and neighbors, they now had to report to village hall at five in the morning when a truck picked them up and took them to the fields.

They worked hard all day but were not allowed to go home when they were dropped off at the village hall at eight o'clock in the evening. Comrade Argesanu required the workers to stay for a meeting, during which he or Lieutenant Ariciu continued to preach the virtues of communist ways. Families were released to go home around ten o'clock. By the time they did their chores at home, they were lucky to get four hours of sleep.

Everyone was forced to work daily during harvest periods. At other times, workers occasionally were allowed one day off a week. Those few precious hours provided a little rest. The unreasonable pace slowed Marin's recovery.

Making matters worse, their lack of sleep was often for nothing. They saw firsthand what they had heard. The new farming practices were dictated by people in Bucharest, 130 miles away, and resulted in unproductive work. Under the communist system, farming was planned through a centralized government. The people in charge didn't take into consideration local conditions. Lieutenant Ariciu required the villagers to plant, plow, and harvest by the central government schedules, which most of the time resulted in losing the planting or the harvest.

This new system resulted in less food produced, which meant less to go around. What little was left wasn't even shared among the villagers. The government took most of the harvest to give to the Soviet armies and people in the cities. Some was shipped to the Soviet Union. The little that remained was supposed to be distributed to the people who worked the fields. However, the corrupt local authorities took part of the grain for themselves, leaving hardly anything for the workers.

If they were lucky, participating families received three bags of corn and three bags of wheat if they didn't miss a day in the field during the year. For every day missed, grain was deducted. The grain they received didn't go far. Prior to the communist takeover, the family stored an average of sixty fifty-pound bags of wheat and corn each year.

Oprita and Marin still had some supplies behind their false wall. They dipped into the precious stores as a last resort. The Dolanas couldn't appear to be healthier than anyone else in the village, or they would be suspected of hoarding or stealing. Any such activity could result in a jail sentence. After supplies ran out and people were close to starving to death, the Dolanas took the chance of being caught and shared some of their stored food with neighbors.

Several months after the Dolanas began to work at the collective farms, Comrade Argesanu and Lieutenant Ariciu took away the Dolanas remaining cow. Two months later, they took several of the Dolanas sheep and goats. For some reason the officials left them two sheep and two goats, so at least the family still had milk for cheese and butter. Families were allowed to keep their chickens, ducks, geese, and turkeys. To have a pig, they had to raise two and give one to the government once it was grown and fattened. The Dolanas accepted that offer.

The missing animals created a disturbing quiet around the house. "How effortlessly and quickly the communists have come in and robbed our country," Marin would often say out loud.

The communist system challenged the peoples' principles. The historically strong work ethic of the people was fading away.

They depended on mental strength to survive, but that, too, was being chopped away.

No one thought things could get worse. But they did. Word spread that the government was going to force everyone to limit the size of their gardens so that everyone would be equal. Realizing that their garden by the church would be seized, Marin decided to give that part of his garden to Tomica, a good neighbor of theirs whose garden was under the size limit. To maintain equality, many acres of potential gardens were not allowed to be planted.

The Dolanas became increasingly frustrated by such idiotic rules.

"Can't the government see that they are significantly cutting the amount of food to go around?" Oprita would say often.

With less from the gardens, fewer animals, and significantly less grain from harvests, the villagers had little to eat. They were always hungry. The weight dropped from their bodies.

During harvest times when guards weren't looking, workers began hiding wheat and corn in their clothing. Adults put grain in their pockets. At first the young boys and girls didn't have a way to hide any food. One day, one of the children came with string tied around his shirt at the waist. The next day all children, including Cornel and Georgica, had strings tied around their waists into which they tucked stalks of grain or an ear of corn. Loose against their thin bodies, their shirts kept their secrets.

These days, Cornel realized his father was angry most of the time. At the table over their sparse meals, Marin would often launch into a tirade against the communists.

"Communists lectured about how life would be better when everyone was 'equal,' " Marin would say. "What communism really means is everyone works harder and gets far less. It means losing any choice in life. It means starvation and suffering." Marin would pound his fist on the table and continue. "Instead of the workers' paradise that the communists promised, they have forced us into becoming slaves in order to create a government paradise for those in power."

PART IV
High School

CHAPTER 12

Summer 1953

MARIN HAD NO CHOICE other than to endure servitude on the collective farm. The days were long and exhausting. He knew the promise of food for his and Oprita's work would not be fulfilled. Only three thoughts kept him going. One was that working on the collective farm was better than being in prison. The second was that he could live his days with Oprita. His final incentive was the thought that at least two of his sons might escape his own fate. Aristotel had found a different line of work, and he hoped he could help Cornel pursue his dreams.

Cornel had finished seventh grade, the highest level of education offered in Rusanesti. Officially, the family had to be a member of the Communist Party in order for Cornel to advance to the eighth grade. Many people did not accept the communist way but joined on paper to receive privileges like education. The Dolanas couldn't and wouldn't join the party. That didn't deter Marin.

"We have to find a way to get you into high school," Cornel's father told him. "I know you despise farming and want to be an aviator."

"But how?" Cornel could not believe there'd be a way.

"I have one idea. Just don't say anything to your friends."

Cornel did not have to be reminded to keep to himself what was said at home. One slip and his father could be sent back to prison. As badly as he wanted to go away to school, he had trained himself not to react when one of his friends bragged that their parents had enrolled them in high school.

Marin's first step was to call on a friend, the woman who had helped their second eldest, Aristotel. When Aristotel had studied theology, he had rented a room from the Dobrescus, a husband and wife in Rm. Valcea. Mrs. Dobrescu became more like a second mother than a landlady to Aristotel. The entire Dolana family considered her to be a good friend.

Marin sent word to her that Aristotel's brother wouldn't be able to continue schooling without her help. A respected woman with connections in the city, she pulled strings with the director of the high school and enrolled Cornel. She offered him a room in exchange for chores and a little wheat from the Dolanas.

Suddenly Cornel had a real chance at a different life. He'd be able to escape field work and the anguish of taking orders from Lieutenant Ariciu in the fields. Cornel loved learning and the idea of adventure. Now he'd be able to explore places he'd never seen. Maybe this new path would lead him to his dream of becoming an aviator, a job Cornel imagined opening the door to the freedom of the skies.

Cornel was eager to make his father proud of him. He saw his father as a hero. Hadn't he built a false wall for their grain so they wouldn't go hungry? Hadn't his father hidden the resister Ion Popescu? Hadn't Marin been strong enough to survive the torture and incarceration that resulted from helping the resisters? Even when Marin lost his land, he had kept his head high and endured the collective farms so his family could survive. Now he had found a way for Cornel to continue his schooling.

Cornel had some work to do before he could be on his way. First, he had to obtain the required government-issued photo identification that he would have to keep in his possession at all times once he left the region of his birth. Marin provided him directions and sent him off on his own to the militia station in Corabia, the capital of the region.

Cornel left in the morning, walked seventeen miles to Corabia, and found his way to the militia station. He reached the locked doors before dark. He sat down, rested against the door and went to sleep. He followed the first person through the doors in the morning, received his papers, and then walked seventeen miles back home.

The day before Cornel and Marin left for Rm. Valcea, they had to notify the local militia. That meant they had to face Comrade Argesanu.

Every time Cornel saw Comrade Argesanu, hate for the man welled up inside the boy. He replayed in his mind all that Comrade Argesanu had done to his family and many other people in his village.

Comrade Argesanu simply logged Marin's and Cornel's names and destination of Rm. Valcea. The militia did not ask people why they were traveling unless their itinerary took them to a border town or village. Cornel was relieved when they walked out of the office.

That night, after a chicken dinner and sweet cake — both special foods to mark a special occasion — Oprita presented Cornel his first pair of dress pants, plus a long-sleeved white shirt and a jacket. His father gave him his first pair of shoes, which were black leather with laces. Cornel was so overwhelmed that he was barely able to squeak out his thanks.

He slipped into his new clothes. He looked down at his pant legs, then stretched his arms and eyed each arm from shoulder to wrist. He decided to look in the mirror, something he rarely did. The small mirror distorted his reflection, but Cornel could tell he looked nice, and that made him smile. He pulled on the black shoes and tied the laces, fumbling a bit with the small strings, but finally finding success with a knot he had often used to tie wheat stalks together. He couldn't believe it — his own shoes. Used to going barefoot or wearing only heavy socks against the cold, Cornel's feet felt heavy. However restrictive shoes might be, he was happy to have them. His first pair of shoes and first pair of pants was an important milestone in his life

Cornel was ready to go.

Late Summer 1953 – Spring 1954

OPRITA, GEORGICA, AND FLORICA waved good-bye as Cornel and his father went through the gate of their yard late that night. The first leg of their trip was a four-hour walk to the railroad station in Studina. They walked barefoot. Their shoes, tied together by their laces, rode on their shoulders. In one hand Marin carried his overcoat under which he had hidden a twenty-pound bag of wheat secreted in another bag so it didn't look like grain. The wheat was to be payment to Mrs. Dobrescu for taking in Cornel. Cornel carried two cloth bags in one hand. One bag contained food to eat on their trip and the second held cheese. In their other hand, they both clutched the feet of a live chicken. Cornel needed no suitcase; he wore the only clothes he owned.

After they reached the small station, they sat on a bench by the tracks and waited. When Cornel caught sight of the train, he popped up from the bench and strained for a better view. As the black steam locomotive drew up beside him, the whistle blew and the brakes screeched. Accustomed to the quiet of Rusanesti and the fields, Cornel jumped back. He wasn't prepared for the hissing noise of escaping steam. The engine roared past him and braked to a stop, bringing Cornel face-to-face with the high side of a passenger car.

Cornel and Marin boarded and found a seat. Cornel sat by the window. They laid their bags on the seat beside them and placed the chickens on the floor. The chicken's feet were tied and the birds sat quietly.

Cornel turned to the window, quickly figured out how to open it, and stuck his head out. He wanted to see the locomotive but had to wait until the train began to round a slight bend. Smoke poured over the top. The force of the air surprised and excited him. His smile broadened as the wind hit his face and blew his hair wildly. The fastest he had ever gone was in a wagon behind a trotting horse. As the train picked up speed, his eyes began to sting and water, and he finally had to pull his head inside.

They changed trains in Caracal. Cornel claimed a window seat again. He kept his face to the window during much of the four-hour ride. Most of the scenery was of woods and fields. As the train slowed and stopped at stations, Cornel stuck his head out the window again. By pushing himself as far as the window opening would allow, he could see the people who got off and on cars up and down the line. Under way again, he rested his forehead against the window, studying the approaching buildings before they flashed by him.

Every once in awhile, Cornel caught a glimpse of the Olt River, but it was narrow and surrounded by hills and mountains, much different than the flatlands surrounding the river near Rusanesti.

As the train pulled up to the Rm. Valcea station, Marin handed a rag to Cornel and pointed to his face.

"Tata, how is that?" Cornel asked after he wiped his face.

"There, right there," Marin touched the bridge of Cornel's nose. "There's still a smudge of that dark soot. We need to put on our shoes now. This is a city, and you want to look presentable for meeting Mrs. Dobrescu."

They left the train station and headed directly to the militia station to report their arrival. The paved streets in town surprised Cornel. A light rain had fallen, which would have created muddy streets in their village. They weren't getting dirty on their walk through the streets. After showing their papers at the militia, they walked the remaining two and a half miles to the Dobrescu home. Marin knocked on the door.

"Welcome to my house," Eugenia Dobrescu said with a big smile.

"Mrs. Dobrescu, this is my son Cornel," Marin said.

"Hello, Mr. Dolana. Nice to meet you, Cornel. You know we are going to get you into school."

"Thank you, Mrs. Dobrescu. I appreciate it very much," Cornel said.

Marin and Cornel removed their shoes before stepping through the doorway. Cornel's bare feet touched the wood floors and the sensation startled him. The slightly rough finish was unlike anything he'd experienced. His house had dirt floors. His school and church had cement floors. It made Cornel feel special that he would be living in the nicest house he had ever seen.

They delivered the grain and chickens to the kitchen.

"Now let me show you the house," she said. As she gave them a tour, Eugenia watched Cornel's face light up at each new discovery. He was a boy on a journey of discovery, finding things he had never seen before.

"You have electricity," he blurted out, pointing at a light bulb.

"Yes, we're allowed to use it three nights a week for two hours each."

Mrs. Dobrescu told Cornel that one of his primary chores would be going to town to turn in the coupons for milk, bread, and meat.

"Mr. Dobrescu and I work for the department of education, but we are limited on the amount of food we can buy and are issued coupons, just like everyone else," she explained.

Cornel grinned, thinking this would be the easiest chore of his life.

The next morning he said good-bye to his father. Cornel felt a pang of sadness as he hugged him. Marin turned from his son, thanked Eugenia Dobrescu and left the house.

Eager to begin his new life, Cornel took the bread coupon to town. He found the store quite by accident when he stopped to ask why so many people were standing in line. He found the end of the line and waited for hours.

Everyone in Rusanesti made their own bread, killed their own chickens, and milked their own goats. Cornel had expected to walk to the store, turn in the coupon, and be given bread — an errand of a few minutes.

Suddenly the line in front of him began to disperse.

"Why are you leaving?" Cornel asked the woman in front of him as she turned away.

"Don't you have eyes?" she snapped. "Why else would I go? There is no more bread."

Cornel didn't want to go back and tell this to Mrs. Dobrescu, but he did.

"We'll just have to do without for a few days. We can only get milk once a week and tomorrow is the day to use that coupon. We're issued meat coupons only once or twice a month. All other days, you'll pick up bread... all they give us is a small loaf," she said. "You'll learn the system. We have confidence in you."

Cornel didn't want to make the same mistake again. The next day he left at three o'clock in the morning, this time with the milk coupon. He wasn't the first in line, but he was early enough to get a bottle of milk. It dawned on him that his chore of turning in the coupons wasn't going to be easy. When school started, he'd have to get up at three every morning to ensure he could procure the household's food.

His first day of classes was his first look inside the school, one for boys only. The building was much nicer than the one in Rusanesti. He felt privileged to enter such an important structure. But he was nervous. He was concerned that someone would ask him how he got into high school, or that he would say something that would give his situation away. During classes, he sat on a long bench with seven other boys. When they didn't ask questions about where he came from, he began to relax. Within days, he had a few friends.

Mrs. Dobrescu made sure Cornel did his homework every day. Occasionally, if Cornel asked, she would help him. Reading and working on his lessons made him tired, and he wanted to doze, but he kept pushing himself. Soon the lack of sleep began to affect his ability to learn. He particularly struggled with the Russian language class, a required subject.

He had a hard time getting through the political science and history classes too, but not because he fell asleep or found the topics difficult. He just didn't like the way the history and political science teachers constantly promoted communism. They said it was making a positive difference to Romanians and that everyone's lives would improve even more. The teachers reinforced the idea that those who fought the communist way would suffer, and those who accepted it would thrive.

Cornel thought of his father and brother who most certainly had experienced the suffering part, so that line wasn't hard to swallow. However, he could not believe life would get better. Everyone had their dogs and most of their farm animals taken away, even if they embraced communism.

He kept his feelings to himself. He didn't want to risk school officials discovering that he wasn't even allowed to be there.

He got a break from the classroom in late spring, but it wasn't a vacation. All teachers and students at his school were required to harvest fruit. In other parts of the country, students had to work the fields. Rm. Valcea sat at the foot a mountain and the main crop was fruit. The teacher and students went to the orchards together and worked until dark. The one positive thing about working the orchards was that teachers didn't give homework.

CHAPTER 13

Spring 1955

IN HIS SECOND YEAR OF HIGH SCHOOL, Cornel tried to talk several of his classmates into sneaking over to the Romanian Orthodox Church to witness the midnight mass of Easter.

"You're crazy," most of his classmates said in one way or another. "They'll throw you out of school. The militia and Securitate will beat you and lock you up."

The large Romanian Orthodox Church in the center of town fascinated Cornel. He had discovered it one morning when he took a different way to school. Since then, every day he walked past the church his steps slowed as he gazed upward. The church's steeple towered five stories high. Stained glass covered the windows. Cornel longed to go inside to see the windows up close, to see the light through them, to look up to the ceiling. Seeing such a magnificent church must be worth a risk.

Cornel asked Mrs. Dobrescu about the church. She told him that this particular church was the center of the diocese.

"But why isn't it boarded up? I see people coming and going. The church in Rusanesti is closed."

"The communists didn't close large churches in cities," she explained. "But we are discouraged from attending. Those who attend high school are not allowed to attend church services." She shook her finger at Cornel as she made the pronouncement; the burn of Cornel's curiosity was evident, especially to wise Mrs. Dobrescu.

Despite the warning, Cornel's interest in seeing the inside of the church, coupled with a chance to attend an important religious service, led him to a personal commitment that he would attend Easter mass. Only his friend George said he wasn't afraid to go.

The two boys agreed to meet one hour before midnight on Easter and walk together to the church.

Easter night was dark, making Cornel feel a little less visible as he met up with George. They were able to hide quickly in between buildings when they saw lights approaching. The only car lights that time of evening would be security guards, and the smartest way to avoid questions was to not be seen.

They reached the church, but waited in the bushes until a few minutes before midnight before going inside. They wanted to be the last to enter. They slid silently through the large doors and stood in the back of the sanctuary where the light was dim. They realized they were the only young people there; even adults their parents' age were absent. Only the elderly, whom the communists couldn't do much to, attended mass. Cornel and his friend enjoyed the services, but it reminded him how much he missed hearing about God's way.

The next day at school, the school director summoned Cornel and George to his office.

"I hear the two of you attended Easter Mass. Is that the truth?" The two boys nodded. "You know that is prohibited," the director lectured. "I have no choice but to expel you from school." He handed each of them a piece of paper. "You will have to go home and tell your parents. How disappointed they will be!"

The two boys left, mortified. Cornel spoke first. "What are we going to do now? I knew we might get in trouble, but I never thought we'd get expelled. My tata will kill me."

"My father will kill me, too."

The boys walked the streets. They didn't talk. Each was deep into playing out in his mind the unpleasant scene awaiting him.

"Hey, wait; I know where a monastery is." George stopped in his tracks, his face brightening. "We can go there and hide out. They'll take us in. After all, our sin is we went to church."

They walked to the train station. They didn't have money for tickets and didn't report to the militia that they were leaving town, so they sneaked onto the train. The boys watched for the conductor. Just before the man entered their train car, Cornel and George walked out the opposite door, climbed the ladder, and sat on top of the train car. They waited long enough for the conductor to make his way through the car and then climbed down and took their seats again. The conductor didn't check tickets again, and the boys rode to the Manastirea Cozia Station.

After walking two blocks to the monastery Manastirea Cozia, they entered the open structure but saw no sign of the monks. George broke the silence, "Looks to me like it is closed. I know of another monastery a few miles through the forest." George led the way. When they reached the base of the mountain, George warned, "You're going to have to help me watch out for bears; the woods are full of them."

Cornel wondered how George knew his way and who had warned him about bears. Too busy listening for the sound of large animals coming at them, Cornel didn't ask. He was relieved when they made it through the woods without encountering a bear.

Cornel looked up across a grassy hillside. As they drew closer, he could see beautiful gardens. His spirits lifted. The boys walked through the monastery's open front door. They continued until they found the chapel where monks were praying.

"What can I do for you?" The voice behind them was friendly.

The boys turned to face a man. "We came here to hide," said Cornel. "The school expelled us for attending Easter services. We're afraid to go home."

They gave the details of their journey, the monk nodding now and then as the story unfolded. "I understand your problem. You had a long journey to get here, and you are welcome."

The monk fed the boys chicken soup, bread, and cheese, then showed them to a small room where they could sleep on blankets on the floor. The next morning, the monks invited the boys to mass. Cornel figured from attendance at the mass that twenty monks lived at the monastery. He knew that they were self-sustaining and that twenty mouths were a lot to feed with their small garden and few cows and chickens. Two more mouths would be a strain. Cornel and his friend weren't getting fed much, but he figured they were receiving as much or more food than the monks apportioned to themselves.

To show their appreciation, they helped around the monastery as best they could. They washed floors, swept the yard, picked up leaves, fed animals, collected chicken eggs, and washed dishes and clothes. The monks didn't have running water, so the boys hauled water to various areas of the monastery.

Cornel and George continued to attend mass every morning and do chores throughout the day. The monks left the boys alone and did not try to influence their thinking.

After a week, one of the monks asked to speak with the boys.

"Do you think remaining here will make it any easier to face the future?" he asked them.

The boys knew he was right. Besides, they'd felt guiltier each day as they ate the monks' food. Cornel and George decided to face their parents. They thanked their hosts and walked back to town. They made their way down the mountain and reached the train station without encountering bears. For that they were relieved, but they still worried about what they would face at home.

They used the same system to sneak onto the train to Caracal as they'd used a week earlier. George got off at Piatra Olt, a station before Cornel's. They wished each other good luck as they parted. As he rode the last stretch alone to Caracal, Cornel worried how to present himself to his parents. When he got off at the station, he still had an eight-hour walk through patches of snow until he reached home.

When Cornel walked through the door, his mother and father were sitting in the kitchen.

"What are you doing home? What happened?" his father asked.

Cornel didn't try to explain, but simply handed him the letter the headmaster had given to him.

"I was afraid to come home. I felt you would be disappointed in me." Cornel looked at his parents, ready to accept his punishment.

"We can't blame you for wanting to attend Easter services. I presume the Dobrescus must be worried. We will have to go there."

Cornel was surprised to find that his parents weren't overly upset. The spanking Cornel had dreaded didn't happen.

Marin accompanied Cornel on the train back to Rm. Valcea and explained the situation to Mr. and Mrs. Dobrescu. Eugenia offered to intervene and meet with the school officials. She returned later that day.

"I was able to get Cornel back into school so he can finish the rest of the year, but he won't be able to attend here next year. That's as much as I can do."

"We appreciate all that you've done for our family and want to thank you for working it out so he can finish this year," Marin said. Cornel shook his head in agreement.

When he returned to school, his friends welcomed him back and wanted to hear about his adventure. Mrs. Dobrescu had warned Cornel not to talk about it even if the boys asked, so he shrugged off their queries.

"Did you get beaten badly?" one boy asked him after class that day. Cornel thought that it was a question he should answer to make his parents look like good communists.

"Oh, yes, I was punished."

Cornel finished the school year without further incident.

CHAPTER 14

May – September 1955

WHEN CORNEL RETURNED TO RUSANESTI, Georgica told him of his seventh-grade experiences. He also told Cornel that he wanted to stay with their mother and father and not go on to high school. Cornel felt sad when he realized it was the last schooling Georgica would receive. He felt guilty about jeopardizing his own education after his father had worked so hard to get him enrolled. Unlike Georgica, he wanted more but wondered if he would now be spending the rest of his life working for Lieutenant Ariciu and Comrade Argesanu in the fields.

Marin, Oprita, Florica, Cornel, and Georgica reported to the village hall early in the mornings. They would visit a few minutes with John and Florina who also reported to village hall, and then they worked the fields all day. Cornel tried to hide how much he hated working the fields, but his father and mother could feel his disappointment and frustration.

On one of their few days of rests, Marin asked Cornel to walk with him to the river.

"I still want you to finish high school," Marin said.

Cornel stopped and looked at his father to see if he was serious.

"I've been considering every reasonable alternative," Marin

continued. "You know that Rm. Valcea is out of the question and anywhere close to Rusanesti is too risky. I think a big city provides the greatest hope."

"Oh, Tata! Do you really think there is a possibility I can go back to school?"

"I don't want you to get your hopes up, but your mother and I plan to ask the Popescus in Resita if you could stay with them and if they would try to get you enrolled in high school."

Cornel couldn't believe his ears. John Popescu was his mother's brother, and he and his family lived in the relatively large city of Resita, 250 miles from Rusanesti. The Popescus had two sons: Daniel, the same age as Cornel; and Ovidiu, who was four years older and living on his own. Cornel always looked forward to Daniel's annual summer visit. The two shared many secrets over the years and had good memories of their times together.

Cornel gave his father a hug. He straightened his shoulders and walked with a bounce in his step as they made their way to the river and took a refreshing swim.

The days went by excruciatingly slowly for Cornel. He couldn't wait for his uncle, aunt, and cousin to visit so that he could find out his fate. Although he only saw Lieutenant Ariciu on occasion, he had to face Comrade Argesanu every day and listen to his propaganda in the evenings when they returned to the village hall.

One evening when the family returned home, they noticed light in the windows of their home. Cornel knew it had to be his relatives. He ran up the path and into the house and greeted Aunt Ruja. He gave her a hug and then took her hand and kissed it. He hugged Uncle John and gave him a kiss on the cheek and then did the same to Daniel. Oprita, Marin, and Georgica joined in on the welcome. They offered food and drink and made sure their company was comfortable in the guest room.

Cornel could hardly sleep that night. They didn't have to report to the fields the next day, and he knew his father and mother would talk with them about the possibility of him attending school in Resita.

The rooster crowed to announce the morning, but Cornel had already finished most of his chores around the house. After breakfast, Cornel invited Daniel to go to the river with him. He hoped this would give the adults time to talk.

When the boys returned, Marin had a smile on his face, and Cornel hoped that meant good news.

"Cornel, despite the risk of persecution, John has agreed to take you under his wing and try to get you enrolled into school in Resita."

"Thank you, Uncle John! You have no idea what this means to me," Cornel said.

"We are proud to do it for you and your family and look forward to seeing you this fall," said John.

The Dolanas never had time to take a vacation, so Cornel had never been to Resita and for him, the end of summer couldn't come soon enough.

Cornel felt fortunate that he'd have a chance to finish high school with a good friend and relative, and to do so in a city. He also looked forward to seeing his brother Aristotel, who now lived and worked in Resita.

Throughout the rest of the summer, Cornel worked long, hard hours with his family at the collective farms.

September 1955

IN THE FALL, Marin informed Comrade Argesanu in Rusanesti that Cornel was leaving Rusanesti to work.

Oprita cleaned Cornel's shirt, pants, and jacket for his new journey and gave him a bag with bread and cheese for the eight-hour train ride. Marin sent two live chickens along with his son to express the family's appreciation to the Popescus for taking in their son.

Cornel's mind wandered with excitement as he watched the scenery go by, and steam from the engine slide past his window. He was off on a new adventure. His energy heightened with the thought of a new opportunity to continue his education. He looked out the window and visualized himself piloting a plane and flying over farm fields, not working in them.

As the train pulled into the Resita station, the sun slid behind a cloud. Cornel picked up the scent of rotten eggs but forgot about it as soon as he saw his uncle standing proudly in his suit and tie. Daniel stood beside him in his white shirt and dark slacks. Cornel was a little surprised to see them and then realized his mother must have written a letter to tell his Uncle John of his arrival time.

"Welcome! How was your trip?" the two waiting relatives asked as they gave him a hug and kiss on the cheek. John and Daniel each grabbed a chicken from Cornel as they started walking toward the Popescu home.

"You'll find Resita much different than Rusanesti," John said. "This is a large city. We have various nationalities, including Germans, Hungarians, and Austrians. So the communists have not been as rough on people here compared to where you live. There are shortages and, like everywhere in the country, we have to use coupons to get bread, milk, clothes, and shoes. We get by better than some others because I still have my job at the school. I guess your parents told you I had to join the Communist Party so I could continue to teach."

Cornel understood that his Uncle John did not believe in the communist system. He hoped his living with them didn't bring attention to John's true beliefs.

This was the first industrial city Cornel had visited. He realized what hid the sun when he entered town was not a cloud but smelly black smoke puffing steadily out of several pipes that set atop the large factory. It bothered him that the smoke hung so thickly in the air that it covered the sight of the sun and blue sky. He already missed the fresh air.

The adults they passed looked the same as at home: they wore the same shoes — Cornel knew all Romanians' shoes were made at one shoe factory — the men's dark suits, the long, naturally-colored or dark dresses of the women. The one difference he noticed immediately was the clothes of young children. In Resita, they wore shirts and pants instead of the long shirts of the children in Rusanesti.

As they approached a building, Uncle John slowed his pace and pointed at it.

"This is the elementary school where I teach all subjects. Our house is attached to the school."

Daniel said with a jump in his step, "This is our home and now yours."

Cornel's Aunt Ruja was suddenly at the door, her arms open.

"Ah, I see you made it. You must be tired, come in," she said as her long arms encircled Cornel and drew him inside. "Daniel, show Cornel where to put his things."

Daniel led Cornel into a small room with one bed.

"Here's our bed. I hope you are a deep sleeper. My mother says I am not, but I'll try not to pull the blanket off you."

"You have electricity." Cornel was impressed.

"Oh, yes. It's on all the time. My father says it's because we live in an industrial city." Daniel said. "We also have running water inside the house. However, the toilet is outside behind the house."

Daniel then took Cornel down a narrow stairway to a cellar.

"This is where we store our food. See, we have carrots and potatoes," he said proudly, pointing to bins of the vegetables.

Next to the bins Cornel spotted a pile of what looked like broken dishes, shoes, parts of chairs, and other rubbish piled in a corner.

"What's all that for?" he asked.

"Oh, I don't know. My mother says you never know when old things might come in handy. She won't throw anything away." He bent over and plucked out an old shoe. "This was mine, but my feet grew before I wore out the shoes. See, there's still some sole on this one."

Cornel dutifully examined the shoe.

Daniel suddenly leaned closer to Cornel.

"Listen, I want to warn you now, while we're down here. My father's still very strict!"

"I remember. When you came to our house on vacation and we got in trouble, your father punished me, too."

"But I mean really strict. I try to obey him, follow his rules, but when I don't…." Cornel watched Daniel's face as his words trailed off. What did his cousin mean?

"Boys, you come up now." Daniel's mother was calling them from the top of the steps.

115

Cornel saw he'd have to wait to ask Daniel what he'd meant about his father.

The next day, Cornel walked four miles to Aristotel's one-room apartment. The two talked all afternoon of Rusanesti and their family. As they parted, the brothers pledged to see each other again soon.

"I hope you don't feel too homesick," Aristotel said, patting Cornel on the shoulder as they parted. "Remember, I'm here."

CHAPTER 15

SCHOOL BEGAN THE NEXT MORNING. Cornel and Daniel left an hour and a half before class began at eight to make their three-mile walk to Liceul Mixt, Resita's high school for boys and girls. As they turned the corner and the school came into sight, Daniel waved to a boy approaching from the opposite direction.

"Radu, come here and meet my cousin Cornel."

"Nice to meet you," Radu said. "Where are you from?"

"Rusanesti."

"I've never heard of it," Radu said.

"It's far away, and it's small, not like here." Cornel almost said that the air of his home didn't smell, but he stopped himself just in time. He didn't want to offend Daniel or his friend.

"What grade are you in?"

"He's going into the tenth grade, just like us," Daniel answered for Cornel. "What's your favorite subject?" Radu addressed Cornel.

"Well, I like geography and math."

"I'm no good in math," Radu shrugged. "Maybe you can help me."

"Sure," Cornel agreed.

The three walked into school and found their classroom. They chose a long bench at the back of the room and placed their pencils and paper on the long wood table. Daniel and Radu waived to several of the boys and girls as they took their seats. Cornel made a quick count of students and came up with twenty-seven.

The morning passed quickly for Cornel. First, the teacher assigned students to one of two classes. Cornel was disappointed when he and Daniel didn't end up together, but the new boy in school felt better when he saw that he didn't need Daniel as his guide. Cornel realized students stayed in their classroom while different teachers came in. His subjects were mathematics, history, chemistry, geography, political science, physics, and the Romanian and Russian languages. Daniel told him that evening that all the students were called into one area for communist instruction.

As the days fell into routine, Cornel found he had no trouble keeping up with the rest of the students, but he was worried about his slow progress in his Russian language class. He had passed Russian in the eighth and ninth grades, but the higher level stumped him. The language made sense to him on paper, but when someone spoke Russian, he couldn't understand it. When it was his turn to speak the twisting words, he struggled to find the right ones.

He could tell that history class, like the previous two years, was going to include very little about Romania; instead it focused on the communist way of life. The teachers talked harshly about America. They took every opportunity to put down capitalism and talk about how America was exploiting people. Cornel thought, *America must be a bad place to be if people there are exploited more than we are.* He wondered why the men visiting his house would speak well of the United States.

One day, the teacher produced a communist newspaper and held it up high.

"This is a story about how Americans went on strike." She handed the paper to the nearest student.

"Look at this picture. They are hungry, and they have no homes." Each student studied the paper and then passed it down the line of hands eager to see what Americans looked like. When the paper reached Cornel, he peered closely at the image of people huddled on a sidewalk on a city street. So here was proof: people were starving in America, too.

"We don't strike here. This is a workers' paradise, so people have no reason to strike," the teacher said as she retrieved the newspaper. She then dismissed class for the day.

Cornel was shocked. He knew why no one went on strike in Romania. It wasn't because it was a workers paradise; it was because strikers would be sent to jail immediately.

He joined Daniel and Radu outside the school, who were talking to their friends Dumitru, George, Florea, and Leana. Cornel had been introduced to them all the first week of school, and he was just getting to feel comfortable around them. Suddenly a loud voice boomed from somewhere, and Cornel jumped. The others laughed.

"What was that?" Cornel said, trying to hide how embarrassed he felt for being startled.

"See the speakers? They use them to announce the news and to play Romanian music," Daniel said.

Cornel had never noticed the speakers, but now realized they were set up about every twenty feet, up and down the street.

"We used to get our news from the radio, but we haven't had radios since the communists took over," Dumitru said,

"Militia prosecute people they find listening to a radio," added Leana.

"We've got to get going or my father will be upset," Daniel told Cornel. They said their good-byes and walked quickly home.

Cornel enjoyed his new life even though days were just as long or longer than in Rusanesti. Even in Resita, no one got enough food and everyone was always hungry. He and Daniel took turns collecting food with the coupons. Lines weren't as long as those in Rm. Valcea, but bread still had to be procured every day. Cornel would get up at four in the morning to stand in line at the market, and Daniel would take his turn the next day. Once a month, either beef or pork was available, and on those days, Cornel and Daniel both went and stood in line as soon as they got out of school. They'd spend the night in the street in front of the market. Cornel didn't mind; he appreciated the opportunity to help out the Popescus.

During the week, he and Daniel studied hard after school and did their chores of cleaning up the house and yard. They were in bed by nine each evening.

Resita offered so much more than other places he'd been. Cornel was pleasantly surprised that they didn't have to spend their entire weekend doing chores and were allowed to meet with friends. The two cleaned themselves up for the weekend, using the inside steel tub.

Daniel introduced Cornel to the art of promenading down the main street to meet girls. Cornel had grown into a handsome young man: six feet tall, hazel eyes, and wavy, light brown hair he combed into a pompadour. He didn't wear it long; it wasn't allowed, and he could be sent to jail for doing so. His naïve and friendly smile attracted the attention of girls, and some stopped to talk, immediately taken by his positive nature.

One day after school, Florea announced, "The cinema

is showing a movie called *Vagabond*. I've heard it's really good. Anyone want to go?"

"I don't think I'd be interested," Cornel said. He wanted to add that all the movies he had seen promoted communism and were total propaganda, but he'd learned to keep his opinions to himself. The communists didn't allow any western movies into the country.

"It's a foreign movie. I saw pictures of actors from India on the billboards at the cinema," Radu said. "Actors don't speak Romanian, but they do run the translation across the screen."

"It sounds better than the movies I've seen. Will Uncle John be upset if we go to the movie?" Cornel asked his cousin.

"Movies are allowed as long as we get our homework done," responded Daniel. "But we have to ask."

Cornel couldn't wait.

Uncle John gave his permission and Aunt Ruja handed Daniel and Cornel money for tickets. Arriving at the cinema, they were surprised to see the long line. They joined three friends to wait their turn to buy tickets.

The movie began with a rich Indian girl falling in love with one of the family's servants. The poor boy and wealthy girl courted secretly and decided to get married. The girl's parents found out and forbid her from following through with it. The young, infatuated couple didn't listen and continued their relationship. The parents became incensed, fired the servant, and sent him away. He tried to come back but found that his lover had killed herself. Distraught, he took off traveling like a vagabond, first to Bombay, then to London, Rome, and Paris.

Cornel had never seen beautiful cities like these with tall buildings and magnificent houses. Cornel couldn't understand the Indian language being spoken, and he didn't bother to read the Romanian subtitles. He didn't want to miss the visual paradise unfolding in front of him; he was discovering the world's treasures.

The Indian traveled to New York City. Cornel thought about the newspaper photograph he had seen and wondered why people would be sleeping in the streets with all of these buildings?

Music filled the air as the Indian walked into a night club. The beat made Cornel want to get out of his seat and twirl through the theater. They'd never played that kind of music where his friends had taken him to dance.

Days later, Cornel still couldn't get the *Vagabond* theme song or the movie's magnificent images out of his head. Everyone talked of it. The movie was having a big impact on the people of the city — and exactly the opposite of what had been predicted by the communists who had vetted it for screening in Romania. People who saw it dreamed of becoming vagabonds. They wanted to travel but couldn't; they wanted to dress like vagabonds and couldn't. They could sing, so they translated the movie's songs into Romanian and sang them repeatedly.

"It sure makes you want to dance," Cornel said as he grabbed Leana and tried to imitate dance moves they had witnessed in the movie.

Vagabond had stimulated Cornel's adventurous spirit. He couldn't concentrate on his homework. He wanted to visit places shown on the screen. He wanted to hear the music.

Silently he questioned what was being taught in history and political science. Losing his motivation to study, Cornel set aside his work and allowed his mind to go on adventures.

When he arrived home from school the next day, he was met by his uncle. Daniel had warned him that their teachers were friends with his father. They evidently told John that Cornel had not completed his assignment. As soon as Cornel walked through the doorway, Uncle John grabbed Cornel and beat him on the back with his belt as he marched the boy to his room. Aunt Ruja tried to save him, to no avail.

"In this house, you get all of your homework done and done well!" John shouted.

CHAPTER 16

Fall 1955

CORNEL TRIED TO FOCUS on his schoolwork to avoid further punishment, but he couldn't get his mind off the cities he had seen in the movie. He wanted to know more about life outside Romania.

At dinner one evening, Uncle John talked about Hungary, a neighboring country that was also experiencing economic stagnation and lower standards of living under communist rule. In talking about news he had heard, John mentioned that some defiant Hungarians were learning what was going on in the world by listening to Voice of America and Radio Free Europe. John noticed Cornel's expression brighten and issued a warning, "Listening to the radio is forbidden! Besides, the communists block or jam the transmissions anyway."

Cornel's mind started to work overtime and thought: *Radios were probably forbidden in Hungary, and communists probably jammed their airwaves, too.* Cornel wasn't discouraged. *If they're still finding out information, maybe I can too. I just need to find a radio.*

Henceforth, everywhere he went, Cornel kept his eyes open for a radio. One evening, he remembered the pile of junk in the basement and Daniel's statement that his mother didn't throw anything away. When everyone was asleep, he quietly slipped out of bed and crept downstairs. Moving past the food bins, he rummaged through the pile of old clothes, shoes, and other items. Nothing. Then, behind an old box, he spotted something square. It was a radio.

He plugged the cord into an electric socket and turned the knob to the on position. The box produced no sound, not even a hiss, and the glass tubes inside the box showed no signs of life. *At least I found a radio. It's a place to start, and I'll figure out a way to fix it*, Cornel thought.

Cornel removed three tubes from the back of the radio and wrapped them in an old cloth he found in a rag pile. Quietly, he put the radio back where he found it.

A few days later he took the tubes to a store where he had trusted friends. They located tubes that would work and didn't ask questions. Cornel carefully wrapped the tubes and tucked them in his pocket. That evening when everyone had gone to sleep, he quietly slipped from his bed and walked carefully to the cellar.

He removed the radio from its hiding place, cleaned off all the dust, and put in the new tubes. He held his breath as he plugged in the radio. He jumped as loud static came through the speakers. He flipped the volume to low and listened for sounds above him. After a few minutes, when he was satisfied he had not awakened anyone, he turned the large dial, searching for a station. Nothing. He swept the dial slowly several times, but still heard nothing but static. He looked again on the back and saw two screws. *It needs an antenna,* he realized. He put the radio away and sneaked back to bed.

The next day, Cornel remembered seeing a junk pile outside the large factory in town. A few days later he found time to go to there. Careful to be sure no one was looking, he scrounged through the pile until he unearthed several long pieces of copper wire.

That evening when everyone was sound asleep, he went back to the cellar and connected his copper wires to the back of the radio. He ran the wires out the cellar window. He crept back upstairs, out the back door and to the cellar window. He carefully pulled the wires behind him to the nearest tree, climbed up as far as he dared, and wrapped the wires to a limb.

He retraced his steps to the cellar and tried the stations again. Music blurted out of the little speaker.

He turned the shortwave dial and heard a foreign language. He turned the dial a little more and heard someone say in Romanian, "This is the Voice of America." A song played, and the announcer said it was the national anthem of the United States. Cornel felt triumphant. Not only had he made the radio work, but he'd proved Voice of America did exist!

The reception wasn't clear but Cornel could hear enough through static. He listened intently to five minutes of news, and then music came on for five minutes more. He hadn't heard this kind of music before, but it made him stand and dance.

A few minutes later an announcer came on with world news. Cornel put his ear close to the speaker. The announcer talked about electrical workers in America striking against a company called Westinghouse. Cornel wondered why America would admit to worker strikes. He didn't want to hear that his teacher had been telling the truth. Then they explained that people were striking to get better wages. *We'd be beaten or put in prison for doing something like that*, Cornel thought. The difference, he realized, was that the announcer was free to tell the truth. *People were striking because they had the freedom to stand up for what they felt was right.*

Cornel knew he'd already pushed his luck for the evening, so he went outside, climbed the tree, and took down the wire antenna.

Back inside, he pulled the wire through the window, coiled it around the radio, carefully hid it in rags, and added two old shoes over the hump. He crept up the stairs and crawled under the bed covers. He'd cut it so close he didn't have time to get to sleep before he heard his aunt and uncle open the door to their bedroom.

During the next few days, Cornel decided he'd better concentrate on schoolwork and get caught up on sleep. He didn't want to draw attention to his evening activity.

As soon as he was back in the good graces of his uncle and felt he wasn't under the microscope, he went back to the cellar. He again ran the antenna up the tree and turned on the radio. This time, picking up a station was a test of his patience. He knew the government worked continually to jam the transmissions. Cornel finally found a station playing a type of music he hadn't heard before, but he loved it. The announcer called it jazz.

He did not tell anyone about his discovery. Every night he waited until he was sure everyone was sound asleep. He climbed the tree to secure the antenna and tiptoed down to the basement to listen to Voice of America. He kept moving the dial and his antenna to find the clearest reception. Some nights he couldn't find it at all. When he did, he listened closely to the news and enjoyed hearing new types of music. A new sound came through speakers, and the radio announcer called it rhythm and blues. It made Cornel get out of his seat and dance around again. Before going to bed, he took down the antenna and hid the radio.

With each secret session in his uncle's cellar, Cornel became more aware of the subtle ways of the communist rule and propaganda — from his teachers' lectures to the street speakers — were manipulating his life. *Feeling hungry while the government tells us we have plenty to eat is blatant, almost laughable, absurdity,* he thought.

But it was dawning on him how the constant diet of propaganda could poison one's mind. He began to feel angry.

Cornel continued to listen to the radio whenever possible. He finally decided to trust his cousin and tell him about it.

"Would you like to listen to some music like you've never heard before?" Cornel asked when they were at the park and far enough away from any ears.

"How? Where?" Daniel asked.

"Your basement," Cornel said watching Daniel's eyebrows shoot upward. "I found a radio and fixed it. I've been listening to Voice of America to hear the real truth."

"How come you didn't tell me before?" demanded Daniel. Cornel realized that Daniel's feelings were hurt because he hadn't confided in him sooner.

"I didn't want to get you in trouble and wasn't sure if you'd turn me in to your father," Cornel said.

"You know me better than that."

"I do know, which is why I'm telling you."

"So when do I get to hear it?"

"Tonight, if you want. I wait until everyone is asleep. I'll wake you up before I go down," said Cornel.

"You won't have to wake me!" Daniel said.

Cornel listened for an occasional snore from his uncle. Once certain the adults were asleep, he lightly punched Daniel, and they slipped out of bed. Worried he'd wake his father, Daniel anxiously followed Cornel to the basement.

Cornel grabbed the antenna wire from its hiding place and ran the line through the window. Outside, he made fast work of placing the antenna. By now he was an expert. Back inside, Cornel unveiled the prized radio to his cousin. After showing him how to attach the antenna, Cornel turned the radio on and was relieved to hear fairly clear music.

A rock and roll song vibrated out of the speaker. Cornel began to dance, and Daniel followed suit. Cornel's body moved with every beat, a silent admission he'd been listening to this type of music for a while.

"I can't believe this," Daniel said after the song was over. "This is incredible."

"I know. I love the music, but wait until you hear what is happening in the Western world," said Cornel.

An announcer began to talk about another strike in the United States. Workers were striking and demonstrating for more benefits and better pay.

"The rumors we've been hearing are true. What they're telling us in class and in the papers are all lies," Daniel said, growing more upset with each word.

Frustration left when another song filled the room. They both smiled at each other and began jumping around to the music. They stayed in the basement dancing and listening to the news for an hour and a half. "We'd better go. We've already stayed longer than I normally do."

After he turned the radio off, Cornel said, "You can't say a word to anyone, not even to our closest friends. It's not so much that we can't trust them, but we just can't take the chance."

Daniel promised to keep the secret.

Cornel and Daniel danced to the music and listened to the news from the West at least two times each week. Now they had a new perspective, and both became increasingly frustrated by the propaganda the communists continued to spread.

CHAPTER 17

Summer of 1956

S CHOOL LET OUT FOR THE SUMMER. Although he had not been worried about his grades in most of his classes, Cornel was relieved that he had passed Russian. Now he could forget about schoolwork for a while — and the communist lies that permeated every lesson.

His uncle found work for Cornel and Daniel at Combinatual Metalurgic Resita, the large metal plant in town and source of the black smoke Cornel couldn't help but notice in his first minutes in the city. His uncle filled him in on the factory's history.

By the end of World War II, the factory had employed 22,000 people, almost the entire adult population of Resita, and was important to the Romanian economy. After the coup to take over the government, the communists took control of the company.

The factory was a foundry. Its products included a wide array of steel goods: machinery, train cars, locomotives, structural building materials, oil drilling equipment, electric motors, and more. Another plant attached to Combinatual Metalurgic Resita distilled chemicals used by the factory.

The two plants stretched from one end of Resita to the other. The entrance to the complex was in the center of town. Looking at the complex as he walked past it on his way to run errands, Cornel had thought of a giant; the entrance was the giant's head, and the stretch of buildings were its several pairs of thick arms groping to engulf the city.

His uncle didn't have to tell him about the smoke; everyone in Resita breathed the smoke, smelled the smoke, lived in the smoke. It came from the scores of stacks that speared the factory roofline. Each tall pipe shot fat plumes of black smoke day and night. The new smoke was quickly swallowed by the black cloud that hung not just above the factory but blanketed the entire city.

The smell was overpowering. Cornel had quickly discovered he could go nowhere within the city to escape it. It seeped into his clothes, hair, and bedding. Some days he even thought he could taste it in his food. The black soot that fell from the smoke cloud dusted the city's buildings and streets. A dark face, grimy hands and smudged clothes marked a person as a factory worker.

Still, Cornel was grateful for the job because it meant he'd have a little money of his own. It didn't matter if he worked at the factory or somewhere else. No one in town could escape the soot or smell.

A few days after he started work, Cornel was told to report to the office of Nicolae Dumitrescu. Cornel walked through the factory until he came to the door to which he'd been directed. He knocked twice.

"Come in." Cornel didn't recognize the man's voice any more than he'd recognized the name.

"Close the door," Nicolae said as Cornel stepped into the sparse room. He came to a stop in front of the man's desk.

"Please sit down," Nicolae said in a friendly tone. "Are you the son of Marin Dolana?"

Cornel said nothing. He felt as if all his energy was flowing into quelling his rising panic, and he didn't trust his voice. If the communists had found out he was the son of Marin Dolana, he'd be thrown out of school. Was this man going to turn him in? Cornel's anxiety must have shown on his face because the man didn't wait for him to answer.

"I was in jail in Craiova the same time as your father," Nicolae said. "I want to help you if I can. I hear you're very smart and good with numbers. I'd like to give you the position of expediter. You'll be responsible for keeping records of the steel pickups and ordering supplies, like wire for the motors. Are you interested?"

"Yes! Thank you!" The words burst from his throat. He couldn't believe his luck.

"Did you know my father well?" Cornel wanted to know all about the man's time in prison with his father, but knew direct questions wouldn't be answered.

"We all knew each other. I think you know how it was. I was released from prison because the government needed me for my management skills and knowledge of engineering and metals." He paused and locked eyes with Cornel.

"You'll need to keep your mouth shut that you know me. We don't want the wrong people to know where you really come from."

Holding his gaze, Cornel nodded.

"Yes, of course, and thank you for this."

Cornel thrived in his position as an expediter, which included supervising others, some of whom were Romanian soldiers. Communists used the soldiers to help reach their quotas at the plant and didn't pay them for their work. Everyone liked Cornel because he was easygoing and always had a smile. Occasionally, he let the soldiers leave work to go to the movies.

Now that Cornel had money, he went regularly to the movies

with his friends. He watched *Vagabond* at least ten times before the next good movie, *Public Enemy Number One*, came to town. The Romanian papers, controlled by communists, promoted the new film because they thought it showed the Western world in a bad light. However, just like *Vagabond*, communists didn't factor in the visual impact of the film.

Much of *Public Enemy Number One* took place in New York City, which gave Cornel another look at this metropolis. The tall buildings continued to amaze him, but this film also showed highways, cars, and junkyards with cars piled high. It was another reminder of his situation. *Here in Romania only top communists had cars*, Cornel thought. *Look at all those cars driven by regular people, and I can't even have a bike, let alone a car. If I could get a car from the junkyard, I would fix it myself.*

In addition to watching movies, Cornel and his friends, including one special girlfriend, Geta, enjoyed dancing at Casa Muncitorilor to tango and waltz music. Cornel wished they'd play rhythm and blues and rock and roll, music he'd heard on the radio. However, he loved all kinds of music and could dance to anything.

Cornel had begun to see North Korean students at Casa Muncitorilor. When North Korea invaded South Korea, the Romanian government brought North Korean students to Romania to study at a special school. The government built and provided apartment buildings for the North Korean students. Some Romanian students resented the foreign students because they were treated far better than Romanians.

The friction between Romanians and North Koreans was growing. Cornel had never felt it personally; he liked everyone — especially girls who liked to dance. Although his dance partners had always been Romanian girls, one evening he approached a

Korean girl. She didn't hesitate to accept the invitation from the charming local.

The two teens threaded their way onto the floor. Cornel had just put his arm around her waist and moved into the dance's first steps when he felt someone grab him and push him from the girl. The next thing he knew, he was hitting a wall. Stunned, he slid to the floor and didn't see the fist coming toward his head. It caught him on the ear. He yelled out and threw his arms over his head, a poor defense against an attacker, but trapped on the floor, it was the best he could do at the moment. A second later, someone pulled the attacker away before he could do further damage. Cornel looked up and saw a group of soldiers he supervised at work and for whom he often bought wine. Two of the soldiers had grabbed the Korean; Cornel watched as they threw the Korean student through an open window. Two other soldiers quickly grabbed Cornel and ran from the dance. They knew it would only be moments before the militia appeared.

Cornel had always been lenient toward the people he supervised. After the incident, if soldiers he supervised asked for days off, he never hesitated to oblige. Cornel always listened to soldiers' needs and tried to find ways to help them. In a communist society, friends in the right places could help you out in numerous ways. The bar incident was a good example.

Cornel felt fortunate to be living in Resita. He was going to school, earning money in the summer, and having fun with his friends at dances and the movies. He was not being forced to work long hours in the fields. He often thought about his family and worried about them. Now that he had a little money, he wanted to help them and was glad when his uncle suggested they visit Rusanesti.

Aunt Ruja, Uncle John, Daniel, and Cornel caught the train after work and rode it to Caracal. From there they walked the remaining twenty-five miles to Cornel's home. They had informed militia of their journey before they left Resita and had to stop and report their arrival to Comrade Argesanu. Cornel hated having to see Argesanu, and his stomach turned when they walked into his office. On the way home, Cornel told his relatives a couple of the run-ins he'd had with the official.

Georgica was the first to see them coming. He ran through the gate and down the street toward the approaching visitors.

"Cornica, oh, Cornica, it's good to see you," Georgica said as Cornel gave him a big hug.

"I can't believe how much you've grown since I've been gone," Cornel said. Georgica hugged his aunt, uncle, and cousin as they walked toward the house.

Oprita was plucking feathers from a chicken when they stepped inside the house. She dropped it and greeted Cornel with a big hug.

"How are you? Is my brother taking care of you?" she said as she looked up at her brother and gave him and the rest of the family hugs. Then Marin appeared from the next room.

"Cornica!" he cried, embracing his son, then his in-laws.

Cornel was shocked how much his mother and father had aged.

The two families visited. Cornel told his parents, "I've missed you both. I've been doing great. Uncle John made me study hard, and I passed the tenth grade. This summer I'm a supervisor at the metal plant. I'll be going back to school this fall and should graduate next year."

"What do you want to do then?" Marin asked

"I'd still like to be an aviator," responded Cornel.

"You know son, it might be tough since you have to be a member of the Communist Party. We found a way for you to go to high school. Maybe there'll be a way for you to go to flying school. Let's just see what happens."

Over the next few days, Cornel caught up on the family news. His older brother, John, now had two girls named Aurelia and Cornelia, and it thrilled Cornel to spend time with them. His sister was also married and lived a half mile away. Georgica, who had grown taller, was working the collective farm with his parents.

They were all thin. Cornel had asked if they still had flour in their false wall. His father had told them that they still had a little, but because so many people were starving, they had shared much of it with others.

As they were getting ready to make the return trip to Resita, Cornel pulled his father aside and handed him money, almost all he'd saved. Marin began to protest and then accepted it gratefully.

"We need it. Thank you, son."

Cornel felt guilty leaving his family. He knew people from small towns like Rusanesti were feeling the brunt of communism far more than people who lived in big cities.

About a month after they returned to Resita, Cornel's uncle announced, "Cornica, a letter has come for you from your family." Everyone enjoyed getting mail, and Cornel was no exception. He tore open the envelope. The family watched his shoulders slump and a deep sadness develop in his eyes.

"Is someone ill?" Aunt Ruja asked.

"No, it's not that," Cornel responded. "Tata has been trying to get me into aviator training after I graduate. He writes that it is going to be impossible because he was an anti-communist and in jail. I'm not allowed to become an aviator."

"Sorry, Cornica," his uncle said. "I know you've talked about being an aviator since you were young."

Disappointment set into Cornel's soul. From the first moment he'd watched the American planes fly over the trenches, the thought of being an aviator had given him a sense of freedom. Now the dream was gone.

Geta noticed Cornel's distress and wanted to help. She invited him to spend the weekend at her home in Caransebes. Cornel accepted and enjoyed the distraction with his girlfriend, but he couldn't overcome the disappointment. He only spent one night, before he took the two-hour train ride back to Resita. Geta stayed with her family.

Cornel contemplated his life on the long walk to the station and during the ride home on the train. Through Voice of America and the movies, he had learned that a better life existed beyond the Romanian boundaries.

His head jerked up as an amazing thought entered his mind. *What I wanted from flying was not piloting a plane, but freedom. I can achieve that freedom by escaping from the shackles of all things communist. I want to live in a free country.*

That was the moment he decided to escape from Romania and communism. Nothing would change his mind.

PART V

Developing a Plan

CHAPTER 18

Late Summer 1956

CORNEL COULD THINK OF NOTHING but his escape plan. There were many details to consider and decisions to be made. How would he escape? How would he support himself once he reached freedom? He made one decision quickly: He would finish high school and earn his diploma before he tried to get out of Romania.

He would either have to escape soon after graduation or figure out a way to avoid serving as a soldier. Once out of school, all males were mandated by law to serve their country for two years.

He didn't want to be in the communist-controlled army. He would gladly have joined the Romanian forces if communists had not taken over his country, but he didn't want to serve an army that forced people to abide by communist laws. Soldiers were also made to do hard labor and received little food under the communist system. No one looked forward to that life.

Cornel got the break he needed.

Daniel knew the family of a recruiter, a lieutenant major whose wife wanted a job at the factory. Cornel was good friends with a man in the factory's personnel department, often bringing him chickens and tuica. Through that friendship, Cornel helped find a nice job in an office for the lieutenant major's wife. He became good friends with the lieutenant major who introduced him to many of the military recruiters, including captains and majors.

He hoped that by developing relationships with the recruiters he could find a way out of the army. He listened to their complaints, frustrations, and needs. He learned they couldn't get gasoline for their military vehicles. A couple of them had personal motorcycles but rarely had the gas to use them. A situation developed that helped Cornel find gasoline.

The plant operated twenty-four hours a day, but offices, including the shipping department where Cornel worked, closed at three o'clock. His duties included preparing materials to be shipped out, figuring tonnage of steel and quotas, and turning in reports. One day as he stayed late to complete some paperwork he heard a truck pull up.

"The office is closed. You can come back at six in the morning," Cornel told the trucker.

"I really need to get my load tonight. I have no place to spend the night. Can you help me?"

Cornel didn't think twice because it was his nature to help people in need. He retrieved the materials, helped load the truck, and completed the needed paperwork for both the trucker and the company.

"What can I do for you?" asked the trucker when his shipment was ready to go.

"I could use some gasoline, if you could spare it," Cornel said. He figured no one would miss a couple gallons out of the large tank.

"That's more than a fair trade for what you've done for me," said the trucker, who siphoned two gallons of gas into a container.

From that day on, Cornel looked for opportunities to help truckers in exchange for gasoline. He stored the fuel at a friend's house. He gave gas to the more influential recruiters and sold it at half price to others. He hoped this would pave the way to keep him out of the army.

The first goals of his plan were falling into place.

Now came the hardest question. How would he escape and where would he escape to?

This dilemma, like so many others he'd considered, opened the door to an overwhelming number of even more questions. His history teachers boasted that all countries surrounding Romania accepted communist rule. So not only would he have to escape from Romania, he would have to find a way to get through another communist country.

He decided he needed an escape partner to help him think through all the challenges. His first thought was Daniel. He had trusted Daniel with the radio, but could he trust him with the idea of escaping? He didn't feel comfortable with springing the question on him yet. He waited for a more appropriate time.

Cornel went for another visit to Geta's home. Her beauty had attracted his attention the moment he saw her at one of the dances. The handmade native costume of Banat she wore to the dances showed off her slender, shapely figure and long, curly light brown hair. Even though he liked Geta very much, he didn't tell her about the radio or his ideas about escaping.

Cornel didn't pay attention to the surroundings on his ride back to Resita that weekend; he was engrossed in his plan. When the train pulled into the Resita station, the conductor announced the stop twice before Cornel realized he should get off.

Approaching his uncle's house, he saw Daniel sitting on the steps outside. Daniel jumped up and motioned for Cornel to follow him.

As they walked away from the house, Cornel was shocked when he saw the liver-colored bruises across his cousin's face and arms.

"One night I was listening to the radio and my father heard it," Daniel said. "He came flying down the stairs and knocked the radio to the floor. Then he beat me. I know how my father can be — you do, too — but I'd never seen him so angry. I'm so sorry about your radio, Cornica."

"What did he do with the radio?"

"He threw it out."

Without it, Cornel wondered how he was going to stay up on news of the West to plan his escape. Cornel tried not to show his disappointment. He knew his cousin had been punished enough and was feeling frustrated too. Cornel decided this would be the best time to bring Daniel into his plan. They had reached the foot of the mountain and the park at the edge of town, a spot that seemed to be deserted. Cornel blurted his question.

"Have you ever thought about escaping from Romania?"

"I suspect it has crossed everyone's mind, but people get killed for trying."

"Are you saying you're not interested?"

"I'm not saying that at all. If we can find a way, I'm with you."

Those words made up for losing the radio.

"Do you know where your father took the radio?"

"I saw where he tossed it, but I think it's broken."

"I'll just have to fix it. We have to have a radio."

"I won't be listening to it. I hope you understand."

Cornel gave him an empathetic pat on his back.

They walked back to the house, and Daniel nonchalantly pointed to the trash pile where he'd seen his father toss the radio.

That evening, Cornel slipped outside and picked it out. He quickly decided on a temporary hiding place: under a pile of scrap wood on the far side of the outdoor toilet, a spot Cornel thought hadn't been disturbed in a long time. After stashing it behind the thickest boards, he stood back to view his handiwork from the vantage point of someone passing by. He suspected it did look recently disturbed, so he scooped several handfuls of dirt and sprinkled them around, taking care to cover his footprints. He decided it would have to do.

He worried his uncle might stay suspicious for a while, so he decided to wait a couple of weeks before he'd chance bringing the radio back into the house. He couldn't, however, wait to discuss his plan with Daniel. They agreed to meet the next day after work at the park, the safest place to talk.

Cornel arrived first and sat down by a tree, well away from the path. When he saw Daniel, he waved to get his attention.

Cornel shared his ideas. "First, we need to find out more about the bordering countries. They're all communist, so we need to consider the terrain, what countries they border, the politics, and how they feel about Romanian escapees."

Cornel drew a map of Romania in the dirt. "Let's just take them one at a time." Dragging a stick to the northeast of his drawing, where Russia bordered the country.

Daniel blurted out, "I guess this won't be an option," They both laughed at the insanity of that plan.

Cornel dug his stick to the east. "The Black Sea...we could swim or find a boat...that's a long shot...it's three hundred miles to Turkey. The only land crossing is to Hungary and Yugoslavia," he said, pointing to the west.

Cornel drew a line on the southern border. "To get to most

areas of Yugoslavia, we'd have to get across the Danube River. We could swim down the Olt River and across the Danube, but we would end up in Bulgaria, which of course is out of the question. We both know it's worse than Romania."

"This gives us some options. Would your father get suspicious if we ask him questions?"

"He's a teacher and likes it when I'm interested in learning more. He'd love for me to become a teacher like him."

"Okay. It's a place to start."

"Just one more thing," Daniel said as he dusted the ground to remove the evidence. "Have you thought about what can happen if we get caught? I've heard my father and others talk about people who have tried. They torture them, put them in prison, and torture them some more. Many never make it. Are you sure you want to go through with this?"

"We just can't get caught. Are you sure *you* want to go through with it?"

"I'm in." The cousins shook hands on it.

At dinner that evening, Daniel looked across the table at his father.

"Someone was saying today that we have it better than people in Yugoslavia and Hungary. Is that true?"

Cornel held his breath. He chanced a glance at his uncle to see if he was suspicious of Daniel's motives. Then he saw his uncle smile.

"I'm glad you are taking an interest in events outside of the classroom."

A wave of relief washed over Cornel.

"Well," John began, "after the war, Hungary fell under communism, and the people were forced to change as we were."

"How about Yugoslavia?" Cornel asked.

"Yugoslavia has a communist government, but they're not in line with Russia. In fact, I've heard that the Americans have some influence with President Tito. They kept him from joining the Soviet camp and Warsaw Pact. Yugoslavia and the Romanian government are not on friendly terms."

The two boys didn't ask about Bulgaria. They already knew that country was a close ally of the Russians.

Two weeks passed, and Cornel couldn't wait any longer. At midnight he got the nerve to try to dig the radio out of hiding. He had to find out if he could fix it. When he slipped out of bed, he heard Daniel stir, but neither said a word. Daniel turned his back to Cornel and was still.

Cornel was careful not to step on the floor boards he knew were the creaky ones. Outside, he let his eyes adjust to the darkness and walked toward the toilet. He realized he had made a smart decision on where to hide the radio. No one would question him walking to and from the toilet in the middle of the night. He pushed aside the boards he'd stacked to hide the radio; it was still here. He grabbed it and made his way silently to the basement.

After switching on the basement light, Cornel carefully examined each tube. None were broken. He couldn't believe his luck. Then he checked the wires and found one that was loose. He reconnected it, turned the radio around, and turned on the power, but kept the volume low. He smiled in triumph when static came out of the speakers; he'd fixed it.

He ran the antenna out the window and quietly crept out of the house. He let his eyes readjust to the darkness and climbed the tree to attach the antenna to a high branch. When he returned to the basement, he twisted the dial and stopped on a station.

Cornel hadn't heard the song before. He jumped to his feet and began to dance, unable to resist the beat or hold back his triumph over the radio. The music helped him release his excitement. The announcer said it was a song by Elvis Presley. As much as Cornel wanted to hear more music, it was time to find a news broadcast.

Over the next several nights, Cornel listened to whatever came in the best. One time the reception on Radio Free Europe was strongest, another night it was Radio Liberty from Germany or Voice of America.

Cornel kept Daniel up on the latest Western news, whenever the two could slip away from the house. They continued to explore options for their escape.

"We could rob a militianu, get his gun, and then when they try to shoot us as we cross the border, we will shoot back," Daniel said dramatically.

"We do need to look at the possibilities of crossing the border by land versus the Danube River." Cornel didn't respond to Daniel's wild idea of getting a gun away from a militianu. "The government keeps tight control over all border towns. You were born in a border zone, so you can legally travel to Lugoj where Romania borders Hungary and Yugoslavia. You'll be able to get close enough to look the place over."

"That sounds like something I could handle," Daniel said.

The following weekend he took the train to Lugoj. Cornel waited at the Resita station. When Daniel stepped off the train, his head was down. He slumped when the two sat on the first bench they found out of earshot of people passing by.

"What is it? What did you see?"

Daniel shook his head. "Impossible! I never got beyond the railroad station. You can't believe how many soldiers and militieni there were with automatic rifles. They were inside the station every two to three meters. Outside the station they were everywhere and checking papers carefully. There's no way to escape from there. The first step we'd make, we'd get shot. A move like that would lead us straight to the grave."

"We'll find another way." Cornel tried to use his voice to shore up Daniel's confidence, but he saw the look on his cousin's face and how Daniel's hands shook.

"I give up entirely. I'm not going to escape," Daniel said.

"You're chicken."

"I might be chicken, but I don't want to be a dead chicken."

Cornel saw his goading hadn't worked. Daniel really was going to give up.

"Better dead than live life this way," Cornel said. "You'll hear from me when I'm free in the West."

CHAPTER 19

Fall 1957 – June 1958

THE DANGER OF ARMED GUARDS didn't dishearten Cornel. His determination grew with each new injustice and lie from the government. He decided to study harder and find a means to escape. He was disappointed that he'd have to do it alone but not discouraged.

In September, Cornel and Daniel returned to school and entered the eleventh grade. Now that finishing high school was part of Cornel's escape plan, he could concentrate more easily. Cornel studied hard and continued to develop his plan to reach freedom.

He resolved that any possibility of escape meant swimming the Danube River. Cornel could easily swim a mile, but he knew that strong currents made it impossible to swim straight across. So he wondered how long he would be immersed in the swift, cold water. He knew he'd have to be in top shape to survive.

Cornel's swimming skills were exceptional. His father and mother had always joked that they were never sure if Cornel learned to walk or swim first. During his years in Rusanesti, he had proven he could swim faster than any of the other boys and girls whether his age or older. Cornel always amazed his friends by swimming underwater for long periods. They never realized how far ahead of the group he was until he came up for air. By that time, no one could catch him. Then, he would join his friends in playing pranks on the girls. Everyone swam nude, the boys in one area of the river and the girls in another. Boys, being boys, liked looking at the girls. They would sneak up on the girls by breathing through reeds and balancing leaves on their heads as camouflage. Sometimes they got caught when one of the boys giggled or someone from the bank alerted the girls to the intruders.

Cornel realized his experiences growing up had prepared him to swim the Danube. He knew about whirlpools. He had developed techniques for holding his breath, swimming long periods under water, and camouflaging. These skills would all come in handy for challenges he might face.

He threw his energy into strengthening his swimming muscles and his ability to hold his breath underwater for long periods of time. He spent as much time as he could at the concrete, spring-fed swimming pool in the park where he and Daniel had met to formulate their plans. He had been there often enough to know when the pool was busy. He was aware that the practice routine he needed to maintain might appear to be unusual. This was not Rusanesti, but Securitate still paid people to tell them about suspicious activities. He practiced every day when the pool wasn't frozen. He welcomed the chilly water because it conditioned his body to the river water temperatures.

While he honed his swimming skills, Cornel attacked other obstacles. He wanted to be able to find work wherever he ended up. He was determined that working the fields wasn't going to be his only option. He enrolled in night school to learn accounting and electronics, which added to his eleventh-grade workload. He believed the two nights a week devoted to classes were a good investment in his chances for employment in a free country. All other evenings, he worked at the factory.

Cornel was the youngest in his night classes, but due to Ion Popescu's tutelage years ago, Cornel grasped the concepts more easily than most of his classmates.

Cornel knew this from watching the man seated next to him struggle the first two weeks of class. One day the man leaned over and asked Cornel a question. Cornel gave him a quick answer.

The two walked out of the room together when the teacher dismissed the class for the evening. The man was about the same height and weight as Cornel, but Cornel guessed he was several years older.

"My name is Porcarin Mihai," he said, following the Romanian custom of introducing oneself by saying the last name first. "I want to thank you for helping me."

"You're welcome. I'm Dolana Cornel." They shook hands.

"I was fortunate that a man who stayed with our family on occasion tutored me when I was young. Would you like some help with homework?"

"I appreciate the offer — and I accept," Mihai said.

Mihai and Cornel fell into the habit of completing their homework together. One spring afternoon when the weather was warm, Cornel suggested they take their books to the park.

As they finished the day's assignments, Mihai suggested a swim. The two shed their clothes except for their underwear. Swimming in the nude wasn't accepted in the city as it had been in Rusanesti. Although a few people wore actual swimming suits, most people, even in the city, didn't have money for this luxury.

"I bet I can hold my breath longer than you," challenged

Cornel. He wanted to practice his routine but didn't want to be obvious.

"You're on. On the count of three: One...two...three." They watched each other underwater. Cornel wondered how many seconds Mihai would last. Once Mihai surfaced, Cornel stayed underwater just a few seconds more, not wanting to reveal his full talent.

"Not bad," Mihai said as Cornel surfaced, barely out of breath. "I think you were under longer than most people could have stayed. So how fast can you swim?"

"Fast," responded Cornel. "Want to compete?"

They swam to the end of the pool, pulled out of the water, then turned and positioned themselves side-by-side on the edge.

"To the other end and back, on the count of three. One... two...three!"

Both made perfect dives. Cornel stroked to the bottom and swam underwater for most of the pool's length. He came up and looked back. Mihai had reached only the mid-pool mark. Cornel slowed his pace, not wanting to discourage his friend. He made the turn and swam just fast enough to make it a close race.

"Where did you learn to swim so well?" Mihai asked.

"I'm from Rusanesti, a small village along the Olt River, and I swam all the time," Cornel said. He shared his story of almost drowning when he was three. "Where did you learn?"

"I grew up in Pristol. It's a very small village on the Danube, and I lived about a mile from the river, near the forest. Of course, I haven't been able to swim in the river since the communists took over. The border guards constantly patrol up and down the banks. We had a small stream and a lake nearby, so I swam there."

Cornel tried not to let his excitement show — Mihai had access to the Danube in an area where the river could be crossed into Yugoslavia. Only those who lived along the Danube, had relatives in the area, or had a special permit from the militia were allowed in border towns. Cornel decided to sound out Mihai on his political beliefs.

"In Rusanesti, before the communists took our land, my family was among the 'rich' people of our village. Now, everyone in Rusanesti struggles. We still don't have electricity or running water. The government takes everything we grow and leaves us with very little to eat. If it weren't for my uncle, I'd still be there."

"It's the same for my village. I feel sad whenever I think of it."

Cornel knew then that Mihai could be trusted and told him the story of how his father was taken to jail for hiding an anti-communist leader.

"At least your father survived," Mihai said. "Some of the people in my village were killed."

"Several from our village never came home, so we're not sure what happened to them. What did your villagers do that was so terrible?" Cornel asked.

"Several people have tried to escape, most of whom were shot and killed."

Cornel's senses went into high gear like a wolf on the prowl. "How'd they try to escape?"

"Some people tried to swim to freedom from the river's edge and some jumped off the ferry. Some tried to use a straw to swim underneath the water. Some of them tied hollow gourds around their waist to help them float."

Cornel thought the gourds were a bad idea. If you needed

to dive to hide from the guards, the gourds would make you too buoyant to be able to go under.

"Do you know of others who've tried?"

"I do, but it's getting late. Let's swim. I'll tell you later."

Cornel tried not to show his disappointment, but at least Mihai had more to tell. Cornel couldn't wait until their next meeting.

They began to meet at the park after class on a regular basis. Over the next few weeks, Cornel felt he was fast becoming friends with Mihai, who was always cheerful and appeared to be good-hearted.

Mihai learned his electronics lessons quickly with Cornel's help, but he didn't have confidence in his ability to take tests. He asked Cornel to take the final exam for him as they neared graduation time. Cornel thought his friend could do well on the test without him, but Mihai's job at the plant depended on it. He took the test for him. Both students received good grades.

In May 1958, about 150 students at Liceul Mixt Resita received a diploma. Almost as important as the diploma to Cornel, recruiters returned the favor of receiving gasoline by placing the files of Cornel, Daniel, Cornel's brother Aristotel (whose time had been deferred), and ten of Cornel's closest friends in the dead file. Later the recruiters provided each of them with identification showing they had served their time. They would never have to join the army.

Cornel's schedule returned to a more reasonable pace when high school and night school ended. That meant more time to swim and prepare for his escape.

Since Daniel had decided against escaping, Cornel had been thinking about a replacement escape partner, preferably one who had access to the border. Mihai could provide both. Cornel held off approaching Mihai until he was sure his trust in his new friend was justified. The Securitate would pay well for valuable information like escape plans. A few days after Mihai had trusted Cornel enough to ask him to take his exam, Cornel decided that was proof enough.

Mihai had just shared another escape story when Cornel got up the nerve to ask. Cornel looked him straight in the eye and said quietly, "How about us?"

"You mean, how about us escaping?"

Cornel nodded.

"Are you serious?"

"I've never been so serious," Cornel said, watching Mihai's expression closely. In an instant, Mihai's joyful face gave Cornel his answer.

"I can't believe it. I can't believe it," Mihai said. He was so excited that he stood up and jumped around. "I'm so happy to find someone else who wants to escape. Even after all the stories I've told you, you still want to escape. Unbelievable."

"I've been thinking about it for a while," Cornel responded. "I had a plan with someone else I knew, but after he saw all the guards and guns and how dangerous it was going to be, he got scared and backed out. I'm escaping even if I have to do it by myself. I'd prefer to have the company."

"No one wants to escape more than I do," Mihai said.

CHAPTER 20

Late June 1958

WHEN THEY WEREN'T AT THEIR JOBS at the factory, Cornel and Mihai met at the park to train in the pool. One Sunday in June, Cornel arrived an hour before they'd agreed upon. He settled on an old bench shaded by a large tree at the top of a hill and pulled a book out of his pocket. The book was a Romanian translation of Jules Verne's *20,000 Leagues Under the Sea*, a gift from the aunt of a friend who knew of Cornel's love for adventure. Cornel was fascinated by Captain Nemo and the Nautilus submarine and didn't want to put the book down. He lost himself in the story, looking up only when he heard someone approaching. Expecting Mihai, Cornel was surprised to see a uniformed man coming toward him.

"Where did you get that?" the militianu demanded, pointing at Cornel's book.

Cornel hadn't realized that the Verne tale was not an approved book, but the reaction of the militianu told him otherwise. Not wanting to implicate the woman who gave it to him, Cornel decided to lie.

"I found it in the garbage, on the street. The picture on the cover caught my eye, so I picked it up to see what it was."

"I need to see your identification."

Cornel stood and fished it from his pants pocket. The militianu stuffed the paper into his shirt pocket.

"And the book." Cornel surrendered it to the militianu's outstretched hand.

"It is capitalist influence. You are under arrest." The militianu grabbed Cornel's left wrist and handcuffed it. Keeping his grip on Cornel's arm, the militianu swung him around as if they were executing a tricky dance step, which ended with Cornel's back facing him. Cornel instinctively pulled away as he felt his right arm yanked behind his back to meet his left, and his wrist was forced into the cold metal clamp.

Something slammed into Cornel's right side. Cornel grunted and lurched forward. Pain exploded from his side and burned across his back. He felt as if all the air had been knocked out of his lungs. He managed to remain on his feet, the cuffs tight against his wrists, his shoulder muscles twisting like wet rags being wrung out by powerful hands.

"Move, move, keep going." As he gave his order, the militianu kneed Cornel downhill. Already off balance, Cornel crashed to the ground. Without use of his arms to break his fall, he hit the dirt so hard he heard the thump. He landed squarely on his right arm. To move away from the pain, he twisted his legs up to his chest and rolled into a face-down position. Still, the pain in his arm tuned up to keep time with the throb along his right side where he'd been kicked.

The militianu grabbed Cornel by the cuffs.

"Stand. Up." He spit out the order in two separate words as he yanked Cornel to his knees and then jerked him to a standing position. Cornel concentrated on not falling so the militianu wouldn't touch him again.

His body was heaving in pain. *Breathe evenly,* he told himself — *like in swimming. Don't faint.* He forced his eyes to open and tried to blink away his dizziness. Slowly he turned his head to the militianu. *The insignia on his uniform sleeve — was that one or two stripes?* Cornel wondered vaguely.

"I'm…I'm up. What…what did I do?" Cornel was trying for the victory of a few seconds so he could be still. He needed time to beat back the blackness that was bleeding into the corners of his vision. He needed time to fill his lungs with air and then expel it.

"You'll find out soon enough, comrade. Go."

Cornel kept his mouth shut, concentrating on not tripping and trying to move fast enough to stay out of range of the militianu. He wondered, *What could communists fear about a fantasy?*

Cornel stumbled to his knees two more times but managed to stand and go on before the militianu could intervene. At the bottom of the hill, the militianu prodded Cornel to turn right. A block later, the militianu pointed left. As Cornel turned, he realized they'd reached the militia station.

The few people in the station looked at Cornel in disgust as he was pushed across the room and forced to walk down a set of stairs.

At the bottom, a wretched smell hit Cornel. He wished he could put his hand over his nose and mouth. The militianu pointed down a hallway, and Cornel walked in the direction indicated, passing by thirty cells already occupied. He stopped when ordered to halt in front of an open door. The militianu pushed him across the threshold, removed Cornel's handcuffs, shoved him deeper into the cell, then backed out and slammed the door shut.

The sharp smell of urine hit Cornel the instant he was inside. He clapped his hand over his mouth and nose and closed his eyes.

When he felt steadier, he surveyed the cell. There was no

furniture — no bench, no cot. The space was small. He could have touched the walls with his outstretched arms, but one glance at the filthy cement dissuaded him from trying. The floor was of the same rough cement as the walls. Above him, a mat of spider webs thickened by dust masked the small square of light outlined by a tiny window close to the ceiling. After a few minutes, when Cornel's eyes had begun to adjust to the cell's dim light, he spotted something on the floor in a corner. Cornel kicked at it. *Bugs. Many, many dead bugs.* Then he saw movement on the walls. *Bugs — live bugs.*

Repulsed, Cornel moved to the center of the room. He resolved to remain standing and not touch the walls. Growing angry, he began to pace but had to turn so often it was more like walking in circles than pacing. Dizzy, he stopped and tried to sort out what was happening to him. Had he really been arrested for reading *20,000 Leagues Under the Sea*? Surely the militianu had made a mistake. Then he realized it didn't matter. If the communists wanted to keep him in jail, nothing could stop them from doing so.

His anger at being dumped into a cell for reading a book had helped him push away the pain, but suddenly he could no longer ignore it. He took stock of his body. First he examined his wrists, which had turned soft and puffy. They were ringed with reddish-blue bracelets as if the cuffs were still there. His hands ached and were smeared with dried blood from the scrapes on his wrists. His forearms throbbed.

He pushed his fingers gently into his ribs on each side — maybe nothing was broken, he decided, but every spot he touched was tender and even slight pressure on his right side made him wince. He gingerly gathered his shirt tails and pulled them up to look at his skin. It was a mass of scarlet-colored scrapes. He was relieved not to see any deep cuts. His shoulders ached.

Without bending, he tried to hike up his pant legs to examine his shins and knees. He could see that his lower legs were scraped, but he couldn't get his pants up high enough to see his entire knee. Still standing, he flexed one, then the other, feeling the skin tighten across swollen tissue. His knees felt like they'd been pumped full of water.

He stood for what seemed like hours. Cornel had only the window light by which to judge time of day. He gave up wondering if anyone would come to tell him why he was in jail and how long he'd be there. As the cell grew dark, Cornel realized he would be spending the night without water, without food. He didn't care about food, but he was thirsty.

His bladder began to nag at him. He waited as long as possible, then finally relieved himself in the corner. Judging by the intensity of the odor, Cornel knew many other prisoners had done the same. He was suddenly so tired he gave up his resolve about sitting on the filthy floor. He lowered his exhausted body to the farthest spot from where he'd urinated and closed his eyes.

He woke suddenly, not sure if he'd heard something or if he'd been dreaming. Exhausted, he fell back to sleep almost instantly. When he woke again, he was curled against the wall, cold and stiff. He turned and looked up at the window. He decided it was morning — the brighter light coming through the small window told him it was past daybreak. Surprised that he had slept through the night, he felt hungry, but his thirst was greater. Cornel stood and banged on the door with his fist. He waited, listening for some sound, then banged the door again. Other prisoners yelled back for him to be quiet. He gave up and sat down, then stretched out and tried to sleep again.

After what seemed like hours, a militianu appeared at his cell door. Cornel sprang up, excited to see anyone.

"Am I being released?"

The militianu said nothing, but motioned for Cornel to follow him. They walked down a hall, through a door, down another hall, and to a toilet that was attached to the building. After Cornel was finished, the militianu led him back to the cell.

"Can I have something to drink?" Cornel asked.

"We'll be by later," the man responded.

"How long will I be kept here?"

The militianu didn't respond and went to the next cell.

A while later the man returned with a bucket. He dipped a ladle into the bucket, filled a small cup that had been sitting outside the cell door, and handed it to Cornel through the bars.

Cornel raised the cup to his nose and sniffed. He lowered the cup and peered at the liquid. *Pea soup?* He poked at a lump and saw it had legs. He fished it out and flung it against the wall, then stirred the soup with his finger, looking for more insects. Finally, thirsty and hungry, Cornel choked the liquid down.

Four days went by. He was taken from his cell and led to the toilet once a day and was provided one cup of pea-bug soup each day. No one spoke to him. Cornel sat in his cell wondering, worried, and afraid. He'd heard of people being put in prison for ten years for just a small offense. Would he be spending his next ten years in this wretched hole? How ironic, he thought, for a young man who sought adventure and freedom from communism not to even be able to walk the streets. He had lost all freedom. If he spent the rest of his life in prison, then Lieutenant Ariciu, Comrade Argesanu, and the entire communist government would have won.

Sitting alone day after day, Cornel reflected on what the likes of Ariciu and Argesanu had done to Romania. They had robbed the people of many things. They had taken away their choices, their voices, and even their abilities to make decisions. They had reduced the amount of food and other resources available to Romanians. They had taken whatever they wanted from the people: their animals — he thought sadly about his dog — their guns, a portion of their gardens, their labor. They had caused many to lose their motivation and, worst of all, their hope.

Cornel's determination to escape grew, but he worried his chance was gone. Even if he were to be let out soon, he likely would no longer have a job. Without a way to earn money, he couldn't save enough to fund his escape. He would have to go home to his parents. He wondered what his parents would say. He suspected they would be distressed, but not disappointed in him. He thought of Mihai. Cornel had been so excited to find someone else who thought of nothing but escape, and he knew Mihai felt the same way. Now, Mihai might go without him, and Cornel couldn't blame him for not waiting.

He filled his hours by working out alternate escape scenarios. On the fifth day, a militianu appeared at the cell door soon after Cornel woke. After the man allowed Cornel to use the toilet, he handcuffed him and walked him upstairs and into a small room where a female judge and male clerk sat as if waiting for him.

"Decadent! You have been influenced by a decadent capitalist society," yelled the judge without preamble. "Where did you get the book?"

Cornel was startled by the outburst, but he was able to repeat the story he'd told in the park.

"I saw it in the garbage. It had a nice picture so I picked it up," Cornel said. "I didn't know it wasn't an approved book until the militianu told me."

"You'll need to pay a fine of one thousand lei, stay two more days and attend the Youth Union of Workers meeting. If I ever catch you again, you'll go to jail for years."

Cornel despaired. He didn't have the money; 1,000 lei was an entire month's salary. While the two-day sentence was a relief — he'd imagined ten years — he wondered what would happen when he couldn't pay the fine.

The prison routine remained the same. The lack of food made him feel weaker each day. His stomach had given up growling after the second day. Cornel suspected he had lost quite a bit of weight. He was thin when he entered prison but now he imagined his ribs felt sharp under his skin.

When the two days were up, a militianu led Cornel out of his cell, this time without handcuffs.

"Your fine has been paid, and so you're being released, but you must go straight to the Youth Union of Workers meeting," the militianu said as he walked Cornel to the main prison door and handed him his identification papers.

Amazed, Cornel took the papers and hurried outside. He was afraid if he stayed to ask who had helped him, that he wouldn't be released after all.

The light of day was so bright that he had to stop and let his eyes adjust. The city air, always so sooty, smelled clean to Cornel, and he breathed deeply. He walked directly to the meeting.

It was already in process when he arrived. Hundreds of people were in the hall, and Cornel tried to take a seat without speaking to anyone. Several men spotted him immediately and told him to stand. Surprised anyone would be expecting him and not wanting to invite trouble, Cornel rose from his seat. They pointed to the stage, so Cornel climbed the steps and turned and faced the audience.

"The militia found this man with a book that has capitalistic influence," screamed one of the leaders as he pointed at Cornel. "It was not to the code of communism."

The members yelled in unison, "Capitalist! Capitalistic influence!"

"Expel him! Expel him! Expel him!"

Cornel silently wondered how he could be expelled from an organization he didn't belong to.

"Throw him out of his job! Replace him!"

So he would lose his job. He'd suspected that would happen, but he was crushed to hear someone say so.

Cornel was relieved when the meeting was over and he had not been hit or kicked. He could deal with the condemnation of the group; he didn't want to be part of it anyway. Outside, he turned in the direction of Mihai's one-room apartment. In a few minutes, Cornel was knocking on Mihai's door, barely mustering the strength to hold up his arm and tap his knuckle against the wood.

The door opened almost instantly.

"Cornel, my friend, I'm so glad you were released from jail," Mihai said, clapping him on the back. Cornel drew back instinctively.

"I'm sorry, I don't mean to insult you, but they beat me. I'm still very sore. You have no idea how bad it was."

Cornel suddenly realized what Mihai had said; Mihai had known Cornel had been arrested.

"So you knew where I was! I wondered if anyone would find out what happened to me. Did you pay my fine?"

"Not just me. We all pitched in — your uncle, your brother, all your friends," Mihai explained that a militianu had told Cornel's uncle about the arrest.

"Oh, thank you, thank you all! I was so afraid I'd be there the rest of my life." Cornel felt like he would cry if Mihai said another word. Sensing Cornel's emotional state, Mihai tried to make Cornel smile.

"Hey, you look skinny! Let's find you something to eat. Sit down, I'll bring you something. Then maybe you'll want to go home and get a bath."

The next day, Cornel arrived early at Combinatual Metalurgic to find out if he still had a job. He had managed a few hours of sleep. It was the first time in a week he'd slept in a bed. Thinking of the filthy cell floor, he shuddered. He had washed, reveling in the clean water and soap. Despite his thinness, he looked much like himself.

Cornel made his way through the throng of workers who always showed up early to buy sips of tuica before going to work. Someone was always at the entrance selling the alcohol. It was poured into a ceramic cup and passed around, everyone drinking from the same cup. Many workers needed tuica to get through the day. Some reported to work drunk. Cornel estimated that 90 percent of the workers were heavy drinkers, and he didn't blame them. They needed a way to forget their suffering, if only for a moment. When they weren't drinking, they'd feel the full force of their situation, so they drank again.

Cornel rarely had a drink before work. His escape plan kept his spirits up. Now, after his time in prison, his resolve was stronger. If he didn't lose his job, his plan could stay on track. If the company fired him, his plan would be in jeopardy.

Cornel made his way immediately to Nicolae Dumitrescu's office and knocked.

"Come in and shut the door," Nicolae said.

"Do you know why I haven't been at work for the past week?" Cornel asked. "Am I in trouble? Did I lose my job?"

"I know what happened. Are you all right?"

"I'm still sore, and I'm tired, but I want to work. Do I still have a job?"

"Don't worry, you do. I took care of it."

Relieved, Cornel thanked Nicolas and went to his desk. His plan could move forward.

June 1958 – August 1959

CORNEL AND MIHAI SPENT EVERY MINUTE they weren't working preparing for their escape. They'd decided their best bet was to swim across the Danube. The practice became a routine: They would dive to the bottom of the ten-foot-deep pool, swim as fast as they could underwater, and hold their breath until they felt their lungs would explode. Each day they stayed submerged a few more seconds. Their capacity to stay underwater was key to the success of their plan; when in the river, the only place to hide from the militianu would be under the surface. They practiced two to three hours a day after work and all day on Sundays.

The second part of the plan was to save every cent they could. Finally, they reached their goal. They were ready. They set a date in August to travel to Pristol.

Cornel returned home in the middle of August to see his

family one last time. *I'll either be dead or free,* he thought, *and I want to say goodbye.*

His parents never knew when Cornel would come home but always looked for him. They greeted him with hugs and questions. Cornel told them about graduating from high school, passing two night-school classes, and working at the metal plant. Last, he told the full story of being imprisoned for reading a book.

They were proud of his accomplishments and troubled by the prison incident. Cornel's mother was particularly upset that the government had put her son in prison for reading. She herself had always enjoyed reading before the communists took over the country. She had educated herself on many subjects but had little time for it now. Looking back, Cornel realized how much she had influenced his life. The French she taught him could come in handy over the next several months.

Oprita told her son she had grown too weak to work at the collective farm but was able to keep house and tend the garden. She related how his father, released from duty in the fields, came to be assigned to run the ferry in Cilieni.

"Even the communists saw we are too old to survive the fields," she said. "But they still expect your father to work. Even the ferry is too much for him."

John and Georgica and Cornel's friends were still working the fields, so he visited with them in the evenings. They all shared glasses of tuica as they talked about girls. Cornel had become as good a storyteller as his father, and they enjoy his rendition of *The Vagabond* and other movies he'd seen. He talked about his closest friends and about the plant where he worked, but he never shared his plan of escape.

His days with his family flew by, and then it was time to say his final good-byes. Cornel's eyes filled with tears as he hugged his father, mother, John, Georgica, and Florica. He had wanted to tell them about his plans, but knew it would be better that they didn't know anything. They were sure to be interrogated when he escaped. Lieutenant Ariciu and Comrade Argesanu would be hard on his family if they were suspected of hiding something. So to protect them, Cornel had decided to keep his plans to himself and couldn't let any of them see how sad he really felt.

He gave his siblings and father another hug, holding on tightly. Then he hugged his mother one last time. Cornel tried to smile as they broke their embrace. He knew if she suspected something was wrong he wouldn't be able to leave without revealing his plans. Or maybe he wouldn't be able to leave at all. He hoped Oprita and Marin would understand later the significance of this particular good-bye, remember his hugs, and be happy for him.

This was the toughest part of his escape plan, Cornel thought as he walked away from the Dolana home and toward the train station. It was difficult to imagine he'd never see his family again, but Cornel knew it was true. Once out of sight of his family, he let tears flow freely.

On the train to Resita, Cornel set his sorrow aside and attacked his next challenge. There was one part of his escape plan that needed to be resolved: Could he come up with a justification that would allow him to visit the border town of Pristol? A person had to have been born there or have a relative living there to have an accepted reason to visit a restricted zone. As a native of Pristol, Mihai had only to show his identification. Cornel had to find some story that would be accepted and approved by the Securitate. His and Mihai's plan depended on it.

A story about visiting a friend would not work, Cornel had

learned. If he claimed to have a job waiting for him in Pristol, the guards would ask to see his work visa. Cornel settled on what he considered to be the only viable plan, but it was flawed.

Cornel had decided he must bank on the fact that Resita militieni wouldn't ask why he was traveling, even if he gave his destination as a border town. Mihai had told him he would be asked the reason for his visit at Turnu Severin and Pristol. The problem was that he didn't know if his story would be accepted until he reached these checkpoints.

The evening after he arrived back in Resita, Cornel walked to Aristotel's apartment. He told him the latest news about the family and shared all the town gossip he had heard.

"I have more news for you," Cornel announced after he finished telling Aristotel about his visit to their family. "I'm leaving Resita to get married."

"That's great, Cornel," Aristotel said. "Congratulations!" Aristotel assumed that Cornel would marry Geta; Cornel didn't say otherwise. They said their good-byes. Cornel left Aristotel in the dark, as he had the rest of his family.

He returned to his aunt and uncle's home, spent the night, and told them that he was going to be leaving the next morning to visit a friend.

PART VI

Pristol, Romania

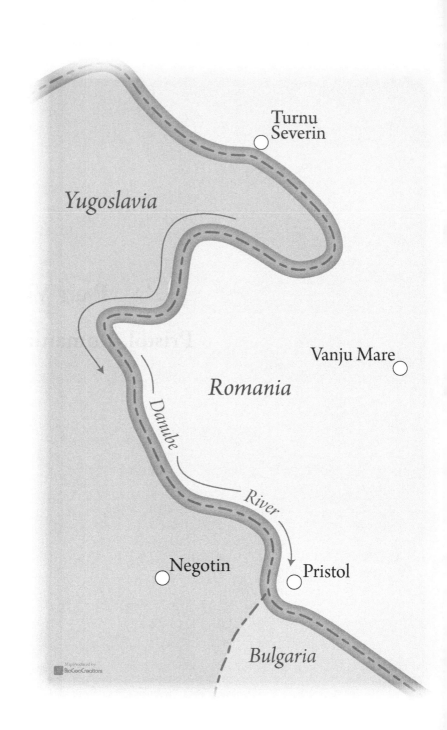

CHAPTER 21

Late August 1959

THE HOT AUGUST WIND that blew through the train window didn't provide any relief to Cornel and Mihai as they set out on the first leg of their journey to freedom. The train stopped at Caransebes where they changed to one going to Turnu Severin. Cornel noticed an increase in the number of militieni on board.

A few miles before they arrived in Turnu Severin, the tracks neared the Danube River. Cornel and Mihai looked intently out the train window. "This section of river is really turbulent," Cornel whispered to Mihai.

"The surrounding mountains narrow the river here, and the current is so strong that even boats avoid this section. Large jagged rocks make it even more dangerous," Mihai explained

"I see what you mean."

The train stopped at Turnu Severin. Mihai and Cornel looked around as they stepped off the train. Border guards patrolled every square foot of tarmac of the depot to make sure people made their way toward town, not the Danube River. The significant presence of guards made everyone tense, but Cornel felt anxiety piled on top of anxiety. He worried his face would betray his intentions if guards looked at him closely.

When it was their turn, Mihai handed over his identification.

The guards then took Cornel's. They let Cornel and Mihai pass toward town. They were relieved that, so far, their plan was working.

At the bus station, they bought tickets to Pristol and left Turnu Severin without incident.

Dust made the miserable heat of the bus worse, and Mihai eventually shut the window beside their seats. Cornel sweated as much from worry about the border checkpoint as he did from the heat.

They stopped in the village of Vanju Mare. He knew the guards would become increasingly strict the closer they came to their final destination of a village near the border. Cornel worried they would turn him back. Twenty-five passengers exited the bus and showed their identification to a Vanju Mare guard before it was Mihai's turn. They returned his identification to him as soon as they saw he was born in Pristol. They didn't question natives like Mihai, but they did stop Cornel.

"Where are you going?" asked the guard.

"Pristol." Cornel said simply.

"Why are you going there and how long do you plan to stay?"

"My intention is to get married," Cornel responded with a big smile.

The guard looked at Cornel's navy blue suit. The government required individuals to buy clothes from a government store; the cost of a suit would have been three months' salary. However, Cornel had bought his suit, shirt, and tie from a friend who secretly did work for people he knew and charged only one month's salary. Cornel was dressed like he was going to get married, and if he was killed in his pursuit of freedom, he wanted to be buried in his best clothes. A trench coat hung over his left arm.

"And I'm the best man," Mihai chimed in.

The guard took another long look at Cornel and then waved them on. Cornel and Mihai got back on the bus.

Cornel took a deep breath as they settled into seats in the back. His excuse had worked here but would it work in Pristol?

"How long to Pristol?" Cornel asked Mihai.

"Only two more hours." They didn't say anything more, content to rest and watch the land slip by.

They continued down the dry dirt roads. Twice more there were stops where people got off and others got on, but these were not checkpoints. Occasionally the two snacked on bread and cheese from the small cloth bag they had packed. Cornel watched the scenery change from the flats to the hills. A sudden shower turned the road to mud, and the bus slid as they rounded a curve too fast. The rain stopped, and the vehicle was again plowing the dust.

In the late afternoon, the bus slowed as they approached the outskirts of a village. Cornel knew they'd arrived in Pristol just by the way Mihai's face brightened. Mihai pointed out a few streets. Cornel thought Pristol looked to be half the size of Rusanesti. The bus stopped, and Cornel and Mihai got off with the rest of the passengers. They stood in the shade of a tree and looked around.

Cornel didn't see any officials. He wondered who was supposed to check their identification. In one way he wanted to get it over with; on the other hand, if his plan wouldn't work, he was in no hurry to be turned back — or arrested.

"I wondered if we wouldn't have to check in with militia," Mihai told Cornel. "Usually they keep a real close eye on strangers here. I think we can wait until morning."

Cornel nodded his agreement. "It sure feels good to get off that bus and breathe some fresh air."

"Oh yeah, that's for sure," Mihai said.

Cornel looked around and realized the only people around were the ones who got off the bus. He commented, "I guess everyone is working the collective farms."

"Unfortunately," Mihai said. "We'll go to my house and rest until everyone gets back."

They walked a mile to Mihai's home, which was on the edge of Pristol. It was a little smaller than the Dolana home in Rusanesti, but the layout was similar. One difference was that instead of a third room, a hallway ran between the two bedrooms. Mihai showed his friend to the room where they would sleep. Cornel was surprised that there were two beds; they wouldn't have to share. They walked out into the backyard. Mihai picked a tomato, from the regulation-size garden, handed it to Cornel, and then picked one for himself.

As the sky darkened, Mihai lit the kerosene lamps. A while latter, Mihai heard his parents come in and greeted them with open arms.

Cornel stood back and watched the joyful reunion of the Porcarins. He noticed that Mihai's hugs for his father and mother lasted even longer than those shared by Cornel's family.

"This is my friend Cornel from Resita," Mihai said. "He helped me in my classes. He's come to get married," Mihai said.

"Welcome, Cornel," Mrs. Porcarin said. "Mihai, make Cornel comfortable while I fix supper."

"We need to run by Ion's place and pick up some bottles of tuica. We'll be back in a few minutes," Mihai announced. When they returned, Mihai poured everyone a glass of tuica, and they enjoyed his mother's homemade cooking.

The next morning, Mihai grabbed one of the bottles of tuica

they had purchased and led Cornel to the militia station. Cornel was uneasy. Even though he had made it this far, the authorities of Pristol could turn him back and spoil their plans.

"What's that for?" Cornel asked Mihai, pointing at the bottle.

"Not for us. Just smile and hand the bottle to the militianu."

It wasn't far to the station. Mihai stopped outside the door and handed the bottle to Cornel.

"Ready?"

Cornel nodded.

Holding the bottle down so his bribe wouldn't be so conspicuous, Cornel stepped into the building. Mihai followed. They were directed to a small room, where Cornel handed his identification to a militianu.

"I arrived in Pristol late yesterday afternoon," Cornel said.

The militianu paged through Cornel's papers, stopping every few seconds to read — which items, Cornel could only guess at. His stomach was flipping.

"What is your date of birth?"

"April 11, 1938."

"What are you doing here?"

"I'm staying with my friend, Mihai Porcarin." Cornel gestured to Mihai. "He was born here, and I want to get married," Cornel said all in a rush as he put the bottle of tuica on the militianu's desk.

"You were born here?" The militianu addressed Mihai.

"Oh, yes" Mihai said, handing his papers over for inspection.

The militianu glanced at them and then put Cornel's papers on the desk. He reached into his desk drawer and brought out a stamp, thumped Cornel's papers with it, and handed them back. Cornel looked at it: a visa for fifteen days.

Elated, Cornel didn't dare look at Mihai until they were halfway down the street. Then they turned toward each other in unison, and their smiles broadened to full extension as their eyes revealed relief and excitement. They had passed the first hurdle. It was a good sign.

"How far are we from the Danube?" Cornel asked after they had walked two blocks.

"It is a short distance out of town. We can sneak through a corn field to get a look at the Danube early tomorrow morning."

CHAPTER 22

MIHAI AND CORNEL SET OUT for the riverside corn fields before daylight. As they threaded their way through Pristol's back streets, Cornel looked up to survey the sky. A few stars winked through clouds to the west.

They walked toward the river. Homes thinned out into fields, and the eastern horizon displayed a tinge of mottled orange. As they rounded a corner, Cornel could make out the unmistakable look of a field of corn. They jogged to the edge, then stopped and listened. A breeze brushed through the field and cooled their faces, hot from the sprint. Cornel heard only a constant rustle, as if the wind was forcing the corn stalks to converse in a language triggered by touch. No one was in sight.

Mihai waved Cornel behind him, and they launched into the sea of corn, the tassels of each stalk wagging high above them as the wind pushed along the row with them. After they were fully inside the field, they slowed their pace and kept their arms close to their sides so they wouldn't make waves that could be detected from afar. The fronds tagged at them as they passed, teasing Cornel into thinking that someone was groping at his shirt from the parallel rows.

After several minutes, Mihai stopped short and dropped to his hands and knees. Cornel followed suit. Mihai glanced back at Cornel, either to give or get reassurance; Cornel couldn't tell which, but he nodded all the same. They crawled forward slowly, Cornel pacing himself so his face was just inches from Mihai's pumping feet. Mihai suddenly flattened to the ground. Cornel dropped down behind him. He guessed Mihai had spotted a guard.

Inching up beside Mihai, Cornel wedged himself between the thick corn plants and his friend's prone body. Mihai shifted to give Cornel more room. They peered down the row to the end, the corn stalks standing sentinel at the opening. Cornel estimated they were about three hundred yards from the riverbank. He could make out the vague outlines of two men and a dog — a German shepherd, Cornel thought, judging by the shape and points jutting from its head. The patrol was on a strip of land between the field and the river. Within minutes, two more guards with a dog joined the others, and they came together in a circle.

It was light enough now that Cornel could see that the two dogs were standing outside the guards' huddle, tails stretched toward the river. Three of the guards lighted cigarettes, cupping them in their hands against the wind off the river.

Cornel froze when the dogs stretched their necks and pointed their noses straight at the corn field. The one guard who had not lit up wheeled and swung his gun up. The other three guards dropped their cigarettes, aimed their weapons, and pivoted to stand behind the dogs. In the growing brightness of the morning, Cornel could clearly see their heads move from right to left in unison, but it was a jerky motion as they stopped every second to get a fix. Suddenly the dogs turned away. Apparently convinced of a false alarm as soon as the dogs lost interest, the guards lowered their weapons and split up into two patrols that set off along the bank in opposite directions.

Mihai jabbed Cornel in the ribs and startled him. They crawled farther back into the row of corn. Mihai stopped and then rose to his knees. Cornel walked himself up with his hands, ending with his lower legs folded under him. Mihai arched his eyebrows and shrugged, then pantomimed the words "let's go." They rose to their feet but kept their bodies bent as they trotted back the way they'd come.

Emerging from the field, they shot across the road and walked a few minutes before they stopped to catch their breath. They slapped at the dirt on their pants and brushed pieces of dried vegetation from their shirts. Cornel pointed to Mihai's hair, then brushed his hand over his own to show Mihai where he needed to remove a small stick. They had instinctively taken time for a brush-off; they didn't want to invite questions from anyone. Cornel hoped their pants would dry before they got back to Mihai's house. Both of them had dark, smudged circles where their knees had pressed into the damp earth. The two men resumed their walk, this time at a leisurely pace as if they had no particular destination.

Nearing Mihai's home, Cornel felt far enough away from the armed guards to discuss what they'd seen, but he kept his voice to just above a whisper.

"Well, what do you think?" he asked Mihai.

"We'd get killed if we tried escaping that way," Mihai stated glumly. "Those dogs would find us within minutes. The sand is about twelve feet wide, and it's so smooth those guards could tell if a bird walked over it."

Cornel nodded.

"I'd been more worried about how we'd avoid the trip wires," Mihai continued, "but avoiding their land mines will be only one of our worries. At least now I'm pretty sure where they've laid the trip wires. It has to be in that brushy area between the field and the sand."

"I don't know how we'd get past those guards and dogs during the day when we could see the wires," Cornel said.

"If we can find out the exact position of the wires, if we timed it just right between their patrols, if the wind is in our favor, and if we pick the darkest night..." Mihai stopped, realizing how long the list of conditionals was getting.

"Yes," Cornel sighed, "so many ifs."

His face suddenly brightened. "But this morning the dogs didn't find us."

"True," Mihai said. He stopped and waited for Cornel to continue, sensing he was getting at something.

"If the dogs had found us, we wouldn't be standing here. We were downwind of them. The wind must have shifted for an instant, and then they could smell us, but we were too far away for them to hold the scent. All we need is a cloudy night with the wind coming off the river. That's usually how wind moves over the river, isn't it?" Cornel turned his eager face to Mihai.

"Yes, it might be true," Mihai said. "We can check each day and see. However, there would be no way to see those trip wires in the dark. It would be pure chance if we didn't hit one."

Cornel remained positive that they would find a means to escape. In the meantime, Cornel knew his story of coming to Pristol to be married might last only as long as the bribe, so he decided not to gamble that the militianu was a slow drinker. Cornel asked Mihai for his recommendations for finding a girlfriend so he'd be ready with some proof.

"The whole village turns out at the field on Sundays for music and dancing. That'll be your best chance of finding a girl," Mihai offered. "Just use your good looks and charm. You shouldn't have any trouble. These girls dream of finding husbands who work in the city."

On Sunday afternoon, Gypsy folk music filtered through the air, attracting people to the field. Everyone was already dancing by the time Cornel and Mihai arrived. Word had spread that a stranger had come from the city with the intention of getting married. No one had to ask who he was. Cornel stood out in his navy blue suit and tie when everyone else was dressed in simple country clothes.

Cornel joined in the circle of dancers and took the hand of a girl next to him. He noticed her smile and her dark hair flowing as her body swayed to the music's beat.

When the band paused between songs, Cornel held onto the girl's hand and led her out of the circle. "My name's Cornel. I'm here visiting my friend Mihai."

"My name is Ionescu Alexandra. It's nice to meet you," she said, smiling.

Cornel and Alexandra danced, and word spread that Alexandra was the stranger's fiancée. When the music stopped, it was mid-afternoon, and Cornel asked Alexandra if he could walk her home. Mihai walked with Alexandra's friends down the one-lane dirt road to her home while the new sweethearts followed and held each other's hand.

Alexandra's gorgeous looks took Cornel's breath away. For the first half mile he wanted to kiss her. Was it too soon? He decided to take the risk. Cornel held Alexandra's hand tightly as he made a quick right turn into a corn field. Once concealed, he put both hands on her waist, brought her body close to his and kissed her. She responded with passion.

Cornel didn't want it to end, but after a few minutes, Alexandra pushed back.

"We'd better catch up with the others," she said. He reluctantly released her, and they headed down the path with an extra bounce to their step.

Ahead of them, Mihai waved goodbye to Alexandra's friends when they reached the sidewalk to the Ionescu home. He waited for the couple, and the three walked to the house together. Alexandra's mother came through the open door, smiling.

"Mihai, is that you? It's been a long time. How is your family?"

"Hello, Mrs. Ionescu. My family is doing well." Mihai turned and gestured at Cornel who stepped forward. "I'd like you to meet my friend Cornel."

"Pleased to meet you," Cornel said.

"Please come in," Mrs. Ionescu said as she ushered the crew into the center room.

Cornel couldn't take his eyes off his new-found sweetheart. He so much wanted to kiss her again. Alexandra didn't break away from his gaze.

Mihai cleared his throat.

"Cornel and I met at electronics school. He's really smart. He tutored me in both math and electronics. We both worked at Combinatual Metalurgic."

Mrs. Ionescu smiled. "Well, we've missed seeing you, but I'm so glad you've made such good friends in Resita." She turned to Cornel and beamed at him.

"We'd better get on our way so we can get home before dark," said Mihai.

Cornel held Alexandra's hands and squeezed them as he said good-bye. He longed to kiss her again, but knew he'd have to wait.

He walked backwards a few steps as he left, not wanting to take his eyes off her. His heart jumped when she smiled and waved good bye.

"What are our plans for tomorrow?" Cornel asked on their way back, hoping he'd have a chance to run into Alexandria again.

"At the dance, I heard about two people about our age who tried to escape. They didn't make it. I know the father of one of them. I thought it might be helpful if we talked to him and see if we can learn anything about escaping by the ferry, which is what the boys tried."

The next day, Mihai and Cornel tromped through several fields to get to the neighboring village. They'd decided it would be wise not to advertise their movements to the militia. On the way, Mihai told Cornel about the ferry that ran from Pristol to the market in Turnu Severin.

"The market is where the peasants go to sell vegetables they grow. The boat stops at every village along the Danube, including Pristol. It leaves here at one in the morning. It takes six hours to reach Turnu Severin."

"But you said it didn't work, that they didn't make it," Cornel pointed out.

"Yet, I think that way might be our best option, so anything we can learn would be helpful," Mihai said. "The road to the landing is the only way to access the river without trip wires, but it probably has more guards than the rest of the border."

They made it to the neighboring village without being spotted by the militia. Mihai led the way to Mr. Grigore's home. After knocking on his door and finding no one home, they walked around the back to his garden. Mr. Grigore came out of a little shack when he heard them coming. The man recognized Mihai, and started to cry.

"You are so like my son, just his age," the man said.

"Mr. Grigore, this is my friend Cornel," Mihai said.

"Please come in. I stay out here to protect my corn. Everyone is always trying to steal from me." The man, now too weak to work the collective farms, walked slowly, slumped as if all hope had left his body. He motioned to Cornel and Mihai to enter his little shack made of corn stalks. They all sat down on a rug that covered the ground.

Mihai said, "We are so sorry to hear about Costica. Can you tell us what you know?"

The man tried to talk but tears made him speechless. Mihai put his arm around Mr. Grigore's shoulder. "We know it's tough for you, and we feel for you and your family."

The man cried for several more minutes. Cornel and Mihai waited patiently.

Mr. Grigore finally began to speak.

"My son and his friend took the ferry to the market and jumped sometime during the ride. We were told that the guards started shooting as soon as the boys jumped, and we think they were killed before they ever hit the water. Securitate agents looked for them, but they were never found. We haven't heard from him. We assume he is dead because he would have tried to get word to us that he made it." His red, swollen eyes filled with tears again.

Cornel felt sorrow for the man and his family. He made a pledge to himself that he'd contact his parents as soon as he made it to freedom. It didn't appear that Mr. Grigore would ever overcome losing his son, and Cornel thought of his parents' grief if he were killed.

Cornel and Mihai expressed their sympathies again and walked from the corn field.

Mihai stopped walking. He looked Cornel straight in the eye and said, "I know we didn't learn much today, but I needed to make sure that you are fully aware of the consequences. I can tell that story really got to you."

"It did scare me. I've always known it wouldn't be easy, but I'm still in 100 percent. How about you?" Cornel asked.

"It didn't deter me. Considering our two options, I think the boat may give us the fewest obstacles. The ferry also takes us up river which betters our chance of ending up in Yugoslavia instead of Bulgaria. The boat runs tonight, and we should check it out. If an opportunity presents itself, we could be on our way to freedom. We could also be dead by morning."

CHAPTER 23

THEY HAD REACHED THE PORT an hour before the ferry was to arrive, so they decided to look around. A half moon provided just enough light for them to see outlines of the trees behind them and the steep bank of the river in front of them. The landing was deserted. Cornel was surprised that no one was guarding the riverbank or the docking area. *Perhaps the guards have fallen asleep. Could it be this easy?* Cornel wondered.

The sight of the massive river made Cornel realize that the swim could be more difficult than he had ever imagined. The river was much wider here than in Turnu Severin. Although the currents weren't as strong, they were still swift. That could make it difficult to dive down against the force of the water in order to avoid penetrating bullets. Then there were the numbing water temperatures and whirlpools...Cornel made himself stop. They'd agreed to take any reasonable opportunity, and he wasn't about to back out now.

Cornel had spotted a speedboat tied to the bank just seconds before Mihai turned to him and pointed at it.

Mihai moved close to Cornel and whispered, "Let's take the boat. The current will takes us downriver, and we can figure out how to start the engine after we're clear from shore."

Cornel nodded. They walked toward the boat. With each step, his excitement grew. When they reached the bank, Cornel was dismayed to see that the boat was actually floating six feet from the shoreline. The bank here was steeper than it looked from their first vantage point, but he thought they could jump down onto the boat deck. It would be noisy but quicker than trying to pull the boat in by the rope. Cornel was still sifting the options when Mihai stepped so close that their shoulders touched. "Let's jump," he whispered.

A voice screamed from behind them, "Don't move!"

Cornel froze. Their upper arms still touching, he felt Mihai's body tense too. Neither one turned around. A light grew brighter around their bodies and barking dogs approached.

"What are you doing here?" Another voice shouted.

Cornel hoped his coat hid his uncontrollable shaking.

As he turned, he jammed his hands under the open flaps of his trench coat and pretended to be buttoning his pants.

"I had to piss." He spoke into a bright light. He could hear dogs whining and panting hard as if straining on leashes. He assumed the guards had guns aimed at them, but couldn't see anything but the light.

Mihai said, "We're waiting for the ferry to go to the market."

"Stay away from the bank. This area is off limits."

The light dropped to Cornel's waist, allowing him to adjust his eyes to see three guards, two dogs, and machine guns. Two of the guards stepped forward and motioned Mihai and Cornel onto the dock. The third turned back to the woods with the dogs.

"Let me see your identification," The guard flipped through the pages of the small gray booklets, then handed them back. Slightly relieved, Cornel took a breath.

Both guards stayed with Cornel and Mihai, but no one said a word.

A few minutes before one o'clock, a man and a woman arrived

at the landing. As the guards checked their papers, everyone turned toward the noise of a motor. Cornel strained until he could make out a dark silhouette of an approaching boat. Three more people arrived just before the boat pulled parallel to the landing.

Cornel studied the boat. It looked to be about fifty feet long. He guessed the painted hull was probably wood. A metal railing rose about eight feet above the flat deck and was covered by fencing. Other than a gate, the fenced railing appeared to ring the entire deck. Five guards stood ready with machine guns at their sides.

The boat swayed in the strong current as the guards secured it with ropes to the pilings. One guard on deck unlocked the gate and swung it open for four tired-looking passengers, papers in hand, ready for scrutiny by the guards on shore.

A few minutes later, a guard on deck motioned to those waiting to depart to come aboard. The guard checked each passenger's papers and asked each to state their destination. Cornel and Mihai boarded last.

They paid their fee, and the guards scanned their papers. A guard stood at the top of a stairway, motioning passengers to go below as the engine revved and the boat headed up river. Cornel took another quick look around before following Mihai down the stairs. They had to duck their heads to clear the ceiling as they descended, grabbing the railing for balance.

They had their choice of seats. Cornel and Mihai selected two under windows on the side away from shore, as far from the other passengers as possible.

"Do you think the guards told those on the boat to watch us closely?" Cornel had to speak up to be heard above the engine throb.

"I watched, and the guards on the ferry didn't really talk to the guards on shore."

Those who had boarded with them stretched out on the floor, stuffed their bundles under their heads, and turned their backs to Cornel and Mihai.

"Try the window, see if it opens. It looks wide enough for us. I'll stand over by the stairs and wave if the guard at the top begins to come down," Mihai said.

Cornel waited as Mihai stationed himself at the bottom of the stairs. Keeping one eye on Mihai, Cornel grasped a lever at the side of the window and pulled. It didn't move, so he knocked it with his fist to try to loosen it. *Maybe it is somehow locked*, Cornel thought. He motioned to Mihai to come back to their seats and whispered that he couldn't budge the lock.

After the second stop, where the boat took on more passengers, Cornel spotted a light on a mountain across the river. He wondered what it was.

The boat stopped ten times before it reached Turnu Severin about six hours later. Cornel felt it pulling up to the dock.

The engine slowed and then cut off. The passengers gathered their belongings and made their way up from the lower level. Mihai and Cornel hung back. A man with a broom clamored down, his broom knocking the stair railing. He began to sweep the floor.

Cornel approached him. "The air is so bad down here. Can you show us how to open the window?"

Cornel and Mihai watched closely as the man stopped sweeping, shrugged, and stepped over to a window. The man held down a button while he flipped the lever.

"Thanks," Cornel said to the man as he and Mihai climbed the stairs.

While they crossed the deck to the open gate, Cornel looked out over the water. The current was fast. Stepping onto the gangway, he looked down onto a rocky bank. Many armed guards with dogs patrolled the shoreline. One of them asked to see their papers.

Cornel and Mihai were silent on their walk into the heart of Turnu Severin and took in the sights along the way as if they were tourists. The beauty of the old city struck Cornel. He had caught glimpses of the city from the train and the short walk to the bus station, but he hadn't seen this section where the buildings, although old, were well-kept. He noted the cobblestone streets. He found he had to watch his step on the uneven stones as they threaded through the growing crowds of a market day.

"I didn't realize how old this city is," Cornel commented.

"I remember studying about it in school," Mihai said. "Turnu Severin is believed to be the oldest city in Romania. In 103 A. D., the Roman Empire built Trajan's Bridge across the Danube where the river is only 800 meters across. Only remnants are left, but the bridge had twenty arches supported by stone pillars."

"I'm impressed by how much history you know," Cornel kidded him. "If I'd known what a history buff you are, I would have asked you to tutor me in history after I helped you in math."

Mihai laughed. "No way. I guess I just paid attention to the section on the bridge; it's the engineering, the wonder of how bridges could be built across huge rivers like the Danube, even in Roman times. It's amazing that they had a bridge that long ago and that there isn't one here today."

Mihai's mention of the river drew their eyes to the Danube, which now they could see only in the distance. Cornel wanted to talk about their escape options, but knew not to discuss it in the open.

They found the peasant market where they purchased food and surveyed their choices of where to spend the night. Mihai chose a very small hotel and paid for two nights. They closed the door behind them and sat down, facing each other, on the two single beds in the room.

Cornel blurted out, "When we were in Pristol, I thought we were on our way to freedom. Then, all of a sudden, I thought we were dead when those guards came out of the woods and saw us near their speedboat. What if we had jumped in that boat?" Cornel was still unnerved by the incident.

"They would have killed us on the spot."

"They almost did anyway. They scared me to death," Cornel said.

"Guards on the boat didn't seem as serious as guards on the pier."

"We could loosen them up with tuica," Cornel suggested, smiling.

"Maybe." Mihai smiled back, more in gratitude for Cornel's attempt to lighten their mood than at his stab at humor.

"Remember the light on the mountain?" Mihai was serious now, Cornel saw as he nodded and waited for him to continue. "It was about halfway between the second and third stops. We should make our jump from the boat when we reach the light. It looked like a good stretch of river to swim. It's wider, and the current isn't as strong, and the current runs in the direction from Romania toward Yugoslavia. That's what we need, and the light gives us something to focus on."

"Okay," Cornel said, amazed how Mihai had figured all this out.

"I think going back by bus won't be as obvious as going back by the ferry," Mihai continued. "We've also paid for two nights. If we return too quickly, people might suspect something."

They rolled their coats to use as pillows and stretched out on the thin straw mattresses. Cornel closed his eyes. Almost instantly, the scene of German shepherds and guards surprising them on the pier replayed in his mind. His eyes popped wide open.

"I can't sleep," he complained to Mihai.

"Me either, and I'm so tired," Mihai lamented. They talked late into the evening, turning each aspect of their escape plan over until they felt they'd touched on every detail.

For the next two days, they took in the sights, walked around the market, and bought and ate their meals there. They both liked the watermelon, cheese, and onion the best, and it was within their meager budget. In the room's privacy, they relived their experiences again and hashed out all the options for their planned escape.

CHAPTER 24

BOTH MEN HAD CALMED DOWN by the time they boarded the bus back to Pristol. Cornel was disappointed that they weren't able to escape, but the thought of seeing Alexandra again gave him something to look forward to. He was still a little concerned about the checkpoint in Vanju Mare. He had his visa, but they could still reject it. When the bus stopped in Vanju Mare, Cornel saw that the guards were not the same ones who were there when they came through the first time. He showed them his visa, and said he was going to see his fiancé. The guards phoned the Pristol militia and received approval to let him through.

When they returned to Pristol, Cornel learned that the peasants wouldn't have to work the collective farms on Saturday. Cornel set out happily on the half-hour walk to Alexandra's home. She saw Cornel coming up the path and ran to wrap her arms around him.

"I'm so glad to see you," she said.

"I'm happy to see you too."

Mrs. Ionescu saw Cornel from the kitchen window and went to the front door. "Cornel, welcome back. You're just in time for lunch."

At the table, Cornel listened to their talk — mostly of people he didn't know — but he was polite and smiled, happy to be sitting across from Alexandra where he could gaze at her face, watch her hair shine, and absorb just how beautiful she was. He was lost in her face when he realized Mrs. Ionescu was addressing him directly.

"We're so glad you'll be our son-in-law. We'd like for you to stay at our house until you're married."

Taken aback, Cornel's mind blanked in panic. How could he respond to that? He had never mentioned marriage to Alexandra. She was his sweetheart, and he was falling in love with her, but he didn't want to make promises he knew he'd have to break.

"Um…That's very nice of you, but Mihai expects me back."

"We insist," said Mr. Ionescu. "It will give us a chance to get to know each other better."

"I'll stay tonight, but I'll leave tomorrow. I can't see you while you're working the collective farms, and I know you'll be tired when you get home," Cornel chocked out his excuse. Before the "son-in-law" statement, Cornel had planned to spend time with Alexandra in the evenings, but the situation was making him nervous.

That evening, Mrs. Ionescu showed Cornel to the guest room. Standing by the bed, he wondered how he was going to get himself out of his predicament. Perplexed, he stayed awake long into the night.

After breakfast, Cornel expressed his thanks to Alexandra's parents and then announced, "Alexandra and I are going to the field to dance. I'll probably see you next weekend."

"Have a good time," Mrs. Ionescu said.

Alexandra and Cornel followed the music to the field and danced all afternoon. Cornel couldn't get enough of Alexandra. He loved every minute his arms were wrapped around her.

Cornel looked for Mihai throughout the afternoon, but he never showed up.

Cornel walked Alexandra home when the music ended. He

insisted on saying goodbye at the gate, not the house. Alexandra wrapped her arms around Cornel's neck and kissed him. He responded by gently caressing her. She made it clear that she was enjoying the affection. This time, it was Cornel who pulled away. He wanted so badly to stay and be in her arms, but he had to see Mihai.

"I don't want to go, but I have to."

"Stay tonight," Alexandra requested.

"I'll see you in a few days," Cornel said. Once again, he had to leave someone without letting on that he didn't know if he'd ever see them again. It was hard to walk away, but he waved, turned, and left.

"I started to get worried about you," Mihai said when he saw Cornel, skipping over a greeting and getting straight to his fussing. "I imagined the militianu...."

"Sorry. I didn't intend to stay over. They called me their son-in-law and insisted I spend the night. I've never mentioned anything to her about marriage."

Mihai rolled his eyes. "You didn't have to. With rumors of why you're here, everyone, including Mr. and Mrs. Ionescu, already assume that you'll marry Alexandra."

Cornel felt mixed emotions. He was falling in love with her. She had a lovely heart, a sweet nature, and a beautiful face. She had become more than just cover for his escape, and he didn't want to hurt her. Under different circumstances, he would have married her. But nothing was going to interfere with his escape from communism.

"Her parents want me to stay there all the time. I gave them an excuse. We're running out of time."

"And money," Mihai said.

"We have to make a move soon. We now know how to open the windows. I've been thinking of the best way to slip through them, so we can use our feet to push out from the boat."

"We'll need to wait another day or two or they'll get suspicious of us returning to Turnu Severin so soon."

"That means I'll need to renew my visa. Do you think I'll have a problem with that?"

Mihai grimaced. "I think there's enough money for a couple bottles this time. However, we'll have to cut back on something else."

"I just hope they buy the same excuse I used before," Cornel said. "It's probably going to be the same militianu, too, isn't it?"

"I think you should let the tuica do most of the talking," Mihai grinned.

They bought four bottles of tuica from Mihai's friend. Cornel entered the militia station armed with two of the bottles and his old visa in hand.

"I'd like to renew my visa. I'm getting married," he said, pushing it across the desk to the militianu on duty. It was the same one as before, and Cornel smiled to hide his dread that this was the time he'd be turned away.

"Congratulations," said the militianu, his eyes brightening as Cornel handed him the two bottles.

"I'm planning a trip to go home and tell my parents and get their permission."

Cornel was counting on the Romanian custom of youth asking their parents. He hoped his stated intention of observing the practice would be enough so the militia didn't question him.

He didn't. The militianu reissued Cornel's visa for another fifteen days.

Cornel had longed for one last kiss from Alexandra, and so he walked over to her house one evening. She made the trip worth while. The two walked to a secluded spot where they kissed and caressed each other. Cornel didn't want it to end but knew she had to work the next day. When they said their goodbyes, he told her he was leaving town for a few days and gave her a fictitious date when he'd be back.

Late that night, a light rain started to fall as Cornel and Mihai arrived at the boat landing just a few minutes before the ferry was due to arrive. They had decided it was best to leave as little time as possible for border guards to question them. They had on their buttoned up trench coats, but underneath, their shirts and pants were unbuttoned. Now they could more easily shed their clothes when they made their move to jump.

Clouds covered the moon and stars. A low fog drifted over the water, adding a moist chill to the air and muffling the sound of the boat's engine as it approached. Cornel couldn't see the ferry until it pulled next to the landing. Mihai at his side, Cornel moved to be beside the boat so they could scan it for any possible escape route. As before, the guards checked their papers as they boarded, and the guards ushered all passengers down to the lower level.

Mihai and Cornel took seats next to the same windows. Most of the other passengers spread out on the floor to sleep. The boat pulled away and made its way up the river.

After everyone settled down, Mihai and Cornel stood up and assessed the situation. They were about to open the window when voices filtered down the stairs. Cornel's heart stopped as he turned to see the guards clamber down into the seating area. They stood apart, shaking the rain from their coats.

"Look, it's really coming down out there," Mihai said loudly.

"Well, it will probably pour for a while," Cornel chimed in, catching on to Mihai's cover story, their reason for being the only passengers standing at the window.

Two guards took chairs near them.

"I'm getting married in a couple of weeks," Cornel told them. He reached down and took a bottle out of his bag and handed it to the guards. "I'm already celebrating. She's beautiful."

"Congratulations," said one of the guards.

"My fiancée's parents plan to throw a big wedding party. If you're in Pristol, you're invited to come." Cornel was inventing the party. He hadn't heard Mr. and Mrs. Ionescu planning one, but a large or multi-day party was Romanian tradition.

The guard nodded. "We don't get much time off to go anywhere."

"Her parents want me to stay at their house even before we get married. I like her parents, but I needed to get away for a few days, you know?"

The guards chuckled and nodded knowingly.

"That's what happens when you get married," said a guard as he accepted the bottle from another and took a drink.

After joking around for a while, a guard looked out the window and said to the other guards, "Looks like the rain is letting up a little."

Cornel asked for directions to the toilet, which he already knew was accessed from the deck above them. With most of the guards downstairs, Cornel thought this might be the best time to look at the situation up on deck.

"It's up the stairs and around the corner." The guard pointed. "But it is still raining."

"Rain doesn't bother me."

Sensing an opening to find out how heavily guarded the upper decks were, Cornel made his move.

"I'll bet the captain is getting wet. I hope he can see to navigate through this rain."

"Naw, he's in an enclosed wheelhouse. He gets to ride in dry comfort. If he needs anything, he sends the guard out to get it."

A bonus, thought Cornel: *Now we know there's a guard with the captain, and probably up so high, the guard can see off any side of the boat.*

The guard followed him up and through the door. When Cornel got to the top, he saw there were three more guards. One fell into step with Cornel. The rest followed his every step with their eyes as he, guard in tow, made his way to the toilet. When Cornel emerged, the waiting guard ushered him back down the narrow stairway.

The point where they wanted to jump had passed. Cornel and Mihai could sense each other's frustration and disappointment. They thought this would be the day. Unfortunately, it would be another week before they could try again.

They disembarked in Turnu Severin and went straight to the dingy hotel where they had stayed before. Cornel had told Alexandra that he'd be gone for three days. They'd have to stay until then so there wouldn't be any awkward questions.

"When I went to the toilet, I saw another way that might work. I think we can climb the railing and jump from there," Cornel said. "It's covered with mesh fencing, so that will actually give us something to hold on to."

"It'll take too much time to get up and over, and they're likely to see us," Mihai responded.

"But it is possible!"

The next few days went by slowly with nothing to do.

Chapter 25

MUSIC FILLED THE AIR as the bus approached Pristol. It was the weekend, but it wasn't Sunday, so Cornel wondered what instigated the special occasion. When the bus rounded the corner, he saw a crowd of people.

Cornel didn't see Alexandra until he was on the bottom step of the bus.

"My parents decided to surprise you with a wedding party," she said, looking up at Cornel.

Cornel forced a smile but hesitated before stepping off the bus, trying to recover from the shock of such a surprise. Yet she was so pretty, he put his arms out to bring her to him as he stepped down. Alexandra grabbed and held him for a long, intense hug. A chorus of yells erupted from the crowd, and Gypsy music filled the air as the couple embraced.

Alexandra's parents put their arms around Cornel and led him down the street. The crowd followed, the Gypsy band bringing up the rear.

"Where are we going?" Cornel asked Alexandra's parents, shouting over the music.

"Home, of course," said Mrs. Ionescu. "We just couldn't wait to announce the engagement. To only a few people, of course. They've been waiting for us at the house."

What looked like at least two hundred people to Cornel were cheering as they turned into the yard. Cornel noted the militianu in the crowd who had issued him his visa.

"Here is the happy couple," Mihai's father announced. He slapped Cornel on the back, beaming at them both.

The Gypsy band walked through the crowd and settled on the far side of the group. Everyone started dancing. Many of the guests were clearly in an advanced party mood, thanks to the free supply of wine and tuica.

Cornel headed straight for the liquor and poured a drink.

"*Noroc!*" Mr. Ionescu said as he held his glass up to Cornel. "We're happy to welcome you into our family. From now on, you'll be staying at our house."

Cornel clinked the handmade ceramic glass against Mr. Ionescu's, and then poured the warm alcohol down his throat. Cornel had been wondering how they knew he was coming home that day, and it finally dawned on him that it was the fictitious date he had given Alexandra. When he had told her that date, he didn't think he'd ever be coming back.

This has gone too far, Cornel thought. *This wasn't the plan. What am I going to do?* He missed Alexandra immensely when he wasn't with her. He didn't want to hurt her. He considered telling her the truth and then rejected the idea as soon as it occurred to him. He couldn't take the chance.

Cornel searched the crowd for Mihai and finally spotted him, dancing and laughing, a drink in hand. *He's not going to be much help right now*, Cornel thought.

He poured himself another drink and just had time to finish it when Alexandra came up beside him, took his arm, and led him into the circle. Obediently, Cornel danced to several songs before he felt she'd consent to quit.

He leaned toward her as if to kiss her temple and shouted over the band.

"I want to get a drink."

She smiled up at him, nodded, and whirled back into the circle.

With a drink in hand, Cornel stood by the food table, watching as several men heaved huge joints of lamb up beside a roasted goose.

All this food for this party that shouldn't be happening, Cornel thought. Wedding celebrations were always one of the most special occasions of the year. He wished he could enjoy it.

As if someone had announced that dinner was served, the guests quickly crowded around the laden platters, scooping potatoes, cheese, stuffed cabbage rolls, and lamb into their mouths.

Cornel and Mihai had eaten very little while in Turnu Severin because their money was running low, so Cornel filled a plate high. He edged up to Mihai and elbowed him, quickly motioning with his head for Mihai to follow him. They moved into a quieter corner, out of earshot.

"They're insisting that I stay at their house from now on," Cornel whispered, his frustration turning his voice into a hiss.

"Maybe you should stay and get married. Maybe you weren't meant to leave now."

Cornel shook his head.

"You've got to get me out of this."

"Look, there's nothing we can do this minute. Why don't you just try to enjoy the party? The food's great, the liquor's great…"

Before Mihai could finish, the pretty girl he'd been dancing with came up and tugged at his arm.

"Dance, come on, let's dance again!"

Zeroed on Mihai, Cornel's eyes pleaded his case; Mihai shook his head at Cornel and went with the girl, leaving Cornel to his own devices. He drank tuica as the celebration continued.

Cornel turned over. He opened his eyes and then shut them tightly against the brightening day. He dragged his body into a sitting position, pried an eye open into a slit, and saw he was outside on the ground. He rested his elbows against his bent knees, and propped in his hands his heavy, aching head. He didn't look up until he heard a moan nearby.

Cornel and the moaner weren't alone; others were scattered across the Ionescu yard. Cornel remembered that the party was still going strong when Mihai left about three in the morning. Cornel couldn't remember much past that.

A few more people were moving, apparently about to wake up. He looked up at the house for any signs of life. He struggled to his feet and headed straight for Mihai's home.

He found Mihai sprawled on the bed. Cornel knew it would be a few hours before his friend would wake up. Cornel crawled into his own bed and quickly fell back to sleep.

A throbbing head woke Cornel. He stumbled into the next room, where he found Mihai with his forehead resting in his hands his fingers wrapped around the top of his head.

"We're running out of time, money, and chances," Cornel said in a whisper. "If we don't escape this week, they'll have me married off next week. We don't even have enough money to go back to Resita."

"Please, not now. I can't think. Go away."

"Mihai, I'm in trouble here. All our plans, all our work, all our training. I can't get married!"

"I thought you liked Alexandra."

"You know I care for her, but nothing is more important to me than getting out of Romania."

"All right, let's figure it out." Mihai sat up, swayed, and blinked at Cornel. "We're just going to have to make it happen this time. I say you talk to Alexandra and tell her you'll have to go home to get your parents for the wedding. We'll take the ferry on Sunday and find a way."

"I'll tell her I have a lot to do to get ready for the wedding so I can't stay at her house. That way, I can be back here every night. Sunday, we have to escape!"

CHAPTER 26

September 19-20, 1959

FREEZING TEMPERATURES ISSUED an ominous warning to Cornel when he walked outside Saturday morning. It was September, 19 so temperatures would continue to fall. The water of the Danube would be warmer, but just for a few more days before it cooled to match the air.

They had set the date and vowed to escape. Just after midnight, he and Mihai would be on their way to catch the ferry, and in the first hours of Sunday morning, they'd have to find a way off the boat to swim together to Yugoslavia.

The past week had been tough on Cornel. As each day had ticked by, his fears compounded — would their chance slip by? Would they be caught?

He also was on edge from the effort of inventing new excuses to give Alexandra for not setting a wedding date. At the same time he was manufacturing excuses, he had to stand guard against the impulse to confess his secret. If he could come clean, he wouldn't feel so guilty about leaving her behind.

His nights had been just as stressful as his days. He had lain awake for hours after pulling the blanket over him, picking apart the escape plan. He would mentally scan through it, stopping when a *what if* came to mind. As the possible hitches occurred to him, he worked out ways to handle them. Then he would flip back to the beginning of the plan to see if he'd missed something else.

When they were alone, Cornel and Mihai repeatedly hashed through it to be sure they were both on the same page. Their review had become a litany.

"When we see the light on the mountain, we jump," Mihai said. This time he was the one to launch the sequence.

"And first we try the window when the guards are on the deck above us," Cornel took his turn. "If the guards come down to the passenger section, we'll tell them we need to use the toilet. That puts us up on deck."

"I insist you go first," Mihai blurted out. "If you get a chance, do not hesitate."

That was not part of the recital. Perplexed, Cornel peered at Mihai and said, "Why? Do you think I wouldn't jump after you?"

"I just think you should go first." Mihai was firm. "Someone has to go first. We can't stand at the railing and argue about it. Besides, you're the better swimmer."

"Maybe I am, maybe I'm not. Just so you aren't afraid that I'll get scared and back out."

"You won't be any more scared than I will be. We just need to get this straight now, not later. Someone has to go first, and I think it should be you." Mihai spoke quickly, as if he were holding his breath until the last word came out of his mouth. He exhaled loudly and waved his hand to dismiss further discussion on the point. "Let's keep going."

"If we're forced to use the toilet option, we'll get separated because the guards will allow only one person on deck at a time. And yes, I'll go first."

Mihai nodded his thanks to Cornel for settling the question. "You stay in the toilet and count down two minutes. I'll be at the top of the stairs, pretending to wait my turn. I'll count down two minutes, then sprint across the deck and follow you over the railing. We'll swim from the boat and stay underwater as long as we can. Each time we come up for air, we'll look for an island and each other. If at any time I don't see you, I'll keep going. If you don't see me, you'll keep going...."

"We'll meet up and rest in the shallows of the first island we come to," Cornel interrupted.

"Stay low and watch out for the guards."

"And then, together, we'll make for the Yugoslavian shore."

"If we can't find each other at the island, we'll wait only as long as we dare, then strike out alone. We'll find each other in Yugoslavia."

Mihai had reached the end of the plan's basic steps. Cornel took the opening to bring up one of the many worries he'd chewed on the night before.

"Do you think the guards will be suspicious of us — watch us every minute — because we've taken so many trips?"

"Their job is to be suspicious of everyone. I think we have to assume they'll be keeping a close eye on us. Our advantage is we've proven we aren't the type to make trouble, so I think they'll tend to pay more attention to new faces."

They rested throughout the day, inviting sleep, but not really expecting it. In the middle of the afternoon, the weather deteriorated. The wind kicked up and a rainstorm came after it. Cornel hoped the wind would keep up — tougher to swim in, but tougher still for the guards to pick them out against a ruffled water surface.

It was past midnight, time to leave. Cornel fought waves of

panic as he and Mihai walked the dirt roads to the river. It was now or never.

Cornel turned up the collar of his trench coat; the rain was coming harder, and the wind pierced through his clothes. Cornel saw Mihai scanning the sky, and he did the same. Judging by the heavy cloud cover, moonlight wouldn't be a problem for them. Cornel took it as a sign that things would go their way.

They reached the landing a few minutes before one o'clock. The rain had turned to a drizzle, the wind settled, and fog was forming over the water. Three other people emerged from darkness and stood by them at the landing.

As the boat tied up, right on time, Cornel and Mihai took their places in line. When it was their turn, the guard only glanced at their papers and waved them through. When they stepped onto the boat, the guards on board also checked their papers, shining their flashlights on the well-worn pages. Mihai and Cornel handed over their fees and climbed down the steps to the passenger area. They found their usual seats by the windows.

They sat quietly, lost in their own nervous thoughts during the first stop. When Cornel felt the ferry turn toward shore for another stop, his stomach churned. A few more minutes and he would have to make his move. No one got off the boat, but four more people came down the stairs as the boat swung back into the river channel.

All their fellow passengers, as they'd hoped, had curled up on the floor. Cornel and Mihai stayed in their seats and kept their eyes glued to the windows, searching for the island's light. The fog had grown thicker. They could tell it was still raining by the fat drops that smeared against the windows as the boat made headway. The fog was too thick to see the light, Cornel decided, but they had to be close. He stood and reached for the latch of the window. Mihai punched him in the leg. Cornel quickly dropped his hand and sat down.

Guards filed downstairs, wiping water from their faces. Cornel trembled. Had they seen him at the window? He glanced at the guards, who were shaking water from their coats, grumbling to each other about being wet. Apparently they hadn't seen what Cornel had been up to, but he worried this was going to be a repeat of their last trip.

Mihai and Cornel looked at each other and nodded a silent agreement to turn to the second option.

Cornel stood and walked over to a guard. "I need to use the toilet."

"It's raining too hard; I'm not going up there now. You'll have to wait until the next stop," the guard said.

Another guard came over to Cornel, laughed, and said, "Hey, there's the groom."

"That's me." Cornel smiled and handed the man their last bottle of tuica. The guard accepted the bottle. Cornel kept his grin steady, stuffing his hands in his pockets, hoping that would be enough to hide how much they were shaking. Mihai helped him out.

"Another one lost to matrimony!" Mihai slapped Cornel on the back. "Wouldn't catch me doing it." He winked at the guards.

Cornel returned to his seat. The churning engines matched the churning in his stomach. Mihai leaned close and whispered, "We go at the next stop. Be first in line for the toilet."

211

CHAPTER 27

THE ENGINES SLOWED, signaling they were pulling into a landing. Cornel and Mihai hurried to the stairwell. Two guards were at the top. Cornel pulled his hood over his head and emerged into the pounding rain. The guard nodded in the direction of the toilet, but didn't follow him this time.

Inside the tiny room, Cornel started counting down the two minutes. He tried looking through the window, but couldn't see anything. He slipped off his coat and unbuttoned his shirt and pants. He stuffed his identification papers into a plastic bag that he'd had in his pocket. He tucked the package into his underwear, then stayed put for what he decided was the agreed upon time.

He pushed the door open and looked both ways along the deck. The closest guard was turned away from him, checking in the people boarding. Cornel couldn't see Mihai but hoped Mihai could see him and that he was ready to make his move.

Cornel sprinted to the railing, dropped his coat, and slipped out of his pants and shirt, not worried about where they fell. The rain pelted his torso and instantly soaked his underwear. He grabbed the mesh fencing, pulled himself to the top rail, and swung his legs over, all in one quick motion. He felt the cold rush of air as he shot toward the water. The river swallowed him whole, the warmer-than-air water blanketing him as he entered feet first. The force of his plunge shot him toward the river bottom.

He almost opened his mouth to shout, *I did it! I did it!*

He pulled and kicked away from the boat until his lungs began to ache. He hadn't been able to take in enough air to stay down long. Cornel stroked upward, forcing himself to slow down so he wouldn't splash as he surfaced. He broke through, took a breath and spun around, hoping to see Mihai.

What he did see were search lights from the boat scanning the waters. *So they know we've escaped,* Cornel thought. He knew it was wishful thinking that they would have jumped from the ferry without them knowing.

He saw the search light coming his way. He looked for Mihai again, then dove before the light reached his location.

Cornel was moving with the current. He felt the urge to surface and craned his neck before he broke through to see if there was anything above him. Nothing. On top, he filled his lungs, breathing as quietly as he could, and then dove again, hopeful he was heading away from the boat and could find the nearest island.

He wanted to surface, but pushed himself to last longer. When he broke through again into the sweet air, he heard an engine in the distance. He sank lower, holding just his nose above water, his ears half in and half out. The noise didn't sound like the ferry, but water warped sound, so it was difficult to tell. He strained to hear. It sounded like several engines. The throbbing grew louder. He dove, kicking furiously against his natural buoyancy to force his body down quickly.

The next time he gave in to his lungs, he let water drain from his upturned face as he twirled in place, trying to see, to pinpoint the source of the sounds. He couldn't spot the boats, but he could hear barking dogs accompanied by louder engine sounds which meant the boats must be dangerously close. Then he felt a rush of hope when he spotted the silhouette of an island. Cornel folded his body into a dive, careful not to allow his disappearing feet to create a telltale splash.

He fell into a rhythm: swim, come up for a few seconds, find the island, and then dive. He could feel his body begin to fatigue and was glad the island was not far.

Mihai and Cornel usually practiced for two hours in the pool. From the way his body felt, Cornel figured he had been swimming for at least that long when his hands brushed against something. He groped to find the thing again and found it. It was hard, probably a big rock. Then his hands found another and another. He used them as handholds, pulling himself along until his back felt the brush of air. *Shallow water at last. Now I can find Mihai and rest awhile,* Cornel thought. He let his legs sink so he could try standing. Just his head and shoulders were above the water.

A light illuminated Cornel's position, and three search boats zeroed in on him. Cornel pushed out, dove, and hit bottom, whacking one hand against a rock. *It's too shallow to dive!* Cornel realized. Lights followed his movements. He heard bullets penetrate the water, saw their bubble trails. He felt a burn across his stomach and flinched but kept moving as fast as he could. He skimmed the river bottom until he reached water deep enough to get his entire body well below the surface.

The light suddenly disappeared. He could hear the boats nearest him beach on the island. Cornel was surprised they didn't continue to follow his movements with the light for they could have clearly done so. He figured that the guards thought he would come ashore. He had planned to come ashore to rest. Now that wasn't an option, and he hoped his training would provide him the stamina to survive the remaining swim.

He pulled himself along from rock to rock, trying not to let any part of his body break the surface. He guessed he couldn't be more than three feet deep. Then there was a new murmur, but from a different direction — and another. Boats were coming from all directions. Cornel couldn't track them. He didn't know which way to go.

One rock gave him the leverage to pull himself several inches deeper just as a propeller whizzed over his head.

He needed air, but was afraid to surface. He kicked hard as another dark mass shot over him. Desperate for air, he surfaced to hear gun shots on the island. They weren't coming toward him, but Cornel worried they might have found Mihai. His friend had given him orders to wait on the island only as long as he dared. Cornel struck out away from shore.

His decision pumped adrenaline into him. He kicked hard until he felt the current move him away from the island.

He wondered how long he'd been under the water when he finally surfaced. He listened, treading water and turning a complete circle to check for boats, lights — or Mihai. He heard nothing but the river, saw nothing through the light fog.

Where is Mihai? What is happening to him? Cornel prayed Mihai had escaped, and they were just too far apart to find each other.

Suddenly he felt alone.

He decided he had to swim on the surface where he could make more headway. He used a breast stroke at a transverse angle against the current, which he figured was in the direction of the Yugoslavian shoreline. He listened for engines. He knew once they didn't find him on the island that boats would be sent to search for him in the river. He tried to maintain a steady pace, adrenaline propelling him forward.

After some time, his body ached for a rest. He could no longer feel his feet or hands. He realized the numbness meant he'd been swimming a long time in the cold swift waters, so he hoped he wasn't far from the Yugoslavian shore. He stopped and treaded water while his eyes searched around him and his ears listened for any sound. Then he resumed his swimming stroke.

He gasped for a breath as he felt something drag him under. Panicked, he kicked furiously and clawed with his hands, but the river would not let go. He felt his body being pulled deeper, and he struggled harder. The river held him. Cornel, starving for air, feared he was being forced into a deep, dark grave.

Cornel finally realized what it was. *A whirlpool!*

His father's words, "You can't fight a whirlpool!" came to him. He commanded his body to stop resisting. His muscles obeyed and loosened up. At first, he felt the whirlpool pull him deeper, but then the water seemed to relax its hold and release him. He kicked and pulled to the surface.

He broke into the chilly night air, inhaling deeply while stretching his neck up to avoid swallowing the rushing river water. He forced himself to breathe slowly and tread water to stay upright. The current pushed and pulled at him. He was confused. He had to start swimming again. *But which way?* He knew the whirlpool could have turned him around. In which direction was Yugoslavia?

He could see nothing and heard only the rush of the river. He made his choice, ordered his arms to pump and legs to kick, and set out. Each stroke was a cold agony. Again, he fought the panic that came when he encountered the force of the current as it pushed his body downstream. Was it taking him farther away from the Yugoslavian shore? Was it taking him too far downriver where he'd end up in Bulgaria instead of Yugoslavia? He had trained hard for this day, but his body had given all it could. He estimated that he'd been in the water at least another two hours since he left the island. Fatigue seized and strangled his muscles.

He could not let freedom slip away and dismissed the thought that he might not be making any headway toward shore. Trying to stay positive he thought to himself, *I'm strong, and the river already said it wouldn't take me today.*

Bushes brushed against his hands, and it startled him at first. When his legs touched slimy rocks beneath him, relief washed over him. He realized he was in shallow water. He grabbed the rocks and looked up. The sky was pale. If dawn was near, then he had been swimming five hours, much longer than he had thought it would take.

A sound or a movement made him turn his head. Terror engulfed him as his eyes focused on three AK47's aimed at his head. In the silhouettes against the half-dark sky, the soldiers' uniforms appeared to be Romanian.

Cornel wanted to weep and thought, *I must have swum the wrong way when I came up from the whirlpool and ended up back in Romania. How did I do that? How could I have made a mistake like that?*

Cornel dreaded the thought of what was about to happen. *They are going to shoot, that's the end of me.* He braced himself for a bullet.

PART VII

Facing Authorities

CHAPTER 28

THE BLAST CORNEL EXPECTED didn't occur. Waves bounced Cornel's body around as he opened his eyes just enough to figure out what the guards were doing.

One of the armed men spoke, but Cornel couldn't understand what he said. The man spoke again.

They didn't speak Romanian, they didn't speak Romanian! The thought repeated in Cornel's mind, and a slight sliver of hope returned. *That's why I'm not dead right now, because they are not Romanian.*

Cornel attempted to stand up but found he could not. Both legs were completely numb. He tried to drag himself onto the bank with his hands, but he didn't even have the strength left for that. Two guards waded into the Danube River and pulled him to shore. A third guard stayed back, keeping his weapon aimed at Cornel.

The guards helped him get to his feet. They let go, and Cornel managed to stand on his own. He wrapped his arms around his shivering body, his sodden underwear the only thing between him and the freezing wind.

One of the guards who had fished Cornel from the Danube pointed at Cornel's waist. Cornel looked down at his body. Blood was oozing from a tear across his midriff. He then remembered he had been shot.

The guard said something, and Cornel looked up to see him

still gesturing. He looked back down and was amazed to see a corner of the plastic he had used to wrap his identification. He had not lost it to the river. He pulled it out and surrendered it. Returning his hand to his stomach, Cornel touched his wound with his fingertips like he was testing the handle of a hot pot on a stove. Apparently the bullet had grazed him. The wound didn't look serious.

What did look grave was his current situation. He had just been captured by another communist regime. He didn't know if he was in Yugoslavia or Bulgaria. He had been in the water long enough that the currents could have carried him all the way to Bulgaria.

Cornel was terrified. But at least for the moment, he was still alive.

The guards led him to a vehicle and drove him a short distance to what looked like a military base. They stopped in front of a small building, motioned for Cornel to get out, and escorted him through the building and into a room. There was a chair, and Cornel sat. They put a blanket around Cornel's still shaking body and handed him a cup of hot tea. His face lit up as the liquid heat warmed his mouth.

He was almost finished with the tea when a soldier entered the room. The man looked at Cornel and asked in Romanian, "Where were you born?"

Cornel was glad to hear a language he could understand. "Rusanesti de Jos, Romania," Cornel said.

Cornel knew that would be the first of many questions the soldier would ask. He decided to tell the truth.

The man wanted to know his date of birth, all of the places

where Cornel had lived and worked, why he escaped, and about his father, mother, and siblings.

When the questions stopped, Cornel asked, "Can you tell me where I am?"

"You're at a military base near Negotin, Yugoslavia," the man responded.

Cornel breathed a sigh of relief.

What happened next surprised Cornel. One of the men removed a soldiers' uniform from a hook on the wall and motioned for Cornel to put it on. The dry, warm cloth felt good. They also gave him a pair of shoes, the likes of which he'd never seen. The soles were made of rubber and the tops of light canvas. When he had finished tying the laces, the military guards and the soldier who spoke Romanian led Cornel back to the vehicle and drove back to the river. The entire incident confused Cornel at first.

Cornel spotted five Romanian search boats close to the bank, and his heart sank. The boats were close enough that Cornel could see Romanian border guards, guns in hand, searching the water around them. After a few minutes, he realized that the uniform he wore made him virtually invisible to the searchers.

"They're looking for you. They probably think you've drowned and want a body to take back and show off," said the soldier who could speak Romanian.

"Do you know that this is a very rare thing that has happened? Very few people escape the way that you did. Only two other people have made it before you. We watch most people get shot by the Romanians before they make it," the soldier explained.

"Did you pick up anyone else last night?" Cornel was hoping for news of Mihai. "I escaped with someone else, but we got separated."

"No, we saw no one else. That you survived is very rare," the soldier repeated. "We need to know exactly how you did it."

Cornel hesitated for a minute. He had no choice but to tell the truth, so he pushed aside his suspicions — what were these soldiers getting out of keeping him safe? Why did they need to know the entire story?

Cornel scanned the river surface as he told his story. Maybe he would see a sign of Mihai.

The soldier continued to ask questions. Cornel decided that some of the questions were being asked to make sure he wasn't a spy. Yugoslavia wasn't that friendly toward the Romanian government. The difficulty of escape made it necessary for guards to confirm that Romanian boats had not dropped him off.

After the questioning, the soldier finally said, "Enough." Cornel searched the waters one last time for his friend before he turned toward the vehicle. This time guards drove past the military installation to the town of Negotin, entered the gates of a prison, and turned Cornel over to the militia.

One militianu handed Cornel a shirt, pants, and shoes and asked him to change out of the uniform. Another opened the plastic bag of Cornel's papers. As Cornel dressed, he glanced at the officer who was paging through his identification papers. The man put most of the papers in a file but tossed one piece of paper to the floor as if he wasn't interested in it. Cornel stooped to tie his shoes, picked up the paper and put it in his pocket.

They gave Cornel a cup of soup and then locked him in a small room with bars on the door and a blanket on the floor. The tasteless soup did little to stop his stomach from growling, but he was thankful for it. Despite not having slept in the past twenty-four hours and his exhaustion from five hours in the river, he was too nervous to sleep. He sat on the blanket, wrapped his arms around his legs, rested his head on his knees, and wondered what his captors planned for him. The old shirt and pants given to him by the militia gave him hope that he would not face death immediately.

The following morning, three militieni led him out of his cell to a vehicle. One drove while Cornel sat between the other two in the back seat. One man spoke enough Romanian to let Cornel know that they were taking him to court to appear before a judge.

A man in a coat and tie sat behind a table at the front of the room into which Cornel was escorted. He spoke to Cornel in Yugoslavian, and Cornel couldn't understand a word. When the judge finished speaking, a militianu took Cornel back to the vehicle. The militianu who spoke Romanian told Cornel that he was charged with passing the border without documentation and would have to go back to jail.

They placed him in a cell with twenty other prisoners who appeared to be hardened criminals. The inmates spoke Yugoslavian, and Cornel could tell they were talking about him by the way they kept glancing and gesturing at him. He kept quiet and claimed a small area of the cement floor with his blanket.

Guards brought food and water a short while later. The ceramic dish handed to Cornel held a piece of white bread and a metal cup of soup. Cornel took a sip of the broth with a hint of potatoes. The awful flavor made Cornel choke at first, but he forced it down. He was hungry and managed to finish it. He tried a small bite of the bread. "Mmmmm," he said out loud as he savored the flavor. He had never tasted white bread before and loved it. Guards brought the same food twice a day.

On the third day, a militianu came to the cell and took Cornel to a car where two other militieni waited.

Cornel became concerned and wondered, *have arrangements been made to send me back to Romania?* The car pulled up to a train station and parked. The men motioned for Cornel to get out. They waited on the platform until a train pulled up and stopped. Once on board, a militianu opened the door to a compartment, and the four took a seat.

The militianu did not say a word to Cornel so he didn't know where they were taking him. The train pulled out, and Cornel sensed they were heading away from the Danube. He breathed a sigh of relief. The uncertainty of what was in store weighed on his mind, but he knew that any option was better than being sent back to Romania.

Cornel began to think about home as the miles passed. Would he ever learn what happened to Mihai? His eyes moistened when he replayed the last time he'd seen Alexandra. What had leaving her gained him? He might never experience freedom, and pursuing it, he had left someone with whom he could have spent the rest of his life. He worried what his disappearance would do to her. Were his parents going to find out? What would Comrade Argesanu and Lieutenant Ariciu do to his family because he escaped?

He hoped that by not telling his family or friends about his plans that they would not be prosecuted. They might anyway. He prayed they would not.

Watching out the window, Cornel could see houses, signs, and large buildings come into view. He wondered if they were pulling into Belgrade. *Maybe they're going to process me here and send me back to Romania. Or maybe they'll let me stay,* Cornel thought. He tried to prepare what he could say to convince the officials to keep him here.

The train screeched to a slow stop at the station. Cornel peered out the window, searching for the station's sign, and saw his guess had been right; they were in Belgrade. A militianu escorted Cornel into the hands of the chief of militia and two men whose uniforms were similar to the Romanian Securitate. When Cornel saw them, he began to shake with fear. He had personally experienced the wrath of the Romanian Securitate, and men like Lieutenant Ariciu was one of the reasons Cornel wanted to escape. He figured that the Yugoslavian equivalents were just as bad. Cornel learned later that the men who looked like Securitate were referred to as *Sluzba drzavne bezbednosti* — SDB for short.

They drove Cornel a half hour out of town and through the large entry gates of a jail. After they registered him, a guard, who seemed to know a few words of Romanian, asked Cornel to state his name, where he came from, where he was born, who his parents were, and how many brothers and sisters he had. Cornel told the truth again. During the questioning Cornel was told he was at a jail in Poncevo.

After Cornel answered their last question, the guards led him up a stairwell. At the top, they walked down an aisle surrounded by cells. Cornel counted five cells. The cells had three solid walls with bars on the front. His cell contained a metal bed with a thin mattresses and one blanket. He learned quickly that when he had to use the toilet, he needed to bang on the bars.

The next day he was allowed to walk in the secure prison yard that was surrounded by tall buildings on all four sides. He was one of ten prisoners in the yard that day but kept to himself. From the yard, prisoners were escorted to a small area to eat. The room contained one long table with benches on each side. Cornel couldn't help smiling when he saw the white bread that came with their cup of soup. Cheese was a welcome addition. The soup tasted better than that of the last prison and included more potatoes.

One of the ten men at the table asked Cornel where he was from. The man spoke Yugoslavian, but Cornel had heard the question enough times that he knew what he meant, and he responded only by saying, "Romania." He stayed quiet the rest of the day and listened intently trying to figure out the language.

Cornel was pacing in the yard when he saw prison guards escort five teenagers into and then out of the yard. When he returned to his cell, two of the boys were seated on his bed. Cornel knew from their appearance they had been to the West. They wore bell bottom pants and leather jackets, a rare sight. Their long hair hung on their shoulders. The teens yelled and swore at the guards in Yugoslavian and then spoke to each other in Italian. Cornel listened intently. Many Italian words were similar to Romanian, so he could follow some of their conversation.

From their accent, Cornel figured they must be Yugoslavian, and from their dress and knowledge of Italian, they probably had been picked up in Italy. They must have done something wrong since the Italians sent them back to Yugoslavia. Cornel decided not to let on that he understood them for two reasons. First, he didn't want to associate himself with those who were disrespectful to the guards. Second, he couldn't be certain they weren't a plant to encourage him to reveal his real intention, which was to escape to Italy or another non-communist country.

On the fourth day, Poncevo prison guards gave Cornel a bucket of water and soap. A guard led him outside to an area surrounded by a short privacy fence that appeared to be about four feet square. The guard pointed to the bucket and pantomimed washing himself, then left. Cornel hung his clothes over the fence and scrubbed with the soap and cool water, pouring the remaining water over his body when he was finished. A wind whipped through the fence's cracks and quickly dried his wet skin, chilling him. The cold didn't bother him; the water felt good.

The next day, a guard came to his cell and motioned Cornel to follow. He took him to a waiting vehicle. Cornel figured he was going to a new facility. They drove toward downtown Belgrade and stopped in front of a beautiful building. A sign on the building identified it as the militia headquarters. They walked up a set of stairs and down a long hallway. The guard slowed, stopped, and knocked on a door. A tall, dark-haired, clean-shaven man dressed in a tie and coat spoke to Cornel in Romanian.

"Welcome," the man said as he shook Cornel's hand and offered him a seat in front of the desk.

Cornel stood frozen in fright. He wondered if his native country had sent someone to take him back.

CHAPTER 29

"How are you, Cornel?" the interrogator said as if he were a friend.

"Fine."

"Are you treated well? If you have any problems, you let me know. They'll be taken care of."

Cornel didn't sit down, so the man asked him in a kind, calming voice to have a seat. Cornel did so apprehensively. The man looked at Cornel quizzically.

"Not too many people escape from Romania. Don't you know that, Cornel?" The interrogator's question was more of a statement. Cornel didn't know how to respond. He thought the man was saying that he hadn't truly escaped and would be taken back.

"My name is Yarsovich, and I'm with the Yugoslavian militia. I'll be working with you for a while and asking you a lot of questions. You have to tell me the truth."

Cornel still didn't relax. Cornel suspected the man was pretending to be on his side. Yarsovich spoke too much like a Romanian native; Cornel couldn't trust that he was truly Yugoslavian.

Yarsovich began asking him questions about his life. Yarsovich wanted to know where Cornel was born and places where he had lived. He even wanted to know where their house was located in the small village of Rusanesti. He asked Cornel to draw a map of Resita with all the streets. Cornel drew a map of the entire city and showed where he worked, where he went to school, and where he lived with his uncle. Yarsovich took detailed notes.

"Why did you want to escape from Romania?"

Cornel had been waiting for this question. He worded his answer carefully so he did not reveal his intention of going to Italy or Austria.

"Life is very tough in Romania, not like here in Yugoslavia. I heard that people have some freedom here. I want to go to college, and I wasn't allowed to do that in Romania. And you have white bread. Romania doesn't have white bread." Cornel added a smile when he mentioned the white bread.

"Cornel, that will be enough for today, but I'll be seeing you shortly." Yarsovich stood and told the guard at the door that Cornel was ready to go.

When he got back to the jail that evening, the young Yugoslavians were gone. Cornel figured they must have been there for processing, but wondered what the militia would eventually do with them. He was back in time to spend an hour in the yard before dinner and then followed others to the kitchen.

He started to take a bite of his white bread when a beautiful woman entered the room. Her thin and shapely frame looked sexy in her long beige pants, pink-and-yellow pullover top, and open black jacket. Cornel estimated that she was about five and a half feet tall. The men's eyes followed her as she sat down at their table. When her brown eyes met Cornel's, he couldn't help but grin. He almost melted in his seat when she smiled back. Cornel wanted to talk but couldn't catch his breath enough to speak. He was glad when another prisoner asked her name and where she was from.

"My name is Natasha, and I'm from Poland," she said in Yugoslavian, adding nothing else.

Early the next morning, guards took Cornel from his cell and back to the militia station where Yarsovich sat waiting in the same small room.

"Hello, Cornel. I hate to do this to you. They don't know where they put my notes from yesterday, so I have to ask you the same questions again."

Cornel had already sat down this time. He knew that the interrogator had not lost his papers. This had to be a technique to find out if he was telling the truth. He knew the man planned to compare notes from the two days. He wasn't too concerned since he had told the truth about everything except for his intentions to stay in Yugoslavia.

The next day, Yarsovich had a new set of questions for Cornel.

"Who do you know in the Communist Party in Resita?"

"I didn't know any communist leaders personally."

"Name some of the communist leaders."

Cornel recounted some of the more familiar leaders' names, but again insisted he didn't know any personally, although that wasn't entirely true.

"Who do you know in the army?"

Cornel couldn't answer this question truthfully either. He didn't want to take a chance of involving any of his friends from the army. He had never discussed his escape with them, but it could mean trouble because they had done favors for each other. Whatever he said, he had to remember exactly. He knew all questions would be repeated.

"I met a few people at work who were from the army, but I didn't know them well."

"Tell me about the factory where you worked and what they made."

"They made metal parts, including propellers for warships, electric motors, and locomotives."

"What do you think of the Romanian Communist Party?"

"I do not like Romanian communists. They took our land, put my father in jail, and put me in jail for reading a book. They wouldn't let me go to school."

"Why did you choose Yugoslavia?"

"I heard it was better than Romania. Everyone in Romania says it's better. After what little I've seen, I believe they're right. You have white bread, and people are happy."

Cornel knew he had stated this the day before, maybe a little differently, but he felt his statement was truthful. During his trip to the militia station, he had seen people in the hallways smiling. He had heard people laughing, the sincere kind of laugh of people enjoying a good joke.

"What is your intention here?"

"If I'm released in Yugoslavia, I plan to stay here. I came to Yugoslavia to live. That is it. I would like to learn the language, go to school, continue my studies, and find a job."

"I want to stay here," Cornel added for emphasis.

"What if you don't like it here?"

"I'll make myself like it. No place could be worse than Romania."

Yarsovich asked new questions over the next five days. Every once in a while he'd throw in a question Cornel knew he'd already answered. The following week, Yarsovich started over, asking the same questions again, but in a different order. Cornel tried to duplicate his previous answers, but worried about those where he had strayed from the truth. Cornel knew if he were caught in a lie his future would be in peril.

Monday through Thursday, the sessions ran three to four hours a day. Friday sessions were shorter. At the end of each day's interrogation, Cornel was returned to the prison. Some days he would return to see that some prisoners had been replaced with new ones. Two Bulgarian men and Natasha were the only ones who remained.

Cornel was always glad to see Natasha and became comfortable enough with her to talk a little more each day. Cornel was impressed with her intelligence and self-assurance. He appreciated that she would spend time teaching him Yugoslavian, and he would teach her some Romanian. With her help, he began to understand enough to communicate.

Time for Cornel seemed to drag more each day. Evenings in his cell were especially excruciating. His mind worked overtime as he thought about his life and the people he had left behind. He constantly wondered and worried about Mihai, still praying that somehow he had made it to Yugoslavia and that somehow they could make contact or at least get word to each other. Cornel's mind continually searched for a way.

One day, a guard came into the cell block with an armful of books. Cornel got a glimpse of several of the book titles and saw they were in various languages. He selected a book in Romanian, and started to read when he had an idea. *Mihai would probably pick out this same book if he ends up here; maybe I can use it to get a message to him.*

He had noted that one of the other prisoners had a pencil and Cornel asked if he could borrow it.

As soon as Cornel returned to his cell with the pencil, he turned to the middle of the book and wrote in very small letters between the lines: "Look for me in Italy, West Germany or France." He hoped he'd picked an inconspicuous place in the book so the guards wouldn't see his note when they flipped through pages. Once he finished his message, Cornel flipped back to where he stopped the day before and began reading. He loved to read and appreciated the diversion in prison.

Trips to meet with the interrogator continued for three weeks. Cornel dreaded the thought of another session, but at least the trips to the militia station got him out of the prison. For the few minutes he was in the open air — cooler each time as the fall days crept toward winter — he breathed deeply.

Yarsovich remained calm and cordial as he continued to ask the same questions, but posing them differently. It amazed Cornel how the man was able to state a question as if he were asking it for the first time. Yarsovich would say, "Oh, I missed this portion," and go back to ground they'd covered.

"We are finished," Yarsovich said one Friday after questioning. "You will be moved to another area. If you pass all of your tests, you'll eventually be processed to stay in Yugoslavia." Yarsovich gave no indication how long that process might be or what Cornel would still have to go through before being released.

Cornel had been worried that his answers had deviated too much and that he'd be sent home. Cornel tried to process what Yarsovich said, and some of it gave him hope. It sounded like he would *not* be sent back to Romania. Was that a hint he'd be freed? Or did it mean he'd remain in a Yugoslavian prison?

Chapter 30

A GUARD UNLOCKED CORNEL'S CELL early in the morning and announced they were moving him to a new prison, but didn't say where. Apprehensively, Cornel followed the guard outside to a vehicle. Cornel's heart skipped a beat when he saw Natasha already seated inside. He smiled with his eyes and noticed her eyes brightened as well. Once Cornel slid into his seat, a militianu slid in beside him while a militianu and two SDB agents piled in the front.

The vehicle pulled up to Belgrade's railroad station, and a militianu motioned for everyone to get out. The two SDB agents told Natasha to come with them; one held her arm as they led her away. Cornel's eyes followed her. A few steps away, she turned her head to search for him. As their eyes locked, he felt his face fall as he detected the fear in her eyes. SDB never had good things in store. Cornel wondered where they were taking her. He had hoped they would be traveling together to the same facility.

More than an hour passed. Several trains arrived and departed. Cornel was confused why they were just standing around at the station.

Then he caught sight of Natasha returning with the SDB agents who had taken her away. He felt flushed with hope; maybe they would be going to the same prison. Cornel smiled at her, but she didn't smile back; instead, tears ran down her face. Cornel had always admired her spirit, despite her difficult circumstances. Her spark was now absent, her shoulders slumped, and her feet dragged with each step. She had the same look on her face as women from his hometown after the Soviets made their mark on Rusanesti.

A train pulled up and distracted their guards. She took the opportunity to confirm to Cornel what he had feared. The two SDB agents had raped her.

They boarded the train and entered a compartment. Two new SDB agents replaced the two who had raped Natasha. The four officers sat on a bench on one side of the compartment and motioned for Cornel and Natasha to sit opposite them.

The officers talked to each other as the time passed, but the men gave looks of disapproval when Cornel and Natasha said anything. The two kept quiet for the long journey. Cornel wished he could take her hand and show he cared. He was deeply concerned about her.

His stomach turned as he imagined the torture his friend had just endured. It made him remember the time many women in his hometown experienced the same suffering. Were things no different in Yugoslavia? He decided it didn't matter; he had no plans to stay.

A small window provided a view of the landscape as they sped along the track. Cornel tried to pick out clues to guess their direction. He figured the train was heading west, closer to Italy or Austria. Small towns and large towns seemed to rush up, then fly past as if they were moving, not the train. Flat land changed to hills, and hills to mountains. Cornel focused on his dream to reach freedom. Every hour on the train meant less walking when he finally escaped.

The train slowed and came to a halt. Cornel looked out the window and searched until he spotted the station sign: Zagreb.

As they exited the train, he saw a parked vehicle and two militieni standing beside it.

Their new guards motioned them into the back seat. They started on a new journey that eventually took them up a mountain on winding, rutty dirt roads.

The temperature dropped as they made their way up the mountain. The guards wore heavy coats and left the front windows rolled down. The cold wind blew to the back seat where Cornel and Natasha shivered. Natasha wore a light jacket, shirt, and pants. Cornel only had the thin, worn shirt and pants that had been given to him at the border.

Deep ruts in the road were impossible for the driver to miss, and all passengers were tossed in the air and from side to side. Cornel began to feel nauseous. Relief came when they met another vehicle and pulled over to wait for it to pass on the narrow road. Later, their vehicle lodged in a deep rut, which gave them another needed break.

"Get out and push," insisted one of the officers.

Cornel was glad to stretch and put his feet on solid ground. His stomach was still up in his mouth. The time it took to push the wheels out of the hole helped to settle his insides.

They continued to climb higher up the mountain, and the road narrowed even more, hardly wide enough for the four wheels. If the road gave way, the vehicle and everyone in it would plummet down a 2,000-foot drop. Cornel dug his fingers into the seat when he felt the wheels slide. He imagined the vehicle plunging into the depths and what a free-falling crash over the drop would be like. Suddenly he was panting. Cornel realized only then that he'd been holding his breath.

After two hours of zigzagging and being thrown from side to

side, he leaned forward and asked the driver to stop. The guards laughed until Cornel vomited on the floor.

"What are you doing? Stop it!" The guard began to cuss at Cornel.

"I can't help it. I feel like I will again." Cornel barely got the words out when vomit erupted again. Suddenly Natasha was leaning over and adding to the stench. The driver finally stopped and handed the two prisoners paper to clean up the back seat.

The next time Cornel warned the driver, he pulled over. Cornel got out, but his stomach felt better as soon as they stopped. The guard ordered Cornel back into the vehicle and warned him not to lie to them again. Cornel tried to explain that he wasn't lying, but the guards told him to be quiet.

A few miles later, they reached a plateau, and Cornel could see a prison that he figured was their destination. A guard at the prison opened the barbed wire gate to allow them through the entrance and then shut it once the vehicle was inside.

One of the militianu asked Cornel and Natasha to wait in the car while the other officer went to the jail. He came back with a bucket of water and rags.

"Now clean up your mess," he demanded.

After they cleaned up the vehicle, Cornel and Natasha were taken into the prison. Their pockets were checked. They answered questions about who they were, where they were from, names of their family members and more. The guards completed pages of paperwork and then took Cornel and Natasha in different directions.

Cornel's guard showed him through the prison grounds and pointed out the toilet, mess hall, and prison yard. The guard talked as they walked.

"Breakfast is seven, lunch is at noon, and supper at six. Between meals you can go out into the yard. You must be in your cell before eight o'clock when we turn out the lights."

Cornel liked the idea of spending time in the yard, even if it was cold.

The guard led Cornel into a larger building. From a table, the guard grabbed a towel and a blanket and then took Cornel to a cell. He handed the short stack of linens to Cornel, topping it with small hunk of something.

Cornel sniffed at it. Lye soap, he decided. He surveyed the cell. It contained only one metal bed with a thin mattress. He poked at the straw mattress and stroked the cotton cover. He sank onto the bed, bone-tired after the trip. He felt relieved to have a cell and bed to himself. It meant he'd be able to get a better night's sleep, which would help his energy level, his attitude, and his spirit. Cornel's cell also had a small window through which he could see mountains, another bonus. He studied the view, trying to figure out in which direction he'd have to travel to reach Austria or Italy.

The next morning at breakfast, Cornel counted sixteen men at the one long table. Cornel saw Natasha come through the door and watched the men's reaction as she joined them. The pink-and-yellow pullover top and open black jacket were crumpled and dirty but were still doing the job of accentuating her figure.

Again, it turned out that Natasha was the only female in the prison. Cornel watched the other prisoners stare at her. He couldn't blame them. Her beauty captured everyone.

The men talked through the meal. Cornel now knew enough Yugoslavian to understand conversations and learned that the other prisoners had been caught while escaping from their respective countries. The prison didn't house local criminals.

Natasha joined Cornel in the yard. They walked and talked for hours. He felt proud as the other men saw him with the beautiful woman. He was also thankful for the opportunity to get to know her better. They both opened up to each other more than they had in Belgrade, but skirted the topic of the rape.

"How did you get captured," Cornel asked Natasha.

"When I was in Warsaw, a friend of mine who had a high position in the government obtained a fake passport for me. So I decided to try and leave Poland and the passport worked. I traveled through Hungary and then came to Yugoslavia where they caught me."

Cornel shared his story of escape, and then they both talked about how tough life was in their countries. She told him she grew up in a small Polish town but went to school in the capital city. Cornel often wondered if she had been a spy.

Cornel studied every inch of the prison as they walked. It was less of a fortress than the Poncevo jail had been. There, he hadn't been able to see anything but the sky from the yard because it was surrounded on all sides by buildings. Here, it was more open. A watch tower guarded the prison from the corner. Three barrack-type buildings stood within the compound. A double barbed-wire fence surrounded the buildings. Lack of a solid wall allowed a full view of the plateau on which the prison perched and of a mountain that spiraled into the clouds.

He decided to be on his best behavior in hopes of convincing the authorities that he could become a model citizen of Yugoslavia. He found out within a few days that the guards demanded good behavior from everyone. The guards dealt strictly with anyone who screamed or fought. Cornel wanted to differentiate himself from others, so he smiled at everyone and was polite and respectful, especially toward the guards.

After a week, Cornel asked one of the guards if he could be put to work. He was assigned to the kitchen.

Even though he sweated, Cornel smiled as he cleaned tables, washed dishes, and scrubbed the floor. He first used a broom and then got down on his hands and knees to wash the floor with a rag, a little soap, and a pan of cold water. The prison didn't have running water, but the kitchen did have a hand pump, so he didn't have to haul water a long way. The work was a welcome diversion, something to help pass the hours.

The inmates' rations were meager. The small servings consisted of bland soup with two tiny pieces of bread and only water to drink. Prisoners never left anything on their plates, but occasionally someone would unknowingly drop a piece of their bread. Cornel picked up any scrap from the floor and ate it.

A guard asked him to clean up the officers' mess hall two days later. Cornel soon realized that this assignment had added benefits. The officers had their own mess hall where they ate meat, sometimes steak, and lots of bread. The first time he saw a piece of meat left on a plate, he couldn't believe his eyes. He looked around to make sure no one could see him. He picked up the meat, put it in his mouth, and let the flavor reach its full potential as he chewed it slowly. He finally swallowed it. It made him crave more. He kept the officers' kitchen immaculate so they would let him continue this duty, plus hopefully give him additional privileges.

Cornel's hard work and positive attitude continued to pay dividends. Three days later, a guard approached him as he was finishing his morning duties.

"You're coming with us."

Cornel had no idea where they were going but didn't sense

trouble. Another guard joined them, and they walked outside of the building and through the barbed-wire entry.

Cornel couldn't hide his excitement at leaving the prison. A bounce in his step, he followed the guards down a path. After a long walk, a village came into view. Cornel felt embarrassed when people stopped to look at him as he walked, flanked by the guards, through the street. He wanted to tell everyone he wasn't a criminal. He smiled at the gawkers, hoping a friendly face might be enough to stop their stares.

They turned a corner, and Cornel caught a whiff of the unmistakable, heavenly scent of a bakery. His mouth began to water with each step taken in that direction. Cornel followed a guard through the bakery door, the other guard close behind him. There, in a corner of the room, was a mountain of crusty loaves stacked on a bench. A guard pulled out a cotton bag, opened its mouth, and fed into it thirty loaves, counting each as he dropped it. He paid the baker, who glared at Cornel. He returned the look with a big smile.

The guard handed the bag to Cornel, and they headed back up the mountain. Cornel threw the bag over his shoulder to help distribute the weight. The return trip took a little longer than the trip to town since they were going up hill, and each had their own load — Cornel with the bread, and the guards with their rifles. Cornel smiled all the way up the hill.

Back at the prison, Cornel helped them store the bread and noticed how filthy the guards' boots had gotten from the four-plus hours of walking the dusty, muddy path. Cornel pointed to their boots.

"I would be happy to clean your boots."

They smiled and seemed pleased by the offer and by the shiny boots when Cornel finished.

"I appreciated my trip and working in the mess hall," Cornel told them. He hoped he would get asked again to go to the village and still be able to clean the mess halls. He didn't want to lose the food he could scavenge.

The next morning a guard approached Cornel and spoke in Romanian, "You need to accompany me to obtain supplies."

Cornel appreciated being spoken to in his native language and was thrilled to leave the prison two days in a row. The Romanian-speaking guard talked to Cornel and was pleasant to him throughout the long walk. When they returned to the prison, Cornel thanked the guards again and said he'd like to shine their boots in appreciation of the opportunity.

Each day, two guards, but not the same ones, asked Cornel to go to the village. He looked forward to days when the guard who spoke Romanian was one of the two. He called Cornel by his first name and treated him with respect. The other guards treated Cornel roughly, demanding he do this or do that.

The routine continued: work in the kitchen until after breakfast, a trip down the mountain, then back to work in the kitchen after supper.

On each outing, Cornel studied his surroundings as they walked around the prison to reach the dirt path. He noted the contours of the landscape and each peak of every mountain.

He didn't know exactly where he was and in which direction the neighboring countries were. One day, feeling comfortable enough with the guard who spoke Romanian, Cornel tried to find out, feigning mild curiosity.

"I have no idea where we are. These mountains, are we close to

Romania?" Cornel knew they were some distance from his home country, but knew he should play dumb.

The guard stopped, turned to face the mountain and pointed at the peak. "Italy is in that direction." Then he pointed about thirty degrees to the north. "That way is Austria."

Cornel shrugged. "This is such beautiful country," he said, sweeping his arm to encompass the landscape around them. "I hope to eventually get approval to stay in Yugoslavia. I really like it here."

Cornel had what he needed. Back in his cell that evening, he began to devise a plan to escape.

Chapter 31

CORNEL KNEW HE HAD TO make his move soon. Dropping temperatures meant rougher weather ahead. No one could survive a long winter walk through the mountains, and he realized that every delay reduced his chances. He would have to wait another four to five months if he didn't escape soon, a fate he did not want to think about.

Italy would be his destination. He didn't know for sure but thought Italy was closer. Just as important, the Italian and Romanian languages were similar, so he felt he'd be able to communicate once he crossed the border.

Food for a long journey was his first concern. He decided to start saving some of the scraps he picked up from the mess halls instead of eating them at the time. Cornel stashed only a tiny piece of bread the first time, the second time two small pieces. He worried that the guards might notice the food through his thin pants if he took too much. He knew he could be severely punished for taking these morsels, but it was a necessary risk. With every trip to clean the mess halls, he pocketed what he could. Each time he was successful, he carefully hid the pieces of bread in the folds of the blankets at the corner of his bed. Escaping would only be possible with food and even the most meager of scraps would help.

Next he had to figure how to get past all the guards. He began studying and timing their movements. He memorized the guards' schedules, their duties, break times, and when they met other guards. He studied paths they used to get from one place to another and which guards talked to each other. He constantly listened to their conversations and watched, even following them when possible.

Warmer clothes were another obstacle. Temperatures could reach zero degrees Fahrenheit. Cornel possessed only the light-weight shirt and pants provided to him when captured at the Danube. The well-worn fabric was thin and would not provide protection against the elements. Freezing rain, snow, and wind were definite possibilities. He had spent many nights in the fields when he was young, but then he could always snuggle into his mother's heavy, handmade wool or hemp blankets. He knew he needed another layer of clothes to give him the best chance for survival. He was thankful that he had been given canvas shoes which would provide some protection from the cold.

He had no idea of the distance between the prison and Italy, how long it would take him to get there, and if he would have the endurance to climb several mountains. The daily trips up and down the mountain to the bakery helped keep him in shape and prepare his muscles for the steep slopes. After finishing his lunch and supper duties, he walked briskly in the yard, usually accompanied by Natasha. He enjoyed talking with her as they walked, but didn't tell her about his decision to escape.

Temperatures continued to fall; even daytime temperatures seemed to chill him. Standing in the yard one day, the wind cut through his shirt; he shivered just thinking of the cold air he might have to face during his escape. A German journalist who had been arrested in Yugoslavia after escaping from East Germany noticed that Cornel was cold and offered him a jacket. Cornel thanked him over and over.

So he had a jacket, his store of bread was growing, but he still had not determined how to get around all of the guards.

The jacket felt good the next day on the trip down the mountain. As they walked, Cornel wasn't paying attention to the guards until he heard the word "party."

"I'm looking forward to the party," one guard said.

"Me too," said the other guard. "There is always a lot of liquor on the Yugoslav Republic Day."

"That's for sure."

This could be my big break, Cornel thought. *If they all participate, it could mean a lot of drinking and posts unguarded.*

When Cornel completed all of his duties, he went back to his cell and checked his bread supply. It wasn't much but it would have to do. Next he thought about how was he going to get out of his cell. He knew the party would take place late in the evening, and the prisoners would be locked in.

While Cornel was cleaning the mess halls after breakfast, the guard who spoke Romanian approached him.

"November 29th, the guards are having a party. We need you to help serve. You may have to work late into the evening."

"No problem," Cornel responded trying not to show his high degree of excitement.

Cornel had a hard time remaining calm the rest of that day and the days that followed.

The moment he heard he could work the party, his mind started working through every detail of his plan. The mess hall, where the guards planned to celebrate, was the building closest to the prison's entrance. He could watch them until he saw an opening and then slip away.

When he slept, he dreamed that *he* was the one partying, partying in a free country.

November 29, 1959

THE MORNING OF NOVEMBER 29, Cornel retrieved his stashed bread, tucked the pieces in his pockets, and put on his jacket. The buildings weren't heated so it wasn't unusual for prisoners to wear their coats indoors.

He went through his usual routine of cleaning the mess halls after breakfast, accompanying guards to pick up the loaves of bread, shining shoes, and returning to the mess hall after lunch. His work detail completed, he paced the yard. His plan ran continually through his mind. When Natasha appeared and fell into step beside him, he was tempted to tell her. He longed to trust her, but trust was a luxury he could not afford. He trusted no one. At supper that evening, he sat next to her. His eyes followed her when she left the room. He knew he might never see her again.

When he lost sight of her, the realization struck him. *I'll be escaping soon. Freedom … here I come*, Cornel thought as his nerves shook in anticipation.

He made himself focus. He couldn't let his intentions show through in his expression. He cleaned the small mess hall after supper and immediately started to help with the party. He carried food to the pass-through window of the officers' dining room, lingering as long as he dared while he set up the plates of food. The guards were already passing around wine, vodka, and *Slibovitch*. Cornel counted the number of guards in the room and made mental notes of who they were.

Alcohol was taking its effect on the guards by the time Cornel cleared the first group of plates. Their loud songs, shouts to each other across the room, and guffaws at their own jokes made Cornel long for the parties he used to attend.

Cornel salvaged every piece of food left on plates and stuffed the bits into his pockets. Between washing sink loads of dishes, he delivered more food to the pass-through window, lingering an extra moment each time to evaluate the guards' progress toward inebriation. His mounting anxiety tempted him to sneak a shot or two of alcohol for himself, but that was against the rules and would only attract attention to him. Even if a bottle had been offered with assurances of impunity, he would have turned it down. Keeping his head clear was too important.

By three that morning, the majority of the guards were drunk enough not to pay attention to anything but keeping their glasses full. Cornel collected another stack of dishes and brought them to the kitchen. The guards wouldn't expect him back for a while.

This was his moment.

He simply walked out the door.

He instinctively dropped to his hands and knees, scanned as far as he could see, and listened. A guard could have slipped outside to relieve himself when Cornel was in the kitchen. He saw no one. He scrabbled past the window and its square of light. The muffled din of the party through the window glass gave him hope that every guard would be inside. He crawled to a spot where he could see the gate.

He couldn't believe his luck. There were no guards at the gate, and the gate had been left open a crack. From where he crouched, Cornel decided the opening was just wide enough to slip through.

But to get to it, he had to cross open ground, in full view to anyone who happened to glance out a window.

He hesitated only long enough to take a deep breath. He stood up and sprinted to the gate. He squeezed through and took off in a run to quickly cover another hundred yards of open space. He reached a stand of trees at the edge of the forest and flattened himself behind the largest trunk. His breathing was fast and hard. He chanced a look around the tree. No one had followed him.

He knew guards would be on his trail as soon as they sobered up and realized he was gone. He knew he still had a long way to go to be free.

PART VIII

Fleeing Across Northern Yugoslavia

YUGOSLAVIA

Chapter 32

CORNEL LOOKED BACK toward the prison one final time before leaving the cover of the tree trunk. Seeing no one, he ran until he was camouflaged by the forest. It was about three o'clock in the morning when he had last glanced at the clock in the kitchen. He figured he would have only a couple more hours before morning rounds, when his absence was sure to be noticed.

At the tree line, the plateau turned into a steep mountain. Cornel began the uphill climb. Tree branches, fallen logs, big rocks, and thick ground cover made maneuvering in the dark difficult. After the first slap of a tree limb, he learned to keep his arms up in front of his body. Each time his arm or hand encountered a tree's searching finger, he gently pushed it back so it would not snap. Freshly broken branches would leave an easy trail for the guards to follow.

He tried to step quietly, an almost impossible feat in a night-darkened forest, and he felt his caution was slowing him down. Resolving that distance was more important than stealth, he picked up his pace as much as the uphill climb and forest would allow.

An owl hooted, followed by a crashing sound. Cornel froze his motion as a cold chill ran down his spine. Listening intently for the source, he heard only silence. He worried that if someone was behind him, that person could have stopped too. Cornel didn't move for several minutes. He finally concluded he had just disturbed the owl, and the explosive noise had been the great bird taking flight, the whoosh of its beating wings amplified by his fear. He took a deep breath and swiped with his jacket sleeve at the rivulets of sweat running down his face despite the chilly air. He set out again.

A dim light filtered through the trees, a fact he faced with mixed emotions. He liked moving under the cover of darkness. On the other hand, daylight meant he could move more quickly and reduce the possibility of tripping or stepping off a cliff. Any injury would slow his progress, but a broken leg would likely mean capture or even death. Death could come from starving, freezing, or being torn apart by wolves.

The ground cover thinned halfway up the mountain. While that meant a more trouble-free walk, guards could easily spot him and possibly get a clean shot with a rifle.

Cornel's body already ached with exhaustion from trying to keep a quick pace for the long distance. The air at the higher elevation made his head throb and his lungs tighten. He stopped by a small windblown tree, sank to the ground, and felt in his pocket for a piece of bread. He savored the small piece in his mouth as he listened for sounds — voices, dogs barking, footsteps, or animals. Safe for the moment, he concluded.

The sun's rays penetrated through the trees and warmed Cornel's body, a very good feeling after an anxious and cold night. The terrain grew steeper, and he was thankful he could maneuver through this area in daylight.

He came to a section of rock facing where he had to make a vertical climb. He studied the rock wall and reached for a crack to get a handhold. He pulled his body up as his toe searched for a foothold. Once his toes were secure, he reached for another handhold.

At one point he made the mistake of looking down. He closed his eyes and held on tightly. He started thinking about falling and how it would feel to land on rock. *Will death be instantaneous or will I lay there and suffer and become a lesson to other prisoners?*

Still frozen in place, Cornel reflected on Natasha's slumped body after the two SDB agents had raped her. Anger welled up inside him as he willed his fingers to reach for the next handhold. He eventually pulled himself up to a level shelf.

He took a short break to study the terrain. Quickly deciding there was no way to know the best route over the mountain above him, he turned in the direction that looked clear.

After a short while, another cliff loomed ahead of him, this one too sheer to climb. He backtracked and headed downhill until he found a way to walk around the cliff. He continued until he saw a route that looked promising. The climb would be steep but possible.

Cornel labored with each step. When he finally allowed himself to rest, his legs throbbed. His calf muscles radiated pain downward to his feet. He longed for water. He licked dew from brown leaves to wet his tongue and felt surprised at how good it tasted.

The summit, almost like a mirage, seemed to grow farther away. After what felt like days instead of hours, the sun dropped in the sky, and his precious light began to fade.

Cornel believed that the guards, even in their hung over condition, would have sent out a search party. Because their bodies were healthier than his, they would be able to move faster. As he made his way in the darkness, Cornel found himself listening intently. The wind whipping around the rocks and trees was the only sound.

He relaxed for a moment and stretched his muscles. His stomach growled. He reached into his pocket for bread, taking inventory of his stores by touch before he drew out a small piece. He had a long way to go, and the little scraps of bread would have to last for several days.

Cornel forced his tired body to climb the remaining excruciating steps. He tried to breathe deeply, but his chest and body screamed for more oxygen.

Suddenly, he could see the night sky in every direction he looked. He had reached the summit. Stars pinpricked the heavens above him, a sight that brought back the memory of walking from the fields late in the evening with his father. Marin would say, "If you look to the sky, God's light will lead you. Cornel, do you see that bright star with several little stars following it? We call that mother chicken and her chicks. The bright mother star, *luceafarul*, is always in the North."

Cornel found the bright star. He was now confident on the path he needed to take down the mountain. After a few minutes of rest, he started down the northwest side of the mountain, keeping an eye to the North Star. He hoped to find a place with thick enough vegetation for concealment, so he could stretch out and sleep.

The terrain turned steep. Hiking down a mountain was more difficult than climbing up. He chose each step carefully, but when his slick-bottomed shoes glided over a patch of loose rock, he fought for balance and then went tumbling through space. He hit the ground on his back and like a greased sled, he slipped downward over bumps and sharp edges that tore at his clothes and banged at his body and head. He grabbed a branch to stop his fall.

Both his hands clutched the branch, his chest heaving with the effort of his upper body muscles to hold himself in place. He slowly rolled to his stomach and dug in with his toes and elbows.

He mentally scanned his body, stopping at each throb of pain. He decided there probably were no broken bones. He attempted to rise to hands and knees and position himself along the traverse of the hill. His body seemed to be in one piece. He inched to a patch of scrub, away from loose rock.

Cornel stood up and saw in the distance a large building surrounded by a high secure fence. He hoped his fall had not aroused the attention of someone at the facility. When he reached the cover of a tree, he stood and watched the compound for any movement. Seeing none, he continued on his way.

He came to a patch of thick vegetation and crawled under the densest scrub. After moving a few large branches and brushing the stones aside, he curled up. Cornel was close to twenty-four hours into his journey. Feeling safe enough to allow his exhaustion to rule, he slept.

Rays of sun filtering through the trees woke him. He lay quietly while listening. He decided to stay hidden during the daylight, worried he could be easily spotted. In addition, he was exhausted and needed a rest. He slept again. He awoke several times throughout the day from unidentifiable sounds. When the light faded, he crawled from his hiding place, stood, stretched his stiff muscles, and started down the steep slope.

With each step, his toes pushed hard against the tips of his shoes and at times felt like they would break through the thin canvas. He placed each foot with studied care; he didn't want to slip again.

Cornel licked the dew from leaves, but that wasn't enough to quench his thirst. Finding water became his priority. He altered his course from straight down to a traverse route across the hillside. As if placed there just for him, he found a small creek. He gratefully cupped his hands and drank. He reached into his pocket and pulled out a piece of bread. It was so stale he had to hold it in his mouth to soften it. His impatient hunger begged him to swallow the entire piece at once, but he resisted, taking sips of water to help the bread dissolve until the last bit could be consumed with a satisfying crunch. He rested a few minutes at the creek and drank again before he left.

Walking became increasingly difficult as the vegetation grew thicker. He eventually came to a gravel road. He took a long look before deciding to gamble on taking the road to make better time. He walked quickly and made good progress for the first mile. The sky grew lighter, but Cornel thought he'd try to stay on the road a little longer. He calculated that this was his third morning away from prison.

A noise stopped him in his tracks, and he concentrated on the sound. He could hear wheels grinding on gravel and instinctively dove into the ditch. He thought of how it would be if guards found him — *They'll arrest me, surely beat me and return me to prison, that is if they don't kill me first.* Cornel knew that prison guards didn't like the idea of chasing down escapees. He'd be at their mercy, especially when first captured.

A bush provided him cover as the wagon wheels came closer. A farmer, with his horse-drawn cart full of hay, rounded the corner and kept going.

Cornel moved farther off the road and hid in a tangle of fallen branches. He watched another horse-drawn cart round the curve. He waited, and another plodded by. Each time he heard something approach, a cold chill ran down his back.

After a long silence, he fell asleep, waking when he heard a rustle in the underbrush. *Small animals, not guards*, he thought after listening intently, but it could have been anything. It was still daylight. He decided to wait until dusk to go on. He knew he couldn't use the road. He dozed off wondering how many mountains he'd have to climb before reaching Italy.

CHAPTER 33

HIS SHIVERING WOKE HIM from a sound sleep, and he wondered how long he had been sleeping. The darkness told him it was way past his intended target of dusk. He rubbed his arms, reaching to his legs to slap them awake. *I've got to walk to warm up*, he thought. As he stood and stomped to warm his feet, he threw back his head to search for the moon or a star. The sky was completely black, and he worried whether he'd be able to maintain the northwest direction without the stars for guidance. He began to climb and chose a direction he guessed was toward his intended destination.

He could tell the land under his feet sloped upward, but that was all. He couldn't see what was in front of him, couldn't even see his hand when he brought it to his face, but he kept moving. Branches tore at his skin and clothes. He continually worried that he was simply circling rather than heading straight up.

Blessed rising sunlight helped orient him on his fourth morning. He stopped just long enough to eat a piece of bread, and then headed northwest, down the mountain. Half-light showed the way through the trees.

After a couple hours, Cornel decided to stop and rest. He spotted a fallen tree with the top of one long branch dug deeply into the earth. He crawled under the limb, chancing that some animal had claimed the shelter before him. Hardly caring if he shared, he curled up and slept.

He woke at the sound of footsteps on dry leaves. He held his breath and listened. He turned over slowly and peered out from under the limb. Again he heard the noise, this time a fast rustling. He scanned the ground just in time to spot a squirrel as it leaped up onto a tree trunk where it seemed to stick, frozen except for its darting eyes and pumping tail. Cornel thought the squirrel's eyes found his just before it scampered up the tree. After listening to make sure the squirrel was his only company, he relaxed and thought what a scrumptious meal the squirrel would make and wished he had a gun.

He slept very little and decided to continue on during the daylight. Cornel was able to scale another mountain. His body had taken a beating. His clothes were torn, and his skin was scratched and bleeding. He wanted rest and water but talked himself into going just a little farther.

He kept walking. Suddenly he was aware of the faint ripple of running water. Encouraged, he rapidly headed toward the sound, stopping to listen every few minutes and turning in the direction where it seemed loudest. The very thought of a long, cool drink lifted his spirits.

Soon he found the source: a river. He plunged his scratched face into the cool water. When he came up for air, he drank deeply and then sunk back onto the bank.

The water revived him. He drank again, ate a piece of bread, and used his wet fingers to rub the blood off his face and legs. His jacket had protected his arms and upper body, but the holes in it allowed the cold wind to penetrate. He moved away from the river, hunkered down under bushes, and closed his eyes, just to rest.

He slept. When he woke, the sky was darkening. The clouds cleared and stars shined brightly. He searched the sky for the constellations that looked like the mother chicken and her chicks to find north. Then he turned slightly to what he figured was the northwest. This direction would take him over a smaller mountain, for which Cornel was relieved. Before he set out, he walked back to the river for a drink, the cold water reminding him of his hunger. He allowed himself one of the smallest pieces of bread left in his pocket, but it did little to ease the pain in his stomach. He thought of the prison soup. Even that would have tasted good now.

He checked the North Star's position and walked into the dark forest. After fighting through dense trees for several hours, he happened upon a small path that snaked up the mountain. Cornel took it, welcoming the easier footing. He suspected the trail was used by firewood gatherers, but didn't think anyone would be out that late doing chores. He walked the path to its end. He stopped to rest just long enough to catch his breath, then stood and stretched.

Clouds had covered the moon and stars. He took a deep breath and walked off the path, fighting his way to the mountaintop against the branches, which never seemed to let up their assault on his clothes and body. All of a sudden a hard impact made him cry out. He quickly realized that he had walked directly into the trunk of a tree, his head smashing against the rough bark. He stood still, waiting for the pain to subside.

Feeling a little dazed, he forced himself to move on. He knew this mountain was not the equal to others he'd already climbed, but it was beginning to feel higher. His hungry, hurting body struggled up the slope.

He stopped to rest at the top, ate a piece of bread, and reached for another but hesitated. Finally deciding he needed it now to give him enough energy to go on, he placed two small pieces in his mouth.

The next leg of his journey was downhill and morning light helped him find his way. Near the bottom, he came to another gravel road. He decided to take a chance and follow it, hoping he could get off it in time if someone or something approached.

He hadn't been on the road long before he heard an engine. He dove for the ditch and flattened himself against the brush. A truck rolled by. The encounter convinced Cornel he must wait until dark if he wanted to stay on the road. He walked into the woods and found a hiding place.

He slept, then woke and marveled at the beautiful sunset, which confirmed he had been traveling west on the road. He remained stone-still as he watched the sun disappear below the horizon. With the protection of darkness, he returned to the road.

The road followed the rolling hills. Cornel hiked a continuous series of ups and downs. As he strode to the top of one hill, the pinprick lights of a city were spread out far below him. Relief flooded over him; he wasn't lost, and he hadn't been walking for days in circles. If he could learn the name of the city, he could determine how far he had to go to reach the border. He stayed on the road and walked toward the distant city lights, the morning still a couple of hours away.

The road took him past a small group of houses perched on a hillside. A rooster crowed. Soon cars and farmer carts would be on the road, so he set out through the fields and headed toward the larger city.

He reached its outskirts late that afternoon. The cobblestone street was busy with horses and wagons, buses, trucks, and a few cars. By now, too cold, exhausted, and hungry to feel fear, he decided to walk through town because he didn't think the militia would notice him surrounded by so many people. Cornel approached an older man and asked for directions to the bus station. The man looked at him strangely but said nothing as he pointed down the main street.

Cornel walked past a bakery and a clothing store, wishing he had money to buy something from each. He spotted two old buses parked on the street in front of the station. Inside, he scanned the walls for what he fully expected to find: a map. There it was, a large country map pasted on the far wall. Cornel didn't hesitate to walk to it.

An arrow on the map told Cornel he was in Rijeka, near the Adriatic Sea. Trieste, Italy, represented freedom. Cornel's eyes followed the path he needed to take. If he were a bird he could take a direct route, but that direction meant many more mountains, which his body could no longer endure. The other route followed the coast, southwest to Pula, north to Umag, and then northeast to Koper, the closest city posted on the map near the Italian border. Cornel's heart sank when he saw the distance he had yet to travel. He'd long ago eaten the last piece of bread. How could his already exhausted and starving body survive that long a journey?

Riding the bus was his only hope, he decided. But he had no money. He'd have to hitch a ride. The schedule showed a bus leaving in about an hour for Umag.

Cornel walked outside, stepped up onto the bus, and looked down the long aisle. He didn't see a bus driver. He walked past six seated passengers and stopped at the back of the bus. Two people swiveled to stare. Their looks of disdain didn't surprise Cornel. He knew he was dirty, and his clothes were ripped.

When they turned back to face the front, Cornel crouched down on the floor in front of an empty seat. He heard a few more people board the bus and prayed they would select a seat near the front. No one came close. Cornel sighed with relief when the motor started. The bus jumped a time or two before the engine smoothed out and the bus picked up speed.

The bus driver announced the first stop. Cornel peeked around the seat and watched as three people got off. At the next stop, two more people left.

A while later, the driver announced they were arriving in Pula. As soon as two people boarded the bus, it proceeded down the road. Cornel could hear the two new passengers walk and stop. He peeked and saw the feet of two militieni stopped halfway down the long aisle. Cornel turned his head so he could see what they were doing. He saw them look between the seats and ask to see the papers of a passenger. They moved to the next row and did the same. Cornel slowly pushed away from the aisle and tried to make himself disappear into the darkness as they approached the back of the bus. A cold chill of fear ran down the middle of his back.

He heard the boots stomping closer. Suddenly, he felt pressure on his neck. A militianu grabbed Cornel and roughly lifted him out of his hiding place.

Oh no, this can't be. Not now. Not when I've come so far, Cornel cried to himself.

"Let me see your papers," demanded the officer.

"I've lost my papers," Cornel responded, trying not to show his fear.

One of the men shouted up to the driver to go directly to the militia station. The bus stopped a few minutes later. The uniformed men escorted Cornel off the bus, into the station, and then into a small room.

Cornel was shaking — from cold, from hunger, but mostly from fear. He felt as if he were in a nightmare as the first militianu asked Cornel questions. Then another came in and continued the interrogation, followed by a third. The first militianu returned and led him to a jail cell.

Cornel learned later that the prison guards had contacted border guards and militia to inform them that he had escaped. The militia paid locals for information about anyone who looked like a stranger. Evidently one of the individuals who had gotten off at one of the previous stops had notified militia.

Cornel sat on the tiny bed. He hadn't been in the cell long when someone came and gave him soup, bread, and water. Never had prison soup looked so good. He savored every sip and each bite of bread.

As he devoured the meal, he wondered what would happen to him. Dejectedly he thought, *I could be executed. I could be sent back to Romania. I could be in this prison, or one like it, for the rest of my life.*

CHAPTER 34

ELEVEN DIFFERENT TOWNS, eleven different jails, and eleven nights…the militia moved Cornel from one town to the next. The jails looked the same. The food didn't vary, but Cornel appreciated every crumb of the small piece of bread and every drop of the bland soup. He slowly regained his strength, but he remained apprehensive about his future.

The militia didn't offer Cornel another set of clothes despite the fact that his were torn and covered with dirt and mud. They also didn't offer him water to bathe, even though he smelled and his body was caked with dirt and blood.

On the twelfth morning, militia moved Cornel again. It became apparent that this would be a longer trip. He worried they were taking him back to Belgrade and then to Romania. When they rounded a curve and turned up a road, he recognized the way to the prison on the mountain. He now knew where they were going and that he would face punishment for escaping. However, he was thankful he wasn't being turned over to the Romanians. The curvy road made him sick a few times during the rough trip, but not as much as during the first trip up the steep mountain road.

Cornel's stomach turned again as the vehicle reached the front gates. Three guards whom Cornel had not seen before escorted him into the compound, but in the opposite direction from his original jail cell. One guard opened a door while the other two threw Cornel into a room. Cornel didn't have time to catch himself before a guard punched him hard in the head. Another guard kicked him off his feet onto the dirt floor.

"You told us you wanted to stay in Yugoslavia," the third guard said while kicking him in the ribs. "Why did you escape?"

When Cornel did not respond, the guard kicked him in the head again.

The questions, kicking, and beating continued until Cornel blacked out. When he woke, he tried to open his eyes but couldn't. Pain shot through his body. The throbbing intensified with every waking moment, and he finally forced his swollen eyes to open a crack. The room was totally dark. He didn't know whether it was day or night, or how long he'd been on the cold floor. He took a deep breath that caused a sharp jolt in his chest. He knew at least one of his ribs had been broken and hoped it had not punctured his lung.

He checked for broken limbs. He first turned his right hand, wiggled his fingers, and lifted his arm. He repeated the same with his left. Next, he tried moving each foot, then each leg. Every move hurt, but he decided his arms and legs were intact. He tried to sit up, but the pain in his chest and head caused him to pass out again.

The throbbing returned as he gained consciousness. The guards did not return with food or water or to lead him to the toilet. His growing thirst told him he had been in the cell for more than twenty-four hours. The cell was so dark, he could not see his hand in front of his face; his eyes longed for light. He struggled to sit up and then willed himself to stand, which he did cautiously. He worried whether his legs could hold him up or whether he would hit a low ceiling. He reached his hands out to find the wall. He found only air. He scooted his feet slowly, wincing with every move, until his hand touched a cold surface that felt like dirt. He followed the wall until he had touched four corners. From the distance between corners, he estimated that the cell was about eight feet square.

He felt his way back along the wall to where he thought he had felt the cell door. He pounded on it. No one came. To release the tension and fear welling up within him, he paced while keeping a hand to the walls for stability.

The questions ran around and around in this head. *What's going to happen to me now? I was so close to freedom. Why did I let my guard down and try to go in to the city? What are they going to do to me now? How long will I have to endure this?*

His pacing exhausted his still-throbbing body. He lay back down on the cold floor and went to sleep.

Thirst awakened Cornel. He'd gone without food for a long time but had never gone without water for this long. In the woods, he could at least ease his dry tongue by licking the dew on the leaves. He stood and found the door. He pounded and yelled, "Please let me out. Please bring me water." No one came. He was wasting energy, and the yelling made his mouth and throat drier. His head began to spin, so he slipped back to the floor.

He said out loud, "Have you left me here to die? Is this my grave?"

He fell off to sleep, woke, stayed awake for awhile, and then slept again. Darkness, dehydration, and hunger worked on his mind. He lost track of time.

When he heard a noise outside his cell, he wasn't sure if it was his imagination or if someone was really there. He raised his head off the floor and turned toward the sound. He squinted as light penetrated the small room. Two guards entered and lifted him from the ground. Cornel winced in pain from the quick move. He feared they might have come back for round two. He managed to get out the words, "Water. Please, water."

The guards dragged him from the hole. The brighter light burned into his eyes. The guards handed him a cup of water and a piece of bread.

I'm going to live, Cornel thought as the water ran down his throat.

They stopped and entered a room at the left-end of the main prison.

"Now you clean yourself up. You stink," one of the guards sneered.

Cornel welcomed the request with a smile. He gingerly peeled off his clothes from his tender skin, trying to hurry but unable to move quickly. A guard handed him a bucket of water and a piece of soap. Cornel poured part of the water over his head. The wet, cold sensation felt like new life. He lathered his hands and the lye smell was so welcome. He washed his swollen face and black and blue body, flinching as the soap penetrated his cuts. He felt alive again.

Cornel didn't have time to scrub all of the dirt from his body before one of the guards told him to hurry. Cornel picked up the bucket and poured the remaining water over his head to rinse off the soap, then reluctantly slipped into his ragged, dirty shirt and pants.

The guards led Cornel to a cell on the second floor. His spirits lifted when he saw it had a window.

"How long have I been here?" Cornel asked the guards as they closed and locked the cell door.

Both guards had turned their backs to him and were walking away when Cornel got an answer. "What does that matter, your time here has just begun." Cornel wasn't sure which one had spoken.

The next morning, guards led him to the mess hall. The other prisoners stared at him. Natasha wasn't among them. He noted many new faces. He relished every bite and spoonful of his breakfast of bread and watery soup. Cornel didn't speak to anyone, despite his desire to find out what had become of Natasha.

He felt as if all the prisoners were looking at him. Words of their conversations floated to him, and from them Cornel suspected they were discussing his battered face. They probably all had heard of his escape attempt. Yet Cornel kept his mouth shut, still afraid to speak, not knowing who was friend or foe, not knowing, because of his actions, if anyone had been beaten by frustrated guards.

After the meal, the guard who spoke Romanian escorted Cornel out of the mess hall.

"Now I know why you asked me about our location," he said.

Cornel wasn't sure if the statement was an accusation and wondered if the guard had gotten into trouble after Cornel had slipped away. Cornel said nothing.

"I've got to tell you something," the guard continued. "You're going to be in trouble. They might send you back to Romania."

"When?"

"I don't know."

Cornel didn't feel comfortable asking more. The guard still seemed friendly, and Cornel felt relieved at that, but the news he brought could not have been worse. He wondered what the Romanian Securitate would have in store for him. He knew it meant death or worse. He'd heard stories of continual beatings, and not for a few days but a lifetime.

Before this news, Cornel had resolved to escape in the spring when temperatures weren't as threatening and time would give him an opportunity to regain his strength. Now he didn't have a choice. He had to escape soon, even though freezing winter weather and temperatures made his chance for survival slim.

Midmorning, the prisoners were allowed to leave their cells for the yard. Cornel looked for Natasha. He finally spoke to one of the prisoners, picking one who would have known her and who, as far as Cornel knew, didn't harbor any resentment against him or her.

"Natasha — do you know what happened to the woman named Natasha?"

"One day she just wasn't here," he replied, shaking his head. "No one knows what happened to her."

Cornel felt terribly alone.

"We all know you escaped. How did they catch you?"

Cornel told him. When he described the extent of his recent beatings by sweeping his hand from the top of his head to his feet, his fellow prisoner drew back, then nodded, and stepped away, obviously bothered by what Cornel had described.

Cornel looked around the yard to see if there were any changes. He noticed that the rain had eroded a creek bed that ran under the barbed wire fence and wondered if he could squeeze his six-foot body through the hole. He stepped closer to the creek bed where he could see that it was about seven inches deep. Perhaps his emaciated body could fit through.

Within a week, Cornel's body began to heal and regain strength. The guards assigned him to clean the prisoner mess hall. He wasn't allowed into the kitchen or the guards' mess hall. The prisoners ate every bit of food given to them, but occasionally

Cornel found a small piece of bread on the floor. Every crumb found its way into his pocket and then to a corner of his bed, his stash for his next escape.

In the yard, two men approached Cornel. One said he had escaped from Bulgaria and the other from Albania. Both had traveled by land and been captured in Yugoslavia. The Bulgarian knew how to speak enough Yugoslavian for Cornel to understand him.

The Albanian drifted away from the conversation. Left alone with Cornel, the Bulgarian said he was waiting for his opportunity to escape. Cornel thought the tall man, about six inches taller than himself, might be a good escape partner, someone who could keep up, someone who could help him if needed.

The Bulgarian told Cornel he wanted to go to Italy. Cornel decided to trust him and told the Bulgarian that he knew the route to Italy. They discussed their plans a little more each day, but didn't stand together for long. They didn't want to draw the attention of the guards or cause other prisoners to become curious and start rumors.

Cornel had heard guards talking about having another party the third week of December, probably as a way to celebrate the Christmas holidays even though they couldn't do it openly.

The large man told Cornel that he would meet him outside the prison. The Bulgarian did not share his plan on how he would get through the prison gates. Cornel didn't share his plan either. He learned from the Bulgarian that the compound he had seen on the other side of the mountain was President Tito's villa. The man asked Cornel if he had seen a very distinctive rock outcropping, just far enough away from the villa that they would not risk being seen. Cornel affirmed he knew the location, and the Bulgarian suggested they meet there.

They set Christmas Eve as the date of their escape.

CHAPTER 35

Christmas Eve, 1959

GUARDS MADE THEIR FINAL ROUNDS for the evening at ten o'clock. Cornel waited for approximately an hour after guards left the cell block. He gathered up the bread crumbs from the corner of his bed, put them in his pocket, and realized there was far less food than last time.

He tied the ends of his blankets and bedding together to form a long rope and attached one end to the bars of the cell's window. He had determined that his head would fit through the bars and figured his extremely-thin body would slide through too. He stood on the bed, pulled his body up to the window, stuck his arms through the bars, and grabbed the bedding, using it as leverage to pull his head and body through the bars. When his feet fell off the windowsill, he held on tightly to the hand-made rope as his legs swung around and down. He slid down his hand-made rope until the cloth ended, let go, and dropped a story and a half onto bushes below. He lay still, listened for any movement, and tried to determine whether anyone had heard him. Nothing.

Cornel rolled out of the bushes, stood, and looked in all directions before moving around the corner of the building where he could see the front gate. If the gate was unattended, he'd slip through it like he had on the first escape. He put his back to the building, turned his head slightly toward the gate, and peeked. When he saw the gate heavily guarded, he quickly turned his head out of sight from the guards.

He moved slowly and quietly away from the gate toward the spring that ran beneath the barbed wire fence. Ice had formed on the two-foot-wide creek. Cornel stepped on the ice to break it and moved the chunks aside. Snow on the yard side had disappeared from countless footsteps of pacing prisoners, but a foot of snow still covered the ground on the freedom side of the fence.

He dropped down and nestled within the length of the creek bed. Although removing the ice had also eliminated some of the water, there was enough left to quickly soak his threadbare clothes. He turned his head sideways and wriggled it under the wire. Fitting his skull between the taut wire and the ground had been his biggest worry. He felt the wire scrape his ear, but his head slipped through. His buttocks, the highest point of his prone body, hit the wire. He dug through the snow drift in front of him until one hand could claw the ground, reached behind him to hold the barbed wire up another fraction of an inch, tried to relax his buttock muscles, and dragged himself all the way under the fence.

His wet clothes stiffened even as he stood up, making an odd crackling noise as he moved. He turned toward the mountain, the cold of his clothes sucking at his meager body heat. He moved quickly over the open field to reach the trees that could camouflage his presence.

The snow deepened as he made his way up the mountain, his feet drilling repeated holes halfway to his knees. His progress was excruciatingly slow and exhausting. He was leaving tracks a child could follow. He prayed for the camouflage of new snow. He stopped to rest his tired body when he spotted a rock overhang that would protect him from the wind. He grabbed handfuls of snow and sucked on the white ball to quench his thirst as he rested. He soon went on, but stopped every time he saw shelter, which once or twice was a small cave that gave him blessed relief from the wind.

Cornel had broken out of the prison several hours earlier in the day than his last escape and had expected to reach the mountaintop by daylight. Daylight came and the peak was still a long way away. He had hoped for some warmth from the sun, but heavy clouds blocked its rays. An unrelenting wind made the air seem even colder. In fact it was so frigid Cornel could see his breath. The inside of his nose felt like it was crystallizing each time he breathed. His worn canvas shoes, light jacket, and pants provided almost no protection. As he reached the summit, daylight faded and temperatures dropped even more. Cornel knew he couldn't stop and headed quickly down the other side of the mountain.

Going downhill in slippery snow was difficult. There were too many trees to allow himself to slide. He'd had a bad experience of sliding into a tree when he was going to school in Rm Valcea. On a break from chores, he had walked up the mountain and tried sliding down on his feet. He lost control, hit face-first into the side of a tree, and was knocked cold for several hours. If that happened to him on this mountain, he would freeze to death before he regained consciousness.

Cornel spotted the lights of the Tito villa in the distance and found his way to the meeting point with the Bulgarian. Already there, the Bulgarian heard Cornel approach and called to him quietly. They hugged each other, repeating three words: "We made it, we made it."

Cornel rested a few minutes while they went over their next

steps. Each had a different idea. The body heat from walking quickly faded and cold crept back into Cornel's body. He stood and jumped around while they talked.

The Bulgarian, who was not as emaciated as Cornel and had a few more clothes to protect him from the elements, sat on a rock and watched Cornel. "Why don't you sit and rest a few minutes. We have a long way to go," the Bulgarian finally urged.

"I can't. I'll freeze if I sit. I have to keep moving," Cornel responded, his teeth chattering.

Cornel reminded the Bulgarian that they needed to avoid towns and people and then insisted they get moving. The Bulgarian said he wasn't in good shape and needed to rest.

"If I sit here any longer, I'll die," Cornel pleaded.

"Go on without me then. I'm not sure I can make it anyway," the Bulgarian insisted.

"I was looking forward to traveling together, but I have to keep going." With that, Cornel turned and continued to fight his way through the waist-deep snow as he headed down the mountain.

The odd behavior of the Bulgarian tugged at Cornel until he began to worry that the man was an informant and had picked the Tito villa as a meeting spot so he could easily turn in Cornel for a handsome reward or a favor. Cornel was glad the snow was falling steadily, for it would quickly hide his tracks.

The sun had risen by the time he reached the bottom of the mountain, and the snow had turned to sleet. He had survived thirty-hours, but his body was totally exhausted and almost frozen. He found a cave, which provided some protection, at least from the bone-numbing slush if not the cold. He curled up and wrapped his arms around his body. He ate a few crumbs of bread.

The cold dulled his mental sharpness and started to play with his mind. A howling sound created by the wind whipping through the trees made Cornel imagine that the woods were haunted. Cornel believed in ghosts, and his mind wandered back to Rusanesti. Two doors down from his home had been a house everyone said was haunted, and he would often hear rumbling sounds emanating from the attic of the empty building. He and his friends would throw stones against the house and run away.

Cornel dozed off and dreamed of the time when he was twelve and came face-to-face with a ghost. The encounter had replayed as a dream many times throughout his life. The ghost had not shown itself at Rusanesti's haunted house, but outside the primary school around midnight. Cornel had been returning from a visit with his brother. Darkness normally didn't bother him. Usually the stars or moon provided some light, but not that night. Suddenly a bright light floated around the side of the school just as he walked past the building. Cornel froze in his tracks. A closer look at the light made him realize that it was a teenage girl in a white wedding dress. He immediately realized she wasn't a real person; she was a ghost. He tried to scream, but nothing came out. He ran as fast as he could, scared she would follow.

Still dreaming in the cave, Cornel's legs twitched as if trying to run. He wanted to get help, so he headed to his uncle's house and pounded on the door. Dogs barked. When no one came to the door, Cornel tried to try to scream or call out, but he couldn't get his voice to produce a sound. His uncle finally came to the door and let him in. By now Cornel was crying and could hardly breathe. His uncle walked him home after he calmed down.

The wind howled through the cave, and another ghost appeared in his dream. His screams woke him. It took him a moment to realize where he was, that the ghost was a dream. Once fully awake,

Cornel decided he had gained enough strength to continue and that the safe cover of darkness had come again.

He trudged up another mountain. He encountered deep snow halfway up. Every step in the heavy mush was an effort. The depth grew the higher he went, and soon the snow was past his knees. He breathed deeply, trying to fill his lungs that were starved by the low oxygen content of the higher altitude. He couldn't push himself to go faster, for he knew he would collapse. He couldn't stop until he found shelter.

The sky lightened. He had survived his third night out. The sight of a cave lifted his spirits and he rested.

He decided to start back up the mountain in daylight and found a pace that allowed him to reach the top and descend through the snow on the other side. He finally reached dry ground, but it was covered with dense brush. It was not as hard going as snow, but still it slowed his progress.

The cries of wolves made Cornel stop in his tracks. Had they heard or smelled him? Cornel listened, hardly daring to breathe. The wind had been his enemy up until now, but for the moment it was his friend. Downwind of the vicious canines, he didn't think they could smell him. Not sure, he remained cautious. A wolf's howl echoed through the forest, and Cornel estimated its position. A chill ran up Cornel's spine and hair stood on his arms as two more wolves answered with howls, obviously closer than the first.

Cornel had had a run-in with wolves when he was a child, which made him realize the full gravity of the situation. When he was eight years old, he and his brother Aristotel were taking their horse to the pasture to graze as their father had requested. They decided to reroute their path through the forest so they could pick wild apples and pears. They tied the horse to a tree and left to pick the fruit. When they came back, all that was left of the horse was four legs. The wolves had eaten the rest. The boys had been scared they would be eaten too; wolves were known to attack people. Cornel remembered how they had been just as afraid of their father as they had been of the wolves. Their fears were justified: Marin used his belt on their bare bottoms. Later, Marin bartered with corn to buy another horse.

Cornel had worried about running into wolves during the first escape but had buried his fears this time until he heard the dreadful howling. Quietly, he made slow movements in the opposite direction of the wolves, stopping every few feet to listen, hoping he'd hear their approach if they were tracking him. Then he heard a howl. It was farther away.

He reached the bottom of the mountain without further incident and surveyed the next peak in his path. He found another cave that protected him from the freezing rain that had been falling on him for the past three hours. He sat down and tried to rest, but was afraid he'd freeze to death. He paced within the cave. He worried about his deteriorating health; he had become congested. The pacing tired him, and the coughing and runny nose robbed him of what little energy he had left. He allowed himself to sit down the last hour of daylight to rest, but he didn't sleep.

The freezing rain grew worse and pounded loudly outside. Cornel, thankful he'd found protection, watched and listened until the rain turned to a drizzle and eventually stopped. He shifted to stand and realized his body didn't want to respond. He forced each limb to move until he finally stood and began putting one foot in front of the other. He emerged from the cave into the darkness of the night.

Each step grew tougher as he ascended the mountain. He

stumbled often, and his hands took a beating as he grabbed trees and rocks to steady himself. A cold north wind whipped at him. He kept pushing toward the peak, but the wind seemed to push back. Cornel felt his resolve, his hope of reaching freedom, being picked away by the wind. His harsh conditions growing up, playing and walking in the snow, wearing only his long shirt and nothing on his feet, helped him get this far. However, these conditions were far worse than anything he had experienced previously.

Finally he reached the peak, but was not sure what good it did him to be so cold, hungry, tired, and alone at the top of a mountain. Despondent, Cornel looked to the sky and prayed.

"I don't want to die now. Please, help me, God. Let someone catch me. I don't want to freeze to death up here alone. Please, God."

Cornel brought his eyes down from the sky and looked across to the next mountain. He thought he saw a light. He blinked, looked away, and then back. The light was still there. Cornel wasn't certain it was real, but he felt his prayer had been answered. It gave him hope and energy to keep going.

He walked down the mountain and started up the other side, where freezing rain turned to snow. He wasn't sure what was causing the light, and he thought about the possibilities as he walked toward it. He knew the light represented a human and that a human would more than likely turn him in to the militia or the SDB. At this point, he didn't care what happened to him. Nothing could be worse than what he was experiencing.

The light intensified as he moved closer, a beacon of hope and the only thing that kept him going through the blowing and deepening snow.

He smelled smoke before he saw the log house. One word

— heat — pulsed through his head, and he charged to the door and knocked.

No one answered; then it occurred to Cornel that whoever was in the cabin was probably sleeping. He raised his fist to bang on the door just as it opened. A wide-eyed man wrapped in a heavy blanket stared at Cornel who let his fist drop to his side and met the man's gaze.

"Wherever did you come from? Who are you?"

"I'm dying. My clothes are frozen. May I please come in?"

The man motioned him in, and Cornel felt relief from the wind the instant he stepped over the threshold. He walked to the fire in the center of the room and thanked God for the warmth, an everyday sensation that felt like a miracle to Cornel.

The man — skinny, dark-haired, mustached, unshaven and about fifty years old — kept his distance.

"I'm in the middle of nowhere up here, and it's the middle of the night. Now, tell me exactly who you are and what you are doing here."

Cornel told him the truth. "I escaped from jail. About four nights ago. I think. Several mountains away." His sentences were chopped into fragments as he stopped to cough, the smoky warmth meeting the cold air in his lungs. His body was shaking, and his teeth were chattering. "I'm a Romanian trying to reach freedom."

As Cornel warmed, his words came faster, and he told the stories of his escape by swimming the Danube, of his imprisonments, and of both escape attempts.

The man sat and watched Cornel talk, not interrupting, only shaking his head. Whether in disbelief or sympathy, Cornel could not tell.

"They were going to send me back to Romania. I had no choice. I had to try to escape again."

Cornel waited to see if the man would accept his story and accept him. He noted a gun by the wall and a blanket by the fire, probably where the man had been sleeping when Cornel knocked. The man wore a hat made out of lamb's wool; he held a blanket tightly wrapped around him.

The man walked to the corner of the room and returned with two blankets and handed them to Cornel. As Cornel wrapped the precious covers around him and inched closer to the fire, he answered all the questions the man posed. Cornel told him anything he wanted to know. Soon he slipped out of his frozen clothes and put them on sticks by the fire. The man handed another blanket to Cornel and pointed to the dirt floor. Cornel sat down on the one blanket he spread out on the floor next to the fire and wrapped the other blankets around him. Cornel continued to answer questions until the man had no more. Then they slept.

CHAPTER 36

THE TEMPERATURE OF THE sparse one-room cabin dropped when the fire burned down. Cornel half-heard, half-sensed the man slip out of his blankets. The man wrapped his arms around his body, walked to the small wood pile against the wall, and threw more logs into the fire. The wind found the chinks in the wall and toured the room before moving the smoke up and out.

Cornel dropped back to sleep. He woke to see morning light filtering through the hole in the ceiling. The man was dressing.

"We don't have food so I'm going to town to get us something to eat. Stay here, rest, and warm up. I'll be back as soon as I can."

The thought of food produced an ache in Cornel that went deeper than hunger. That, and the knowledge he could stay by the fire, overwhelmed him, and his eyes teared.

"Thank you. Thank you for saving my life."

The man gave Cornel a quick smile and left. Cornel heard the snort of a horse and wondered where the horse was kept. He broke into a long coughing spell and decided to rest a few minutes more, pulling the warm blankets tightly around him. With the logs the man had added, the fire radiated heat that felt like the hands of God. Cornel's eyes closed, and he slept.

His own coughing woke him. When the coughs stopped coming, he closed his eyes again, but the realities of his situation started to creep back to his mind. Twelve hours earlier, when he didn't think he would survive his fourth night in the mountains, he hadn't cared if knocking on the cabin door meant going back to prison. He had been close to death. But that was then, and now that he was warmer and had slept, he had to rethink what he should do. He could not be certain but presumed the man who had taken him in would tell the authorities.

Still tired and weak, he peeled off the heavy blankets and stood to check that his feet and legs were in working order. He was no longer freezing or shaking profusely. His congestion, coughing, and runny nose, unfortunately, had grown worse.

He walked slowly over to his clothes and ran his hand over the warm, worn cloth. Thankful they were dry. He surveyed the rips, evidence of his brutal journey. He slipped into the shirt and pants. The soles of his shoes were worn smooth and thin. The cloth uppers were torn, but at least they were dry.

Alive but not well, he willed his body not to give up and allowed the dream of freedom to return. Staying in the warmth of the cabin meant being sent back to prison and eventually to Romanian torture.

He thanked God for showing him the light and for the ability to warm up and dry out his clothes in the forest cabin. He realized, when he had given up almost all hope, God had stepped in and given him a second chance.

Cold wind hit Cornel as he ventured outside the cabin, but dry clothes meant the effect on his body wasn't as drastic. He plowed through knee deep snow with renewed energy.

He made good time in the daylight hours. The snow depth lessened as he descended the mountain. He was thankful when he reached bare ground where it would be harder for someone to track him. He changed directions to make it difficult to be followed.

Cornel continued walking when the sun set and stopped to rest only when he felt he must. He walked six hours in the dark and eventually reached the foot of a large mountain he would have to climb. His renewed energy now drained, he knew if he pushed himself any more it could kill him. He curled up under a tree and slept.

Sleep didn't revive him much. His cough had grown deeper into his chest and each step up the mountain grabbed what little breath he had left. Though almost starved, the sickness in his body subdued his appetite for the moment.

It was dawn when he reached the peak of the mountain. To his relief, the terrain below appeared to be a series of smaller hills. He hoped the border wasn't far away.

Cornel reached the base of the last high mountain. He took a break and reached in his pocket out of habit. Not even crumbs remained, and his starving stomach longed for any type of nourishment.

The terrain gradually flattened to rolling hills. At the top of one small hill, he surveyed his course and was shocked to see an expanse of water. His heart sank. It was the Adriatic Sea. He had traveled too far west and not far enough north and had wasted a lot of time and miles. Frustration and disappointment set in until it occurred to him that at least he knew where he was. Instinct told him to remain positive.

He turned right and followed the gulf until he reached the outskirts of a town. Now when he coughed, he put his hand over his mouth, afraid someone would hear him. He no longer had to worry about freezing to death because nighttime temperatures were warm along the coast. Lack of food, physical weakness, and his worsening congestion were his enemies.

He knew this was the same area where he'd spent a night in jail in each town. This time he avoided the towns, traveling only at night and keeping a wide berth around any sign of civilization. Thick brush on the hills provided the cover he needed.

He counted down the towns as he walked past them without incident.

A larger span of lights, still showing against the sky in the early morning daylight, gave Cornel hope. It had to be Koper, the town that bordered Trieste, Italy. Freedom wasn't far away.

He climbed a hill on the outskirts of Koper, but even in full daylight he couldn't see Trieste. He found a place to hide and rest. His stomach kept reminding him how long it had been since he'd had anything to eat. He licked dew from a wild cherry tree's brown leaves to wet his dry mouth. He fantasized how he would have feasted on cherries if they'd been in season.

As the sky darkened, Trieste's city lights became visible. He shook as he took his first look toward freedom. This is as close as he'd been, but he couldn't let down his guard now. Border towns were heavily guarded.

Cornel looked around for any movement and then walked down the hill towards Italy. He stepped cautiously, watching that he didn't crack a stick or roll rocks as he approached the border. He stopped to listen after every step. Cornel dropped to his belly at the first sight of moving lights, which he guessed were lanterns that guards held in their hands as they patrolled the area for anyone trying to flee Yugoslavia. One light moved one way, while another moved in the other direction; the guards were keeping tabs on the entire area.

The thought of land minds and trip wires crossed his mind, but he had no other choice. He had to go for it.

For the next four hours, Cornel crawled slowly along, keeping his profile below the lowest bush and his eyes on both guards. He timed their movements and knew them by heart by the time he got closer. He had somehow been able to suppress his cough, but didn't know how much longer he could do it. Freedom was close, but yet, oh so far away. One wrong move and he would be discovered.

The guards reached the point Cornel had determined would give him the maximum time to slip through. He took off, scuttling across the ground on his hands and knees as quickly as possible. He chose a path between the two lanterns. As soon as he was a good distance past the guards, he stood up and ran, calling forth all of his remaining energy.

Cornel caught sight of a watchtower light. He realized and almost said out loud, *Oh, no! I'm still in Yugoslavia.* He asked himself, *How could I make such a mistake when I'm so close?* He dropped quickly to the ground and froze. His heart sank; his nerves shook.

Seconds seemed like hours while he watched the tower to see if he had been discovered. When the light from the watchtower didn't scan in his direction, Cornel believed he was still safe, at least for the moment. The wind blew hard in his face, and he realized that God had saved him one more time. The sounds he made as he ran traveled away from the tower.

Cornel sat tight and watched the tower closely. One guard climbed down the tower ladder and another climbed up. *A changing of the guard,* Cornel realized. He crawled on his belly while the guards were distracted. He couldn't see very well since he was trying to keep his head down. Prickly bushes and rocks tore at his clothes with every move. He tried suppressing his cough, putting his cut and dirty hand tightly over his mouth.

He had moved enough so the tower was now parallel to him, about two hundred feet to his right. He carefully pulled his head up and looked over the bushes and saw a three-foot rock wall about twenty feet ahead. Many questions ran through his head. *Was that the Italian border? Was freedom on other side of the rock wall?* Cornel prayed silently that it was so.

Cornel couldn't stand it any longer. With the thought of freedom that close, he stood and ran flat out, almost flying as he leaped and cleared the rock wall.

Expecting to hit ground on the other side of the wall, Cornel was astonished to be airborne. He kept falling, then hit hard and tumbled, head over heals down a steep hill, bouncing on rocks and against bushes along the way. A stand of thick brush finally broke his fall. Cornel sat for a moment to catch his breath. He knocked grass and sticks from his hair. He shook his shirt to shed grass that had somehow gotten inside it. He stood and realized he was in a ditch by a busy highway.

The cars that whizzed by did not look like the cars in communist countries. *This has to be Italy*, Cornel thought hopefully.

He squinted as car lights caught him, and he looked down at himself. His clothes were ripped to shreds, and his body was covered with blood. He wondered what people thought when their headlights picked him out of the night. Whatever they thought, they just kept going.

A police car drove by — and just kept going. Cornel was surprised that the police car had not stopped.

Cornel started walking toward the lights of the town. Every time a car went by, he stopped, hoping someone would pick him up. Another police car sped by without stopping.

What's going on here? Cornel thought. *If someone crossed the border to take over the country, they wouldn't even know it.*

He saw a sign that told him Trieste was ten kilometers away. He limped every step to town, reaching Trieste at one in the morning, according to a clock he heard strike the hour. He thought about sneaking on to a train to France because it was farther away from the communist country. He had learned French from his mother and thought it would be the best place for him to continue school. In Italy, he'd have to learn the language.

The last part of his journey had taken its toll. He could hardly put one foot in front of the next. He was starving and sick. He kept coughing up phlegm, and his breathing was ragged.

He approached a lady walking in the street when he reached the city limits. He asked in Romanian, "Unde este politia?" He didn't know Italian but the languages were close enough that the lady understood and pointed him in the right direction.

He thought once again about going to Paris instead of turning himself in. The thought didn't last long. His body was destroyed. He hadn't eaten in three days. He realized he'd never make it to France. He walked to the police station.

CHAPTER 37

CORNEL TRIED TO OPEN the police station doors, but they were locked. He pounded. He waited and pounded again. Finally a policeman appeared at the entrance and stared at the skinny, dirty young man before him. His eyes scanned the length of Cornel, whose clothes were half ripped off his body. Bloody cuts and bruises covered his ninety-pound, six-foot frame. A week's worth of beard made him look that much worse.

"What do you want?" the policeman asked in Italian.

"Eu sunt din Romania. Ajutor!" (I'm from Romania. Help!) Cornel hoped the man would understand.

"No posibile (not possible)," the policeman responded with disgust. Yugoslavians caught crossing the border were sent back, so most escapees said they were Romanian. The policeman probably figured Cornel was just another Yugoslavian and escorted him to the captain's office.

Cornel continued to speak in Romanian, and the policeman spoke in Italian, but the languages were close enough that each understood what was being said.

"Your identification," the captain asked while holding his hand out to receive them. "Are you Yugoslavian?"

"I'm Romanian. The Yugoslavian militia took my papers and put me in jail."

"Do you have anything that might prove where you're from?" the captain asked.

Cornel remembered the paper in his pocket. A militianu from Negotin, where he was first interrogated after being picked up from the Danube, had thrown one of the papers from Cornel's identification packet to the floor. Cornel had picked it up and put it in his pocket.

He reached into his pocket and pulled out the mangled and torn four-inch-long piece of paper. It was his train ticket from Resita to Caransebes and Turnu Severin.

The captain studied the paper trying to make out the few words still visible. After a minute, the captain smiled as he recognized the Romanian city names. "My brother, welcome to Italy."

"Thank you so much," Cornel said with the biggest grin he could manage between his coughing, sneezing, and runny nose. Had he really made it? He almost couldn't believe it.

"Have you eaten?" the captain asked and motioned to his mouth so Cornel could understand. "Are you hungry?"

"Yes, food please," Cornel responded.

The captain asked the policeman to bring a sandwich. A few minutes later the man came back with a can of sardines, a sandwich, and water. The starved Cornel, who would have appreciated any morsel of food, was overwhelmed by the spread before him. He puzzled over the sardines as he gulped down the sandwich and water and then put one of the strange fish in his mouth. The salty flavor was pleasing. He stuffed the remaining sardines in his mouth thinking it was the best food he'd ever eaten. As he swallowed, he began to cough and doubled over.

"You're very sick," the captain said. "Tomorrow, we'll get you to a doctor."

Cornel had never felt so sick. He wondered if he would die before he experienced a life of freedom. He'd never been to a doctor and had no idea what one would do. He just prayed that the doctor would help make him well.

"Let's get you into the shower," the captain said. The policeman handed him a package. Cornel opened it to see soap, a razor, a funny little brush with a six-inch handle, and a tube of paste. He followed the police officer out of the captain's office and through the building into a shower room. The man turned a handle in a tiled stall and water sprayed from a spout in the wall. Cornel stood, bewildered. He had never seen a shower.

Cornel removed his clothes and stepped underneath the stream. The water was warm, not cold. He couldn't believe it. *Warm water in a free country,* he kept thinking as the shower washed away grime and blood, exposing his red scars and redder gashes from his fall over the cliff. Despite being weak and sick, he felt better with every drop that ran over his body. He shaved with the razor and ran his hand over his smooth face when he was done. He wanted to stay under the warm water forever and would have liked to have slept in the shower. Not wanting them to become angry, he decided to step out. He felt so light, as if he had wings.

The policeman handed Cornel a towel. After Cornel dried his sopping hair and rubbed his skin, the policeman presented him a set of clean clothes. The clothes felt wonderful against his dirt-free body. He looked proudly at himself in his set of new attire, putting his shoulders back and standing tall for the first time in months.

Cornel asked the man about the paste and little brush that was in the packet they gave him. "Put a little paste on the brush and then run the brush over your teeth," the policeman explained.

The toothpaste had a mint flavor, and Cornel swallowed instead of spitting out the foamy water.

They escorted Cornel to a jail cell and gave him blankets and a cot. The door was left open. Not having to worry about being caught or freezing to death while he dozed, he slept soundly for the rest of the evening.

Cornel spent the next few days in a hospital where doctors diagnosed pneumonia and gave him medicine to treat it. His system was weak from sickness and days of strenuous walking without nourishment. He was so sick that he didn't even notice the nurses who were treating him. All he wanted to do was sleep, and he did so for several days.

With rest and medication, his body responded. He finally noticed that the nurses were cute, and he began to apply his natural charm. They responded by visiting more often and taught him how to speak Italian. He was thankful for his time at the hospital. It was the first time in months that he was treated like a human being. *They have a respect for people here*, he thought.

When he regained his strength, the hospital released Cornel back to the police. The police chief gave Cornel a little money and transported him to a campus for refugees. A man showed Cornel around the complex, which had a room with several beds, a mess hall where meals were provided at no cost, and indoor toilets and showers in a separate building. He told Cornel that the campus primarily processed Yugoslavians who would eventually be sent back.

"A policeman guards the front door to keep Yugoslavians from escaping, but you'll be allowed to come and go freely," the man explained.

The next morning Cornel went straight to a store and bought a postcard to send to his parents. He debated over signing his name. His ego wanted to shout to Lieutenant Ariciu and Comrade Argesanu that he had defeated them by escaping their oppression. He decided not to sign the postcard because he worried what Ariciu and Argesanu might do to his family. He hoped his family would figure out the card was from their son.

Cornel continued to worry about his family and friends. Had they been arrested because he had escaped? Did Mihai make it? How was Alexandra? He missed them all. At times he felt terribly alone, but his positive attitude toward life told him he had made the right decision to seek freedom.

Later in the day, Cornel was sent to appear before an Italian interrogator. The man sat behind a desk. Cornel was surprised there wasn't a chair in the room for him. The man asked Cornel basic questions such as where he was born, his parents' names, where he went to school, and where he had lived. Cornel paced about the room as he gave his answers.

Cornel felt relaxed and wasn't overly concerned about being sent back. He had proved he was from Romania. Listening to the Voice of America, he had learned that Romanian escapees who reached Italy or France were allowed to stay.

"How did you escape?" asked the interrogator. "It's impossible to get out of Romania."

The man was very respectful. Cornel enjoyed talking to him and told him everything. Cornel was interviewed by different interrogators once or twice a week for a month, each session lasting two hours. One was an American who spoke to him in Italian.

No one believed he could have escaped from Romania or

survived the conditions he encountered, but here he was, and his story was checking out. They all told him he was lucky to be alive.

A man from Radio Free Europe came to visit Cornel and took his story. Cornel never learned if it was broadcast or not. The kind man was impressed with Cornel and gave him a little money. Cornel had told him he wanted to go to Paris, and so the man gave him a business card with his address in Paris in case Cornel made it there.

Police eventually transferred Cornel from the refugee holding center to the city of Latina for further processing. There, one of the interrogators asked, "Where would you like to go?"

"I want to go to France," answered Cornel.

"You can't go to France," the man answered. "France is over-populated and they won't take anyone else. Germany isn't accepting anyone either. Your choices are the United States, Canada, and Austria."

Cornel didn't know the English language, but he had heard his family and the men that met at his house talk about America. The Voice of America was sponsored by the United States. *It had to be a good country*, he decided. He filled out the forms that showed he'd like to be admitted into the United States. The man informed Cornel that it would take a long time to process his application, and he'd have to stay in Italy until then.

Cornel bought another postcard to send to his parents. He remembered the devastated man whose son had tried to escape. He didn't want his family experiencing the same pain and had to make sure they knew he was alive and in a free country. This time he signed his real name and mailed it at the post office in the town of Latina. He wanted to come right out and tell his parents that he had made it to freedom, but he was afraid communists would keep such an announcement from reaching his parents.

The postcard read: "Dear Mama and Tata, I send you best wishes from Latina." He signed his name "Cornica," the name they always used for him.

Leaving the post office, Cornel shed a tear wondering about his friends and family. He wished Alexandra could be with him; he hoped that Mihai had made it and was enjoying freedom too; and he already missed his family.

I pray they are okay and that I will be able to see them again. I hope they get my card so they know I'm alive, why I've left, and that I've arrived in a free country. I know they will be happy for me. Tata risked his life so I could pursue a better life. He'll be proud that I've escaped. He'll be overjoyed that I've reached freedom.

Cornel

Two more years of adventure confronted Cornel before he received clearance to immigrate to the United States. His experiences during this time could well fill another book. Cornel spent several months in Italy before making his way to Paris, France, where he enrolled in an electronics school, L'Ecole Central San Fir & Electronique.

The American Embassy contacted Cornel in Paris to let him know that he was being issued political asylum by the United States. However, he first had to find a sponsor. Cornel was fortunate that Baptist Church Reverend Hodoraba, who had befriended Cornel in Paris, contacted the First Baptist Church in Branford, Connecticut, and the members volunteered to sponsor Cornel.

Branford church members Mr. and Mrs. Warren Adams provided Cornel a home for few months and treated him like a son. Warren, a teacher at Branford High School, assisted Cornel in many ways. In return, Cornel did chores around their home to help out.

The Adamses had small children, and the entire family tried to teach Cornel English. In addition, Cornel listened to the radio and television and took a night-course in English in New Haven.

With the electronics classes Cornel had taken in Resita and Paris, Warren found Cornel his first job as a technician making semiconductors for a company called Edal. Cornel shocked the company when he offered to work for free until he learned the terminology and English. They insisted that he at least earn minimum wage of $1.15 an hour. Cornel was just thrilled to have a job in his field.

Mimi, a twenty-year-old woman who worked at Edal, attracted his attention, and they married in 1963. Eventually, they had three children: Cornel Jr., Michelle, and Danielle.

Cornel felt honored and blessed when he became a citizen of the United States in 1966.

He worked at Edal for nine years and sold cookware in the evenings to make extra money to support his family. He held positions with two other companies before starting his own electronics business, which he named Doltronics.

The first big contract for Doltronics was with a phone company that had purchased telephones from overseas, but the phones didn't work in the United States. Cornel worked out of his garage repairing all of those phones.

As his business grew, he moved his operation to a large facility in Branford, Connecticut. Doltronics developed into a prominent electronics contracting firm that employed as many as forty people at a time, including Cornel's family members. The client list included corporations such as Bell Atlantic, Yale University, Ivy Biomedical Systems, Picker International, and ADC Telecommunications. When he retired, Cornel turned the business over to his son, Cornel Jr., and a nephew, Chris Abbatello, who continue to run the company today.

Cornel continued to write to his parents over the two years he was in Italy and France and when he came to the United States. He remained concerned until he heard from them a year after he'd been in America. The letter had been opened by the Romanian government and several lines had been crossed out. He learned his father and mother were okay but that his younger brother, Georgica, was dead.

Cornel also learned that the Romanian government held a military trial in his absence. They charged him with treason and issued a prison sentence of ten years.

Cornel's wife, Mimi, flew to Romania to meet his parents in 1970 and returned again to Romania with their three children in 1971. Cornel was able to return for the first time in 1977; the American Embassy assured him they would help get him out if a problem occurred. He was able to see his mother and father.

Cornel returned again three years after his first trip, but by then his mother had passed away. He continued to go back every two to three years until 2006.

The people of his village still have very little. Limited electricity finally reached Rusanesti in 1972. In 2006, homes in Rusanesti still had no running water or indoor bathrooms. Cornel felt privileged to have achieved the American dream and did not forget the country or the people he left behind. Each time he or any of his American family made trips to Romania, they took with them as many critical items as possible to give their friends and relatives. Cornel paid for stoves or other appliances when such items became available to the villagers.

Mihai

MIHAI NEVER HAD A CHANCE to jump off the ferry the night that Cornel did. His try at a later time sadly failed, and he endured seventeen years of brutal treatment in a Romanian prison. According to Cornel, "The prison guards beat Mihai beyond belief and rammed his head against a steel pole many times." Mihai did survive. He married, has a daughter, and writes beautiful poetry. On some of Cornel's trips to Romania, he was able to visit Mihai.

Daniel

DANIEL, CORNEL'S COUSIN from Resita, became an electrician, married, and had a daughter. He died of a heart attack in 1985.

The Dolanas in Romania

CORNEL'S FAMILY WAS INTERROGATED by the Securitate. Because they could truthfully say they knew nothing about his plan to escape, Lieutenant Ariciu and Comrade Argesanu did not do anything to them.

Marin and Oprita feared Cornel had drowned, and they were devastated.

The family never received the unsigned postcard that Cornel sent from Italy. After six months of no word, the family decided to bring closure and began preparations for their son's funeral.

The signed postcard Cornel sent from Latina, Italy, finally reached his family just before his funeral. Sorrow quickly turned to joy and relief with word that their son was alive. However, the postcard left them confused. They had read the postmark as Slatina, Romania, and wondered why Cornel had taken so long to contact them. Marin went to Slatina to search for Cornel but could find no one who had seen him. He eventually showed the postcard to his niece, and she pointed out that it was from Latina, Italy, not Slatina, Romania.

They were thrilled their son had reached freedom where he

could have a better life. Now they partially understood why Cornel had not contacted them earlier. They would miss him but were thankful he was alive.

After the postcard arrived, Lieutenant Ariciu interrogated the family again.

Georgica stayed with his parents, which is custom for the youngest child. He was eighteen when militia showed up at their house to again ensure they were abiding by communist mandates. During their visit, a militianu shoved Georgica causing him to fall fifty feet down into the well where his head hit rocks. He lived, but two years later died of a tumor caused by the fall.

Aristotel remained in Resita until his death in 1993. He worked as a machinist at the large metal plant in Resita. His first wife died, and he married again. He had one daughter, Fabiola.

John (Ion), Cornel's oldest brother, continued the hard life of collective farming. After the fall of communism, the country restored the ownership of land to the original owners. John's life improved when he could make reasonable decisions about planting and harvesting, but more importantly, the family could keep what they harvested. John married and had two girls and a boy: Cornelia, Aurelia, and Constantine. Cornelia escaped when her dance group performed in Austria in 1969, and with Cornel's assistance, she was able to come to the United States. She now lives in Old Saybrook, Connecticut. John died of a heart attack in 1994.

Florica married and had two girls and a boy: Ioana, Leana, and Aurel. She lived until 1995. Her daughter Ioana was able to get a visa to come to the United States before the fall of communism. She met a man in California and stayed.

Oprita died in 1979 at the age of seventy-eight.

Marin lived through the chaos of Ceausescu's regime, which was a period of communism worse than when Cornel lived there. Marin died in 1990 at the age of eighty-eight soon after the fall of Ceausescu.

Romania

THE ROMANIAN PEOPLE CONTINUED to be isolated from the Western world through the 1980s. Gheorghe Gheorghiu-Dej was succeeded by Nicolae Ceausescu, who implemented a foreign policy independent of the Soviets. Ceausescu borrowed significant amounts of money to erect buildings, large monuments, and statutes of himself. He then forced the Romanian people, through austerity measures, to help pay back the loan. He also sold Romanian goods (such as textiles, wheat, corn, and chickens) and resources (such as oil and coal) to the Soviet Union to pay off the debt. The standard of living, including access to food, had deteriorated once communism was implemented, and it plunged to an unbelievably low level under Ceausescu.

Ceausescu's regime was overthrown in December 1989, and he was tried and executed December 25, 1989.

With the ability to access information from around the world, the standard of living has improved. Supplies of food and other essentials are getting close to the levels enjoyed in Western Europe.

Cornel Dolana   *Ion (John) Dolana*   *Aristotel Dolana*

Georgica, Oprita, and Marin Dolana   *Florica Dolana*

Dolana home in Rusanesti

Mihai Porcarin

Dolana Kitchen

Below: Romanian Orthodox Church in Rusanesti

More photos and background information at
www.nopavedroadtofreedom.com